A King of Mischief & Memories

The Forged Trilogy: #1

Shelby Cuaron

To my husband Tim - for believing in my dream, supporting my writing, and being the inspiration for the spicy scenes of my books.

I love you.

And to you, for picking up this book and reading.

ACKNOWLEDGEMENTS

I have many people to thank for this. I want to give my gratitude first and foremost to my husband, Tim, who was always willing to bounce ideas around until I got to the right one. He doesn't even read fantasy, yet some of the best plot points come from him.

To the community of Bookstagram, where I met six wonderful beta-readers who advanced this novel to the next level with their feedback. My friends. Gabby, Eve, Kara, Missie, Jo, and Ada. To my ARC Readers, for their candor and willingness to help spread the word with their social media reach.

To social media, my personal friend and wicked foe, for giving me the platform to share this book with the world. To my cover designer, Emily Wittig, for bringing the spirit of the book alive. To Chaim Holtjer (chaimholtjer.com), the cartographer who made the Realm of Ignisiem as real as it is in my head.

Lastly, I'd like to acknowledge you. The reader who imagines my world and my characters in your mind, in whatever way that you need to escape for a few hours.

I'm glad you escaped with me.

PROLOGUE
THE FORGE

BEFORE THE FORGE, THERE WAS NOTHING.
AFTER THE FORGE, THERE IS NOTHING.

Magic and its nearly burnt scent bombarded the endless workshop. Steel clanging against steel, the bottles of the soul pouring into the cauldrons of life sprung up a melody that had repeated since the beginning of time. Flickering flames of the Forge cast moving shadows against the stone walls as they worked. Where the fires of creation and the blacksmiths work in tandem to fabricate the beings meant to inhabit the world. The threads that are bound by the Forge determine destiny. Every drop of being they pour into the cauldron decides the character of the soul. Magic can be added, power can be granted at will —but only if the writings of fate demand it.

The Smiths were hard at work creating, molding those who would dwell in the realm of Ignisiem. Beasts of dwarven creatures, larger than the mind can comprehend, with muscles as big as mountains and ancient wisdom of the beginnings of this world. Lines of age plagued their faces, but still they do not grow old and weathered. Grizzly brutes with tangled, wild beards tinged by fire and darkened by ash do not live in finite amounts of time. Rough, mammoth-like hands from constant work made by those who pass on in the realm are always in a state of use. Their lives are in service to creation, to the Forge that calls upon them to create when it is time for new life to ensue.

When the fires roar into the darkness of the infinite underground caves that they reside, the work begins again. New life must be created, as one or many are taken away. The masters of balance, magicians of animation, curators of art. They begin again, disseminating emotions, physical attributes, and most importantly —power.

Once the concoction is created, the Forge brings about life from its ingredients. Greed and Gluttony. Persuasion and Power. Honesty and Beauty. Life and Death.

These incessant traits that mold what is, who is.

Over the cauldron, the Forge wills them to pour empathy and healing into the life of a nurturing soul, who is Gifted with the ability to create life of their own. Electricity and resentment are generously poured into the life of another, whose pride may eclipse their bountiful power. Knowledge and strong-will mixes to create strength, not without an existence that requires much suffering.

Power is not infinite. Every being has their own limit. While many are granted with abundant Gifts of fate, others are plagued with the power that could determine their own end. When the flames flicker, beckoning the Smiths to begin, the Forge does not know what actions the Forged will take. Only what they are given to exist in this world.

Destinies can morph and change like the formations of flames in the Forge. While the Smiths create as the Forge commands, they are not all-knowing. They do not know what happens once the Forged are brought to Ignisiem to live throughout their existence. What exists in the lands of Ignisiem is not for the Smiths to bother.

Swift, ever-moving Messengers bring the Forged to their final place of existence, to the many beginnings, and inevitably, to the many ends. Once the Forged are there, they shall impose their own purpose and conjure their own logic with the tools they are Forged to have.

Good or evil, nothing but Forged Fate can decide.

In the time before, when the Smiths were the only beings to

exist under the will of the Forge, good and evil did not exist. There was only energy.

Now, with the threads of fate so delicately intertwined with the many that inhabit Ignisiem, the Forged have created such an ethos. As they live, they act. As they act, they create new ideas and ideologies that diverge the path of their ever-changing destinies.

Simplicity of life and death is not enough for the Forged, created with such differences that simply existing no longer sustains them.

The Forge is buried deep within the catacombs of Ignisiem, burning white hot in the face of extreme death while only flickering embers remain when life has been replenished. Wars cause great death, while blessings cause new life. Their souls recycled, the energies used to create other life and to accommodate the new beings that will be brought into the world by the Forge's power.

Fairness and the ideas of equality do not exist when the Forge imposes its will and instructs the Smiths to create. Magic does not care about what is fair, only what is given and what is meant to be. All is as it should be, equal in the respect of life and death.

The only two things that matter to the Forge.

CHAPTER 1
THE HEALER

Blueberry pie wafted through the house and downstairs, the sounds of fall cascading through the windows of the small but cozy upstairs above the town Apothecary. The heat of an old gas stove warmed the house as the crisp autumn air threatened to chill the space. Rough, rutted cobblestone roads lined the small ramshackle buildings of Blarra. Burnt orange leaves scattered across the road in disarray, the strong Fall wind ripping them from their trees as the town neared the dregs of Winter. In Blarra, the town named for having the darkest blue lake in the southern realm of Ignisiem, there was a lovely auburn-haired healer who used her Smiths given Gift to rid the small town of their ailments.

Maeve trudged upstairs to grab a cup of coffee from the pot that was roasting on the stove. Once her feet planted onto the top stair, she nearly ran into the creator of the otherworldly scent that spread through their home.

"Morning, Maeve!" Ezra's spirited grin was so wide his pink gums were gleaming in the dawn's soft light. His two front teeth were slightly crooked, giving him a kind, boyish charm that she had always adored.

"Where are you off to, Ez?" Her voice cracked in a subtle

whisper, the scratches of sleep fresh on her throat.

He brushed past her to the bottom of the small metal spiral staircase. Ezra looked up at her with carefree, bright hazel eyes and answered. "I'm off to the garden, harvest time is here and we need fresh herbs for restock and winter, see ya!"

With a slam of the hardwood door, his light feet were padding into the shop that they worked at together and out to the town below. Maeve was the owner and healer, but Ezra had been around since the first day she arrived in Blarra.

Years before, while being handed the keys to her new Apothecary, Ezra had swaggered over to her in his unique awkward grace. He had a spring in his step, and his dark mocha curls were forever on the verge of poking him in the eyes. With nothing but an old mule and a sack of his belongings, he engaged her in conversation outside of her new business.

"Good morning beautiful, you need a roommate?" His soft, yet confident voice brought her warmth. No ill intentions could come from this male.

From then, Ezra became her part-time employee, friend, and roommate. Even if sometimes she believed he yearned for much more. Maeve smiled at the memory, breathing in the fresh roasted coffee and blueberry pie cooling on the counter.

After devouring the slightly oversized slice of mouth-watering pie, she poured herself a cup of hot coffee from the stove. Knowing the Apothecary needed to open in forty-five minutes, she hurried to the shared bathroom and turned on the hot water into their bronze clawfoot tub. There were many things she would be frugal about, but paying the local *aimsuras* for hot water was not one of them. Money could sometimes be scarce, but nothing indulged her more than a steaming hot bath. Discarding her pajamas to the floor, she stepped into the almost-too-hot water and sighed.

This ritual had a calming effect on her, and eased her into the workday. She sipped her black coffee that she kept above the base of the water, exposing her hands to the subtle chill. Dipping down lower into the steaming water, she avoided the sensitive tips of her small buoyant breasts breaching the surface of the water into the cool air.

Peeking at the window, which was cracked, she cursed herself for not closing it. Rough footsteps traipsed down the hallway, and a loud voice rang through the small apartment's bathroom door.

"Hey! I'm coming in," as she was half-way through the door. Petra looked in shambles. She had thick, raven-black, shoulder-length hair thrown up in a loose bun with curly tendrils framing her face. Thick lashes fluttered against her sharp ice-blue eyes, which were smeared with dark, inky liner.

Despite the obvious lack of sleep and violet circles under her eyes, Petra was gorgeous. Her deep brown skin appeared to glow with post-coital bliss, and she exuded such confidence that came with being a *bhiastera* and huntress.

"You look like you had a fun night." She observed as she raised an eyebrow.

Petra splashed water from the pot onto her face to wipe away the night. A sly smile played across her full lips. "Oh, it was more fun for her, don't worry."

Maeve sighed, rolling her eyes. "Right, lucky you. Once again…" It had been ages since she looked even remotely that satisfied.

"You know you could get bedded a lot more often if you actually left your room or the Apothecary. The Forge granted you ridiculously good looks." Petra spoke with such confidence, a compliment from her always brought a smile to her face.

"You have a fair point. Meet the guys, fuck the guys. Can't just skip steps."

"Unless you're me, of course." Petra said sardonically.

They laughed together, and she returned to her bath.

After dunking her hair and lathering in her fragrant lavender soap, she rinsed and stepped out of the tub. Petra handed her a towel, peeking at the tips of her perked nipples.

"It really is a shame, you know." Petra said with a glance back to herself in the mirror, the kohl and excessive night of drinking and sex finally washed away to reveal her striking natural beauty. Petra's comment caused her to shake her head, and she wrapped

7

the warm towel around her to shield from the bite of the chilled air.

She tossed on her loose-fitting tunic that showed off stark, defined collarbones. She had no need for a brassiere, her breasts sat petite and perky underneath the comforting fabric of the oversized sweater. It settled just above her thighs, sticking to her wider-than-usual hips. Petra swore to her it was an attractive feature, despite her own opinions.

She shook on her leggings with a few generous bounces, fitting her curves into the tight, soft material. Throwing her hair in the towel, she walked out to her bedroom, leaving Petra with a nod.

She adorned her bedroom with many candles, the warmth and light soothed her. The room was quaint, with a large blanketed bed tucked in the corner with too many oversized pillows, and a small rickety nightstand. Grabbing her makeup, she looked in the mirror and saw a soft face with lightly tanned skin and a spattering of light brown freckles across her thin nose. Her large, doe-like, bi-colored eyes blinked as she brushed her thick lashes up, adding a bit of black to bring out the bright colors of her irises.

She was in no way overconfident, but knew her eyes were gorgeous. The number one thing she absolutely loved about herself, her two different colored eyes. One curiously intelligent sage green eye, and another glowing amber eye with the lightest flecks of gold rimming the pupil.

Despite being a young, lower-powered Fae of twenty-five years Forged, she felt that this one thing made her the smallest bit of special. Mysterious, even. No one ever expected it when they looked at her, and she enjoyed how it threw others off for that brief moment when they met her gaze. Being created of the Forge, it takes a blessing to be considered special.

She knew that some Fae were Gifted with tremendous amounts of power, and those who are usually go on to become royalty or great warriors in one of the Five Fae Kingdoms. Oftentimes, the Gifted Fae live longer lifespans, but no Fae could live forever, the Smiths would not allow that.

The Smiths had their own plans when creating them. Being Gifted the healing power, and being known as a *helbredera* was a privilege. While her services were limited, she could heal wounds, bones, and minor ailments of the body with her touch. She was charismatic to be more. She read legends of healers whose Gift allowed them to perform resurrection on those who had passed. Her Gifts never reached this caliber, but being able to use them for good was enough for her for the time being. Healing is the best Gift she could have been given. As well as healing, the Forge can grant other Gifts.

Bhiastera, the shifters. They are able to turn into beasts of different shapes, always predators. Petra was Gifted with her saber-tooth form, which she used to hunt game with the hunting legion of the town.

Nadura, those Gifted with a proclivity of nature. They could grow crops and plants with incredible efficiency. Ezra was one of the many who lived in Blarra, using his skills to feed the town and earn a fair wage.

Treaniera, the strong. She had once seen a female pick up a large, brutish male who had tried to touch her inappropriately and throw him across a bar. She envied her.

Spaidera were those Gifted with the ability to attain an unfathomable amount of knowledge. She had only met one who was passing through Blarra, and he did his studies in the Temples to the Smiths. This ability was relatively rare, and many Nobles and Royals sought after these Fae for their wisdom.

Aimsura, the climatists. She had only met a few lower-powered *aimsuras*, who worked to keep the water warm when it left the faucet of the residences and businesses of Blarra.

Cleasiera, those who can change one's perspective. They can alter how those around them perceive things, which was another rare Gift that she had often coveted. She knew of one, Reynir, who worked at the tavern a few doors down from her Apothecary. Though he had never tried to use his mischievous Gift on her, he wasn't afraid to swindle a few travelers out of their wares when the opportunity arose.

There are those who are Gifted no power by the Smiths, the

ganeras. This fate had always confused her, because a life with no power was much more difficult. While she thanked the Smiths for her healing Gift that fulfilled her purpose in this life, she often wondered why they would create those without Gifts if they are able to give them.

Ganeras often served as cooks, laborers, servants, and grunt workers in Blarra and in the Kingdoms. In the Southern Realm, where the Villages of the Forged are spread from the Mountains of Dorcha to the Aeriös Ocean, they did not discriminate as harshly. Not the way the Kingdoms did. Power is everything if one plans to work their way into the folds of one of the Five Kingdoms.

She dabbed a bit of red on the apples of her cheeks to look like she didn't spend most of her time indoors and put away the makeup. The towel unraveled from her hair in a sweep, and her long, damp auburn waves swept across her partially exposed back, tucked behind her sharp ears. She raked her hair to one side, donned her boots, and began the descent to the Apothecary.

This day was just like any other, she would welcome the Apothecary's patients, tend to their wounds, and collect a modest wage from them. Petra assisted her with bandages and simple breaks when she wasn't off hunting or sleeping with beautiful females, but she enjoyed doing most of the work on her own. Today's load was light, with only a few minor injuries that needed her attention.

→» →» «← «←

The sun began to set as the few businesses that lined the quiet streets of Blarra began to shut down. Ezra returned with a large basket of herbs from the Garden, where most of the other *nadura* spent their days using their Gifts to help plants prosper past their natural growth. Ezra would often help create healing ointments and salves for the Apothecary to sell to those who weren't in dire need of a *helbredera*'s attention. Together the three of them lived in the space upstairs and served those they had come to know in the town.

Ezra traipsed into the Apothecary.

"It is such a great year for harvest, look at all of this lavender for your soaps, Maeve…" His voice was flustered from carrying his large basket filled with herbs and trimmings from the Garden down at the other end of town.

Redness found Ezra's sun-kissed face when he looked at her, his hazel eyes lightening in the evening amber light.

She gave him a kind smile. "Oh, thank you! I'm sure these will go to great use."

He smiled at her and took the basket to the cool storage room. Once she finished counting the bronze and silver made for the day, she addressed Petra and Ezra.

"We've been doing very well lately, you each get five silvers and seven bronze…minus rent. I had to heal a few without payment, as they could not afford my services. I hope you guys don't mind."

Ezra cut in, his voice light. "Maeve, you're the healer here. The fact that you pay us for what we do is a kindness in itself."

Petra looked between them, nodding in full agreement with Ezra.

Petra tossed back the one silver for her part of the rent. Ezra set his single silver down on the counter beside Maeve's hand, brushing it lightly. Sometimes she felt strange being the business owner and rent manager, but they had never taken it too seriously. After years of living there together, the trio's bond had strengthened into that of a family. This bond meant so much to her, because many Forged had trouble finding others they could connect with in a world that forces you to be alone.

Not like the Born. Born Fae are granted the most unique Gift, family. While it is not common to birth one's own child, it does happen. All who are Born are almost immediately considered noble and live a privileged life, but those who are Born from parents of two different Gifts are the rarest of all. The only Born Fae she had met were *ganeras*, but she had heard of the royals who were lucky enough to be Born and who gained great power from it. Two Gifts, she could not imagine.

Petra huffed. "It has been a long week, I think we all deserve a little fun. You two up for a trip to the tavern?" She looked at Maeve, hope and excitement shining in her icy, convincing stare. "Come on Maeve, we can open the Apothecary a little later tomorrow. The random guy with a cut on his knee can wait."

Maeve smiled. "Okay, fine… but I am definitely borrowing one of your outfits. This won't get me anywhere." She looked down at her oversized tunic with a soft grimace.

She knew that Petra would more than oblige with her request. She turned the small "open" sign to "closed" and the three of them headed upstairs to their home.

After a small, but savory dinner of broth and chicken, the roommates were getting ready to go out to the tavern. She looked at herself in the mirror, gawking at the tightest piece of fabric she had squeezed herself into.

"You look hot. Like, fires of creation, hot." Petra said, a flirty smile curving her mouth.

She let out a soft laugh, staring at herself. "I feel like it's a little…. Revealing? You know my legs haven't seen the sun in ages."

Eyeing her rounded hips being suffocated by the bright red thigh-length dress, she felt a bit exposed. However, she did love the cutout that showed off the bottom half of her breasts.

Petra spoke with an unprecedented amount of excitement. "Enough. Your legs are light, but they are incredible. You're so going to find a lover tonight. One more thing."

She threw Maeve a matching red lipstick to coat her small, full mouth. Sometimes she felt like Petra was more interested in her sex life than she was. But she was glad for it.

Petra donned a somehow more revealing ensemble, large breasts popping out the top of her midnight blue corset top. Her toned legs were enhanced by criminally tight leather pants that showed off her firm bum, lifted by the sky high heels she had to wear to be the same height as Maeve, who was wearing flat sandals that wrapped black straps up her long legs.

A knock on the door resounded lightly, and Ezra walked in. She caught his eyes roaming over her curves. He was not skilled in hiding his shock. Recovering himself, Ezra quickly asked them.

"Are we ready to go? The band has probably started playing by now."

With a nod, they each headed out the door of Petra's messy bedroom and down the spiral staircase to the bustling street below.

A KINGDOM OF MISCHIEF & MEMORIES

CHAPTER 2
THE EYES

The gatherings in Blarra were usually quaint, since no more than a few hundred actual Fae lived in the village. However, the Inns and the Tavern had seen a fluctuation in guests recently such as traders, nobles, and soldiers due to increasing tensions in the East. While the Kingdoms are large and vast amongst the whole of Ignisiem, the disseminated power amongst its inhabitants varied significantly. Many Fae who were not Forged with Gifts, or who were given a short life span, defected from this way of life and created their own civilization within the mountains of the East —foregoing the idea of levels of power and creating a place of total equality. The Eastern Realm was completely uncharted territory, far from the reaches of Kingdom politics. Their town served as a short rest stop before traveling to the vast mountains of the Eastern Divide.

The Tavern had Fae moving in and out, dancing to the music with lovers and friends, ale spilling over their hands as heads bobbed and bodies weaved through the crowd. The music crooned from the back corner, where a band played echoing drums and an amplified fiddle. The sounds couldn't possibly be loud enough on their own, which is why the singer and *cleasiera* Reynir used his Gift so all could at least think they could hear the sounds booming in the Tavern's stone walls.

His dark blue eyes always glowed when he performed, signaling the use of his Gift. *Cleasieras* could alter perception drastically, and it would not take a very powerful one to make the partygoers in the room think the music was louder than it actually was. A practical use of such power.

She bounced to the beat, feeling eyes on her as her dark auburn hair caught the light while swishing back and forth, bringing about the reddish hue that sparked under illumination. Hearing the strings of the fiddles croon their melodies into the air, the music dragged her into the Tavern.

The room was much larger than it appeared from the outside, with an upper level for more intimate affairs. The ceilings were relatively low, covered in twinkling lights that cast a subtle golden glow on the crowd of dancers. Petra immediately beelined for the bar, where she got Ezra, Maeve, and herself three shots of a suspicious brown liquid. The Tavern was nothing special, with a few wobbly tables and chairs on the edges of the room, the stone walls keeping the space cool amid too much body heat. She enjoyed it for the ambiance and those who dwelled here, but the decor could use an upgrade.

She sighed. "I'm definitely going to regret this in the morning."

The group toasted to a rowdy "Cheers!" and tossed the liquid down. Her eyes and throat burned, but a fueling warmth rushed through her. Music has always been one of her weaknesses, and moving her body brought such catharsis.

Leaning against the roughened wood of the bar, she and Petra looked out at the crowd of lively Fae. She noted a few nymphs, a small female group of fire nymphs that sat in the corner of the space. They were stunning, their various shades of red and orange hair long and flickering from the breeze of the open door. Bright blue like the hottest part of a flame, their eyes smoldered against their dark lashes and features.

Despite their beauty, no Fae would get near them. Not only It would be considered disgraceful of Fae and Nymphs to breed, at least to those who had such prejudice against the Nymphs. As well, it would be dangerous for the Fae who tried. For fear of getting rejected, or burned.

"That fire nymph, the shorter one. She was looking at me. She is ridiculously hot." Petra had leaned in, chatting in her ear.

Literally she thought to herself, her lips turning up at her own humor.

She turned to Petra. "I have never seen them around here, they must be from one of the other villages. They are rather beautiful." She sat on the stool beside her at the bar, her mobility limited by the confines of her tight dress.

"I'm going to bring her home tonight I think." Petra said, a sly smile on her full lips. Her eyes pointed toward the shorter, curvier fire nymph whose skin was the color of deep red wine, her vibrant orange hair framing her soft face in spiral curls. Her blue eyes were large, but pulled up at the edges, making them look sharp and intimidating.

She gave Petra a sharp look. "Are you sure about that?"

Petra laughed. "As sure as I can be. I know you don't have a problem with that, with me being with a Nymph, right?" She asked, her tone laced with amusement.

She scoffed. "Of course I don't care! You know I do not believe they are lesser. No one is lesser." She explained, a hint of seriousness in the press of her lips.

"Well, what is the problem then?"

"I just don't want you to burn the fucking Apothecary down. Or our house, for that matter." She burst into a fit of laughs, and Petra squeezed her arm.

"I love you, girl. Good luck tonight." With a wink, Petra had strode into the crowd toward the group of fire nymphs.

Well, now it was her turn to find a mate for the night.

She attempted to gracefully weave through the crowd, getting closer and closer to the center, beads of sweat beginning to form on her temple. Hips swaying to the beat as fast as she could manage in the red form-fitting dress, she felt at ease as the melodic tunes drifted to her ears and into her blood.

Cleasiera music often had that entrancing effect.

Large hands brushed the small of her waist, sending a

seductive shiver up her spine. She looked back to find Ezra, who had followed her into the crowd of moving bodies that were bunched together in one on one dances.

"Hey you," he said, hazel eyes twinkling under the many golden lights.

"Are you trying to dance with me or something, Ez?" she replied, lifting her eyes and twisting around to meet his gaze. The music may have influenced her actions more than she wanted to realize.

Those green-brown hazel eyes reminded her of a different time. When she and Ezra had first met and became roommates, they instantly had a strong attraction toward each other. Despite thinking of Ezra as an attractive male, she never quite felt the pull of love or romance. To Ezra's credit, he did try. He would bake her cookies and cakes, use his Gift to make beautiful flowers grow, and always grant her the sweetest of compliments. She just couldn't get there, and she refused to lie to him.

One drunken night at home with a few bottles of wine and a card game, she and Ezra shared a brief moment of passion, in a kiss. While it was hazy, she remembered being the one to deepen the kiss, and remembered his hands all over her as they ripped each others' clothes off. He was an incredibly generous lover, and they both left that night more than satisfied.

Since then, Ezra had always wanted more. She never returned the desires, even if in moments like this she remembered how the heat of him felt against her, and how his kiss tasted of spearmint leaves.

"You look incredible by the way." He said into her ear, causing a smile to grow on her face.

"You clean up rather nicely yourself, Ez. Thank you." She said hastily, attempting to keep the conversation platonic.

She pressed up against Ezra, dancing against him while he gently clutched her waist. They had danced together many nights before. Ezra tilted his chin down so they were eye to eye, but his eyes were hungry. She felt the need to shy away from that stare, being that Petra already thinks she leads him to draw conclusions that she does not want to become reality.

His eyes flashed. "I mean it. You are stunning." His hands caressed her arms as they made their descent, planting firmly on her hips.

She smiled softly, looking up into his eyes. He was only two or three inches taller than her, so their faces were nearly touching. "Thank you." She adored him, but not in the way that he was trying to force at opportune moments like dancing.

He knew that she did not return those feelings he so desperately held on to eight years later, but she knew he still wanted to try. Even though many Fae can live for centuries, it is uncommon for anyone to find 'the one' to spend all of that time with. Many married for power or money, for status or security. The majority that she had seen had not needed to get married for something as simple as love.

She just hoped she wasn't the only one he was able to love and he could one day find someone who returned everything he gave. They danced through a song or two, then drifted apart as if their encounter had never happened.

Petra managed to travel through the crowd with the curvy nymph, who was smiling from ear-to-ear as Petra pulled her into a dance. She was impressed by how quickly she managed to seduce a fire nymph, and with no visible burn marks.

She pushed through the crowd to the bar, tossing the bartender a Bronze in exchange for two more shots, this time of a dangerous golden liquid that she paid a little extra for. Ezra had walked over with her, accepting the shot and downing it in half a second with a low and unexcited 'Cheers'.

Feeling the need to drown her thoughts, she drained the large shot glass and looked up to see a set of incredible green eyes staring at her from the table in the corner. They froze her to the spot, their intensity like nothing she had ever seen. The color was unmatched.

He sat there with friends, many with females atop their laps, grinding and bobbing up and down with the music. He just continued to stare, his dark lashes framing the eyes that studied her like a book. A hint of heat found her cheeks, and she felt her stomach turn in anticipation.

She could not make out much of his face in the dark corner, but decided that his stare made her uneasy enough to not pursue the issue. She gave him a solid furrow of the eyebrows, a shrug of the shoulders, and bobbed back into the crowd to dance against a tall soldier. When she turned to meet this tall, enticing male, she found a perfectly handsome face. Deep ebony skin, brown eyes, and black hair with a scar down one side of his lazy smile. On the side of his head, he had a dusting of greying hair mixed with the black that proved he was older. She forced herself to speak loudly, over the crowd and loud music.

"What's your name?" She half-yelled near the male's ear. He peeled back and pulled her closer to him. "Davin, and what's yours, beautiful?" his eyes scanned her flushed face, but he clearly focused on the pushed up breasts popping out of her red dress.

"I'm Maeve, do you come here often?" She asked, hoping that she wouldn't need to see him again after this night.

"I am only here for a few days, but it appears I'm in the right place."

His elaborate charm made her smile, even though she found it lame. She needed another drink if she wanted to take this guy home. Smirking, she asked, "Drinks?"

He gave a charming smile. "Please."

She did really need to find a male to bed, and he was a perfectly acceptable suitor. Batting her lashes up at him, she began to pull him toward the bar. Davin bought them each another shot of that same golden liquid and together they downed the drinks. Her throat burned, but that familiar rush of confidence flowed through her blood as she leaned into Davin, scarlett lips just inches away from his as they leaned against the wooden bar.

Davin's eyebrows rose as he looked into her green and amber eyes, and she decided right then that she could have him for the night, since they clearly both wanted it. She did not usually play the seductress, but a small fire was lit in her tonight. She decided to allow it, and let the spirits do their job and get her in bed with a male. She leaned closer toward him, to lightly brush his parted lips. Pressing her mouth against his, he pulled her body so close to his that she felt his hardening length against her. It had been a long time since she had found pleasure with a male. She was trying to convince herself that Davin was a good idea.

As she deepened the kiss, tongue drunkenly exploring his whiskey-coated mouth, she felt an odd sensation down her neck and rising into her skull. Her eyes suddenly met a set of piercing green eyes across the room, and she pulled back from the aggressive kiss. Something in her lit up, knowing this male still had his impossibly beautiful eyes on her and she blushed bright red. Those eyes made her want more.

He cocked his head, the details of his face masked by the darkness of the corner he sat in. His stare caused a terrible ache in her, and she caught herself fidgeting with her drink and squeezing her thighs together as she stared back.

The male with the emerald eyes lit something in her, but not enough to have the courage to talk to him. Davin was an easier choice, so she peeled her eyes from the mysterious male and returned her attention to Davin.

After an hour or so of more flirting and kissing, she decided to take the male home. She waved to where she saw Petra, the fire nymph, and Ezra with a pretty red haired girl talking around a table of ale. Petra looked up at her, giving her a wink and a kiss. She turned around before looking at Ezra. His expression would not be a happy one if he knew she were bringing a random male into her bed.

When she and Davin reached the Apothecary, she felt the bubbles and shots take over. Her steps wavered on the harsh cobblestone street for two blocks, but she made it to the Apothecary, keys in hand. They nearly made it to the spiral stairs before he took her face in his hands, devouring her and using his hand to feel her wetness between her legs.

She groaned, feeling a sensation already start to build at the apex of her thighs. She allowed herself to escape with this male, letting her stress fade away. It was clear between the two that they both needed to blow off some steam.

Petra had a phrase she used for nearly every situation: "Work a little, play a lot."

While she didn't quite agree with that statement, it had driven her to allow for more freedoms in life. Every once in a while she felt like playing, too.

She let her hands glide over his arms and back as he gripped her round ass. Davin was definitely older, grey hairs peppered through the dark locks. She liked that he was older, and she realized he clearly knew what he was doing as he nudged under her dress to circle around that spot, knowing it would weaken her knees.

"Ready already huh?" Davin asked, his dark eyes glazing over in drunken lust.

A giggle came from her, a sound that could only be explained by the spirits clouding her brain and enhancing her bravado.

"Come," she said suggestively, grazing her bottom lip with her teeth. Holding onto his fingers as she began stepping up the spiral staircase, her body was vibrating with lust.

Up the stairs to the pillow-filled bed in her candle-lit room, she peeled off her too-tight dress, and waited for Davin to take off his boots, trousers, and tunic. He was a fit male, his lean muscles indicative of labor and hard work. Strong forearms pulled her toward him, but she fell back onto the bed, watching as his length sprung from his pants.

She could ignore the inelaborate flirting now, he plenty made up for it in manhood. Feeling his warm, bare body press against hers took her breath. He struck, clumsily pumping in and out until the ecstasies of the night and the spirits she drank cradled her into slumber.

CHAPTER 3
THE GASH

She woke up the next day with an awful headache. Temple to temple, she felt a menacing throbbing that made her curse her decisions the night before. Petra always had a way of convincing her to do things.

Davin had already left her bed and her home, tip-toeing out before the sun began to rise. How thankful she was that he showed himself out, because she could barely get out of bed. She managed to make it to the shared bathroom to wash off the night before. Scrubbing at the leftover makeup made her feel only a fraction better. Despite only remembering a little over half of the night, she knew she had a good time. She just wished it didn't require getting drunk and feeling ill.

In the mirror, purple-splotched eyes looked back at her. Sometimes she wondered if the few times she went out were worth it. Davin kept her company, and they definitely had a great time together, but she did not plan to see him again.

Maybe her standards were a bit too high, but there didn't seem to be a grand selection of handsome, available males in Blarra. No one ever really made her *feel*, but twenty-five years was pretty short in the scheme of things to meet the love of your life. So she was in no rush to find whoever was waiting for her.

She was not sure how long she could live, but she knew that her Gifts were not incredibly strong. Others with similar amounts of power have lived for a few hundred years, which seemed like enough time to fall in love, settle down, and try and move up in the world. Maybe a few more random males could lead to something more. She was never one to have a different guy in her bed every night, but the occasional visitor eased the loneliness that she felt some nights when she laid in bed with nothing but her thoughts.

After leaving Geneza, one of the many First Villages, where she lived in a shared home for newly Forged, she welcomed the alone time. Before turning sixteen, the age where a Forged Fae is considered old enough to go out on their own, she used her Gifts to help those in need.

Geneza is the beginning, one of the many places where the Forged Fae are relocated once they are created of the fires of the Forge. In Geneza, many hold the belief that everyone is equal. This is true until the younglings from the Forge begin to harness their powers. Once the Keepers know of these powers, they can be raised accordingly. The *nadura* children learn to garden, the *helbredera* children learn to heal, and so on, as the Smiths continue to create new life.

She remembered a time when many of the younglings began to get their powers, and then once they were known to be powerful, to be adopted by families with similar powers that had not been blessed with a Born. A young girl with red hair, the Keepers had named her Ruby, was given to a family at the small age of six months. It did not take long for others to realize she was special, when a garden of flowers began to bloom anywhere she decided to play.

Smiling at the memory, she sank into the warm tub, washing Davin's musky scent off of her, her favorite scent of lavender replacing it. Dipping low enough to touch her chin to the top of the water, she closed her eyes and saw nothing other than those bright green eyes staring back.

Who was he? She thought, scrubbing her skin and luxuriating in the warmth of her bath.

→» →» «← «←

Dying to hear of each others' sexual escapades, she and Petra woke early to chat over some coffee and leftover blueberry pie. "It was good, not like the best I've ever had or anything. But we were both pretty drunk." Maeve said nonchalantly as she watched Ezra walk out of his room.

Ezra strode out, tired eyes watching the two females. His solemn expression quickly turned to his usual cheery, carefree smile.

"Good morning ladies!" Ezra said confidently as he poured himself a cup of hot black coffee, she noted his avoidance in looking her in the eyes.

Petra cleared the air. "I managed pretty well for myself last night too, what's her name had an incredible body. Nymphs can get wild. Definitely won't be seeing her again, though."

She took a sip of her coffee, gazing away reminiscing of her night. Ezra rolled his eyes, clearly envious of Petra's record with beautiful females.

"What about that pretty girl with the red hair?" Maeve asked nervously, picking through the crumbs on her plate.

She glanced at Ezra's bored expression. "Right, we didn't make it home together. Definitely not a love connection." Ezra shrugged his broad shoulders.

She decided not to push him any further on that particular topic of conversation.

"Well, it's a Saturday, what's the plan?" Petra changed the subject, boredom growing in her demanding voice.

She looked down, noticing the too-thin silk of her robe, exposing the lines of her torso and her nearly-peaked nipples. She answered, "I think I'll be cleaning up the Apothecary and tend to anyone who stops by." Then added, "I had my fun last night, now it's time to do some work."

Petra rolled her eyes, not having the intention to stay indoors on one of the last sunny, warm days of the month. "Alright, I'll see what trouble me and Ez can get into then. Enjoy your blood and guts." Petra added, sticking her tongue out at her.

Ezra peered at Maeve apprehensively, unsure of whether to go with Petra or not. She said knowingly, "Go and have some fun guys, I promise I'll be fine here." With a glance back, she began the descent to the space below.

After a few hours of diligent work, the Apothecary was thoroughly organized to her high standards. The satisfaction of a clean and orderly store always brought her a small bit of joy. Her stomach growled, reminding her of the half-eaten piece of pie that had been fueling her all day.

"Right, food." she said to her stomach as she hopped off her tall stool behind the shop counter.

The light-blue painted wooden door to the Apothecary creaked open, bringing in a cool breeze and the sounds of townsfolk buzzing past in the Saturday afternoon bustle.

Maeve, slightly startled due to the complete lack of visitors all day, looked up quickly toward the door. Her body froze, noting the same eyes she had watched stare at her the previous night. In the daytime, those eyes were even greener than when she first saw them, if that were at all possible. The male's eyes glittered with flecks of gold, his irises as green as the first bloom of spring. Dark lashes surrounded his hypnotic eyes, his thick eyebrows defining the sharp lines of his face. The male's hair was cut short on the sides, almost to the skin. On top of his head sat a mass of neat yet wild curls that were the color of chocolate. The few tendrils that fell over his forehead highlighted his tanned skin, which glowed in the afternoon sunlight.

His sharp cheekbones moved, and she realized he was talking to her.

"What?" She asked quickly, stopping the male in his tracks.

"Are you the *helbredera*?" the male said impatiently, walking fully into the now cramped feeling Apothecary toward her.

She took in a sharp breath, calmed herself, and replied. "Yes, hello sir. How can I be of service to you today?" She really hoped he didn't notice the edge of nervousness in her voice.

The male raised his thick eyebrows and gave her a half-smile, time passing slowly as he looked her up and down. "I thought it was obvious." he said, glancing down at his bloody wrapped-up arm. His blood had seeped into the bandage of what must be a nasty gash up his arm.

"Oh, shit!" She said with surprise, closing the distance between them. Her instinct to help took over the overwhelming nervousness she felt around this ridiculously handsome male. Biting her lip, she wiped her damp palms on her apron.

"Sit here, please." She gestured toward the overstuffed chair in the corner. He looked down at her, examining her face as if he were trying to figure something out. His piercing eyes met hers and she immediately sped away to get her kit.

The male sat down in the chair, long legs splayed out confidently, his torso upright. She noticed his clothes, which seemed of finer quality than hers, but still worn from travel. He wore a fitted cream button down, which was untucked from his dark brown trousers that showed off his muscular legs. The hem of his pants sat just slightly above his ankles, showing off leather hiking boots. She returned and set her basket on the side table.

"I thought *helbrederas* used their Gift to heal? What is all this?" he looked at her speculatively, with that perplexed look that began to mildly annoy her. She averted his gaze to examine the wound.

"Yes, we definitely do. However some wounds don't require the extent of my Gifts to heal properly. Sometimes natural remedies can do the trick, if you know what you're doing, of course." She worked hard to keep her words intelligible, beginning to unravel his bandages, noticing that the wound looked like it happened overnight, blood had coagulated around the gash. "Oh, this is quite an injury! How did you manage something like this?" She asked, shock growing on her face the more she unraveled his thick, muscled bicep. Her body buzzed as she was painfully aware that she was basically kneeling between this male's knees.

His piercing green gaze found hers, and sarcasm dripped from his tone. "Well, what do you think happened? Your professional opinion."

Her face reddened, the scarlett hue enhanced by her deep auburn locks that shrouded her face as she looked down at the man's wound. "Well, since I am the one fixing you up, I'd at least like to know who… or what tore your skin to shreds. But I guess it could have easily been an animal. This is definitely not a clean sword cut, and if I had to bet it was some sort of beast. Care to elaborate?" She replied keenly, glancing up at the male and batting her long lashes.

"Hm, you're not terribly far off," he said quietly, wincing as she pressed her cold fingers against the edges of his wound. "A Sergeant of mine —who just so happens to be a powerful *bhiastera*— and I may have gotten into a bit of a disagreement." The male explained, one end of his full mouth curling up in an almost-smirk.

Her interest was even more piqued.

"*Bhiasteras* don't usually just go attacking others, you know. You must have provoked him." A curious brow lifted high into the air.

"Nosey, are we? And why should I be telling a random healer I have just met about such an incident?" He asked indignantly, but she sensed an edge of amusement to his voice.

She gave him a wry smile. "I think that's a nice way of saying he kicked your ass."

He shook his head, his lips cracking into an amused smirk. "I'm sure he wishes."

"What're you doing in Blarra anyway? I have definitely never seen you in or around this village." Really, she had never seen anything close to someone like him.

"You are quite oblivious to personal boundaries, aren't you… I do not know your name." Usually, she hated arrogance; however, his flavor of arrogance and sarcasm was becoming oddly tasty.

She began cleaning his wound, possibly wiping at the dried blood with more force than was necessary. She looked up from her work and answered.

"Maeve. If it pleases your royal highness, what is your name?" she answered, cleaning the bloodied rags in the warm water on the table. He attempted to sit back in the chair, but she yanked his wrist back down on the arm of the chair to reveal the wound to her.

A groan left his lips. "Hmph. You're a tad rough for a healer." He exhaled loudly, rolling his shoulder to loosen it up as he answered. "I'm the General of the 22nd Brigade. We just got into town last night, resting the soldiers and gathering supplies."

"And... your name?" She asked, glaring up at him.

"Hagan. It's nice to make your... acquaintance, Maeve," he said with a newfound curiosity looming in his now bottle-green eyes. She spotted a tiny speckle of yellow at the corner of each eye.

"Well, thank you, Prince General Hagan, defeater of wild beasts." She said with a sarcastic flavor on her tongue.

Hagan huffed a half-laugh and watched her work. Hagan's wound was now thoroughly cleaned, and she began to heal it.

Focusing on the gash, she closed her eyes. Power surged through her veins like silk cloth dancing down her arms, ending in tingles at the tips of her fingers. She channeled the energy outward, toward the wound on his muscled arm. A subtle light bloomed from her hands, and she just barely touched the outside of the long gash with the tips of her fingers.

Starting from the bottom, she slid her fingers up the gash. The skin and muscle fibers slowly found their way to merge together, creating a smooth layer of skin before completely sealing over. The bits and pieces of the body were always idle to start, but once her gentle touch coaxed them to heal, they were quick to listen. She continued this process until the wound was nothing but a faint scar, cream colored against his tan skin.

The soft light disappeared suddenly, and she examined her work. She may have taken her time holding his arm and examining the scar, enjoying the feel of his warm skin and strong muscles.

"You're all fixed up!" Her breath hitched as she caught the oddest expression from this male. She could have sworn amazement disappeared from his eyes when he looked away from her.

Hagan examined his arm where the gash once was, stretching it out and touching the newly healed skin. "Excellent. I must say I am impressed with your work. How much do I owe you?" He rose from the low sunken chair.

"A Copper, if it isn't too much trouble." She answered, shrinking back from his immense presence. She walked toward the counter, grabbing the locked chest where they kept the Apothecary funds.

Hagan closed the distance in only two steps, still examining his almost unnoticeable scar.

"I've never gotten an injury healed so quickly and with such a subtle scar." His voice was speculative. "Such abilities are wasted in a town such as this. Why have you settled in the Villages of the Forged, and Blarra of all places?" He continued, his concern for her social-standing made her a bit uncomfortable.

"Well, I was Forged only twenty-five years ago, so I worked for a bit in the First Village after my Keepers released me to get my bearings and save up some money. So I moved to the Second Village two years after that and met my roommates, began renting this Apothecary, and have been thriving in Blarra ever since. It may not be much, but I do love it here." She answered, a sag in her petite shoulders.

She looked up at Hagan, and he was closely scrutinizing her like he did just the night before. Her cheeks flushed and she looked down into the chest.

"You may just be the most fascinating thing Blarra has ever seen." A small smile pulled at his full lips. "It's quite the shame a creature such as you is caged in this place. Your potential could be endless."

Maeve, shocked at the outrageous compliment from this mysterious male, burst into a fit of laughter.

Eyes starting to water, she cooled her laughter and spoke. "Alright your highness, are you sure you didn't lose too much blood? You must be completely delirious. I'll take that Copper please." She shook her head, bit her lip and smiled up at Hagan, but all she saw was the back of his head as he walked out the hardwood door.

Confused, she looked down, discovering a Gold sitting on the counter. Her eyes widened as she looked at three months rent for her and her roommates. She snatched the Gold up and bolted for the door.

"Excuse me, sir... General... Hagan?!" Her eyes darted up and down the street to spot him. She simply could not accept such a grand amount of money for such a simple procedure.

He had disappeared. After peeking down the nearest alleys and into a few businesses, she found nothing. Strolling back to the Apothecary, she walked into the shop and quickly put the money away. Hagan had just paid her an entire Gold for a gash that took her but a few moments to heal.

"What the fuck?" She whispered to herself, walking over to the corner chair to clean up the area that Hagan had inhabited. She smelled fresh rainwater and something with which she was familiar... whiskey. She felt dizzy, but noticed that her post-drinking illness had subsided in his presence. In fact, it was as if she had sipped a new and exciting drink that was quickly making her a completely different type of intoxicated.

Her mind drifted to thoughts like the density of his muscled arms, vividness of his calculated green eyes, and the Gold he left on the counter for her. Definitely intoxicated.

CHAPTER 4
THE GOLD

She bought herself dinner from the Inn that night. The Inn was dark, but homey. Everything in the space was built with old, darkened wood, similar to the tavern across the street. However, tables were crowded into the space surrounding a gigantic hearth that burned bright during the Winter months. Warm, joyful light filled the space and sweet warmth and smells of roasted meats swirled through the air. Travelers filtered in and out, some heading upstairs to the Inn rooms and others surrounding the bar and counter drinking the Inn's famous cider.

Hefty food tray in tow, she carefully headed to the table she shared with Petra and Ezra. She purchased three juicy, roasted lamb chops, smothered in a golden gravy paired with assorted fruits and vegetables and a few slices of fine cheese with toasted bread on one large pan. The bountiful meal had cost her six Bronze, but she decided she earned it considering her living costs were all but covered for at least a month or two.

Before Maeve could grab a plate, Petra put her hands together in a faux prayer to the Smiths. "Thank you tall, dark, and rich." Her smile widened as she and Ezra took their portions and filled their plates. They dug in.

"Tell us everything," Petra demanded, squinting her ice blue across the table at her.

"Everything? I mean it was a ten minute exchange! I healed him and he basically ran away. It was pretty weird, actually."

She looked down at her plate, cutting into the fragrant lamb chop. It was cooked in rosemary, the herb's scent making her mouth water. With a deep inhale, she gave in.

"Okay, so I remember him from the tavern the other night. I couldn't forget how damn green his eyes were. The greenest I have ever seen, almost unnaturally so. He was tall, dark soldier-style hair, and pretty muscular... oh. And he's a General," She said quickly, looking up from her plate to see Petra gawking at her, a bit of gravy on her lip.

Ezra was just feasting away acting like he wasn't listening.

She chuckled. "He seemed like a dick. I mean, like super arrogant and high on his horses. Then after I healed him, he kind of... changed. He complimented me a few times, and I think he was oddly attempting to flirt with me." She took a large bite of the crunchy bread, chewing thoughtfully.

Petra squinted her eyes even more, ripping a piece of bread apart. "You know, really vivid eye colors are usually indicative of a strong Gift. I have to wonder what he was given. Hopefully not a *bhiastera.*" Petra sized up a large chunk of lamb before devouring it whole.

Petra looked at Maeve through long lashes and swallowed. "So, what else? I need details, Maeve. First, we need drinks."

She laughed, her chair screeching against the battered wooden floors as she rose to buy them a round of ciders.

When Petra returned, Maeve leaned across the rough table, eyes darting between her best friends. "He said, verbatim, 'You may just be the most fascinating thing Blarra has ever seen.'" Maeve's face flushed just like it had when Hagan said those words to her. "I know, it's crazy. I've never heard someone speak so highly of me in my twenty-five years of life. He had such a strange way of speaking too, almost as if we were familiar with one another, but also not."

She took a long sip of the cool cider, enjoying the tickle of its bubbles on her tongue.

Ezra suddenly spoke up. "That's wonderful Maeve, and I'm really happy for you. I'm feeling super tired, I'm gonna go home. Thanks for the meal, it was delicious."

Maeve and Petra looked concerned and tried to stop Ezra from leaving so quickly, but he rushed out the door having only taken a few sips of his cider. His jealousy was her least favorite trait.

"I don't know why he always has to do that. I value his friendship so much. I should feel comfortable talking about my life with him." She said in frustration, then took a long drawl from her cider mug and refilled it with some of Ezra's.

Petra shook her head, curls bouncing around, and shrugged. "Well, if the guy would ever get over you, maybe he wouldn't struggle hearing about how awesome you are. I mean, it's all insecurity. He's just mad because your mystery General is someone who actually meets your standard." Petra took a long drink from her mug, and let out an obnoxious belch. "Don't worry yourself, M. You deserve to find someone that makes you excited like this. I have never seen you act this intrigued over a male. The General left a mark on you." Always the positive one, Petra smiled from ear to ear and held up her glass to cheers with Maeve.

With a soft smile, she muttered. "He really did."
She clinked her glass with Petra's. They began chatting about further details of the General and ate and drank until they felt like they could roll their bloated bodies back to the Apothecary.

"Oh my god, I forgot the weirdest part!" She said, bubbles bouncing around in her head from the apple drink. "After he said that, I looked up from the chest and he was gone. I ran out, tried to find the guy to give him change, and just fucking gone like that." She snapped dramatically, to add even more spice to the already interesting predicament.

Petra smiled, her eyes shining bright. "I am never leaving you alone again, that's the only time your life gets interesting!"

A sarcastic laugh came from her, and she winked at Maeve while grabbing a few more bites of the fresh berries on the platter. Petra and Maeve stumbled back to their home together, laughing up until they went up the spiral staircase and to their beds.

CHAPTER 5
THE THUNDER

A week passed and there had been no sign of Hagan, besides the many soldiers fumbling in and out of her Apothecary with minor injuries that reminded her of him. She went about her normal day-to-day routine, and on the following Saturday decided to take a much-needed day off and go somewhere. After donning an old, oversized tunic that exposed a shoulder and a pair of loose shorts, she went into the kitchen and was welcomed by the grand smell of muffins.

Ezra sat on the weathered leather couch and greeted her, a tight-lipped smile on his face. "Good Morning, Maeve."

She smiled at him and walked to grab a muffin and coffee. She took a bite of the warm muffin and groaned. "Pumpkin, huh? Already?" she asked Ezra while still savoring every bite of the delicious baked good.

Ezra laughed a bit and stood up to stand by her in the kitchen. "Yeah, I may have worked a little overtime at the Garden to get those to sprout early. How is it?" he asked, his hazel eyes radiating amber in the morning light. Her mouth was half-full as she managed, "Mmmm," and covered her mouth so crumbs wouldn't litter the floor.

He laughed, and went to pour her a glass of milk. Once she

chewed the muffin down and took a swig of milk, she managed to start a conversation. "What're you up to today? I think I'm going to keep the shop closed if you want to get into some trouble." She smiled awkwardly, realizing the pretense in her phrasing.

Ezra examined her face, searching for something that wasn't there for the briefest second. "I have absolutely nothing planned today." His gaze shifted to the window over the couch of their home. "This will probably be the last warm day of the season. Do you want to go to the Lake?" Hope flickered in his warm eyes.

She nodded. "That sounds perfect. I'll go see what Petra's doing." She smiled, and skipped to Petra's door and banged loudly upon it. Petra growled, clearly she had awoken her in her beast form. A swish resounded from the door and Petra stood in the doorway. She was completely naked.

Her full breasts looked right at her, nipples like eyes staring into hers, but she made it a point to look into Petra's eyes as she spoke. "We're going to the Lake in a bit, would you care to join us?"

Petra smirked and answered "Um, yes!" and began to walk out of the room.

"Woah, woah, woah, aren't you missing something?!" She exclaimed, her hand held out to stop Petra. She realized quickly that she was an inch from touching her exposed breasts. She quickly put her arm at her side.

"Oh, right. Swimming with clothes on. Sounds like fun." Petra said dryly, and walked back into her room.

She walked back to the kitchen, feigning shock toward Ezra as he sat there giggling like a youngling. Petra made her entrance minutes later, wearing a tight blouse and shorts.

"Let's hit it." she said, and they left the apartment, locking the Apothecary and striding down the cobblestone street toward Blarra's darkest-blue Lake.

Through wispy clouds, rays of sunlight bathed the town in a warm glow. About half a mile from town, she, Ezra, and Petra each climbed the smooth rocks over the hill to the Lake. Their hands met the familiar grooves that they could pull themselves down upon. Petra finished the short climb first, her agility gained from being a saber-toothed tiger for the greater part of her day-to-day life. When her feet hit the rough gravel shore, her brows furrowed as she looked out toward the water.

"Looks like we've got company. A lot of it."

Ezra and Maeve hopped down beside her and heard the twenty or so voices looming from the water's edge. Maeve and Petra strode toward the lake shore, heading toward the tree with the swinging rope. Usually, they could come here and have most of the space to themselves, but a large group had gathered on the last warm day of the year.

They laid out a few blankets and set their bags down in a semi-open spot when she spotted him. She whispered in Petra's ear, signaling that the General was only a few stones' throws away from them. Petra quickly whipped her head around, maybe a little too obviously, toward where her eyes strayed. He was quite easy to pick out in a crowd and Petra spotted him, green eyes enhanced by the Lake's dark blue water.

He had foregone his shirt, the golden-brown tone of his skin luminous in the sun's rays, the lines of his densely muscled torso as if he were carved from stone. His hands were behind him, holding himself up as he chatted with a male with darker skin, but a similarly carved form.

Petra slowly looked down and away from him, whispering to her, "Wow. For a male, he is something. His friend too." Maeve laughed, laying down to relax under the warm sun.

Ezra glanced over at where the females were spying on the General, and he undoubtedly rolled his eyes. Propping herself up, she took in the large expanse of the lake, and the tree covered hills surrounding the back side of the lake. The stark contrast of the dark green firs was enhanced by the deepest blue of the lake. Ripples of dark blue water invited her to swim. *You deserve someone who excites you.* Petra's comment replayed in her head from the previous night.

She immediately stood and went for the swinging rope. She couldn't help but notice eyes on her as her hips swished and her generous bottom bounced with a newfound conviction.

Once she reached the rope, she looked pointedly at Hagan and climbed up it, one foot toeing the ground. She pulled back, ran, jumped high into the air, and dove into the deep side of the lake, deep down. She had mastered the jump, and loved the freedom that came with flying through the air for the shortest moment. Usually, she wasn't trying to show off, but considering her audience she found it fitting.

Cold water sent a quick shiver through her as she sank into the deep water, but she soon adjusted, floating up to the top of the calm Lake water. She heard a loud splash and guessed Petra promptly followed her in.

"Quite the performance you put on." A husky male voice said behind her.

Startled, she quickly began treading water and turned to look straight into those striking eyes. Hagan looked a bit different than when she last saw him. His hair was slicked back, curls starting to form at the ends. A sense of lightheartedness shown in his vivid gaze, the dark blue water complementing his green eyes. She liked this more casual version of him.

He treaded water and boasted broad, muscled shoulders that strained holding his weight above water. Her eyes trailed back up to his face and watched his eyes do the same as her oversized white shirt fell down her shoulder, pulling dangerously low from the weight of the water.

She smirked. "I quite enjoyed yours. Do you care to explain why you grossly overpaid me for healing your arm and then promptly disappeared from my Apothecary the other day?"

Hagan returned a nod. "Yeah, sorry about that. I had to return to the camp. Besides, you healed my arm so well I thought you deserved a tip. If the money is not to your liking, I'd be happy to take it back..." His eyes lit with amusement.

"I'll accept the tip, thank you. I do feel like I owe you a bit more for what you paid, though." She said, watching his expression turn a shade darker.

"Hmm, the possibilities." He said, the side of his mouth turning up. "How about a question? Well, more specifically, an answer to my question."

Now her interest was really piqued, though her arms began to burn from holding herself above water. "I can provide that."

He nodded, looking out toward the farther, darker depths of the water. "Are you content with your life as it is now?"

His question took her aback, her breath catching in the back of her throat.

"I guess I hadn't thought about it too much." In truth she had, but had never elaborated it into words. He watched her as she contemplated the answer. She swam to a shallower part of the Lake, until the tips of her toes could brush the bottom and gave her arms a rest. He promptly followed her, strong arms pushing him to her in a few strokes.

She sighed, curling her toes into the sand underneath the water. He inched closer than before, leaning in to listen. "Content. I'm not even sure what that word means to me." Her eyes darted to his, searching for the words. "You know, there has always been a small part of me that yearned for more. I think in some ways I am content, living this life and serving this town. But sometimes I wish I could travel and see every part of the Realm. Meet new friends, learn more about the art of healing, do more with the Gifts the Forge gave me other than superficial wounds. I often dream of what could be."

His eyes were glued to her, and her cheeks heated. Besides Petra, she had not shared so much with someone before. He seemed to put her mind at ease, to coax her truths from her.

His lips parted, eyes still latched to her. "What's stopping you?"

Before she could answer, she noticed a darkness growing on his face. Above, the clouds had gathered in the sky, in a formation that promised rain.

She returned her gaze to his, and prompted. "We should probably get out of here." While a few storm clouds didn't scare her, answering that question did. Before she could say more, a crackle of thunder echoed overhead.

He looked dangerously at her, and clouds filled his eyes. "I asked, what is stopping you, Maeve?"

They weren't just storm clouds.

His gaze burned into hers, and for the first time she felt his power. As if static clung to her skin, the essence of his Gift radiated from he to she. Hagan was an *aimsura*, masters of weather and its dangerous allies. By the excruciatingly delightful warmth and power that was emanating from him, she knew it was a great power.

She realized that the clouds overhead were due to him losing his grip on his Gift, and by the hardened look in his eyes she knew she should give him an answer before she pushed him further.

"I don't know." She managed, purely dissatisfied with herself.

His eyes lightened, and she noticed the clouds also receding and the sky brightening back up. His eyes had the smallest flashes of bright yellow against the now darkened green. Almost as if small lightning bolts struck across his irises.

He was closer now, his height giving him the advantage in the almost-too-deep water. His jaw ticked, but he nodded. "We all make decisions we don't know the reason for. Myself, included."

The corner of her mouth turned up, the tension in her muscles lessening. "My debt is paid, then?" She asked, tilting her head to see his angled face.

He dipped his head, now inches from hers. "For now."

Her heart may have skipped a few beats. She closed her eyes, inhaling his scent.

She gazed upon a lake similar to Blarra's, but a much brighter blue similar to a sapphire. The moon bathed the scene in a soft light, its reflection painting white swirls in the water's ripples. A figure swam away from her, but all she could make out were broad shoulders and well-built muscles glistening from the cool, calm water.

In that brief second where she closed her eyes, she felt her nose hit the water, and she took in a sharp breath.

Water filled her nose, nearing the pathway to her lungs.

She sprung back up, her throat burning from nearly choking on the water. Hagan made the single stroke to go to her, clutching her to keep her above water. She felt his warm, strong hands easily grasp her up by the sides. The bottom of her shirt had floated up, and left her hips and stomach exposed to his touch. If her nose and throat weren't burning, it would feel exhilarating.

The skin his hands grasped buzzed with electricity, but not from his Gift. It was a warm, welcoming hum that spread throughout her body like she had just lit a fire on a cold night. Her eyes met his and she inhaled sharply, all events happening in the briefest moment. Her breath was labored, but she willed air back into her lungs after a few more coughs.

Hagan's burning eyes met hers, a subtle flush spreading across his cheeks. Maeve quickly pushed him off, her hips still warm from his touch. She said a swift, "Thank you. I should be getting back now," and began swimming away breathlessly.

What in the Forged Fuck is happening? She thought to herself, as she made it to the shore and saw Petra staring at her from their spot by the rope. She ignored Ezra's alarmed stare, the vein in his forehead popping out. Petra began before she could even lay down on the blankets to dry out.

"Well, what the fuck was that? He's an *aimsura* then? If I could take a guess, the Forge blessed him with a lot of power, those clouds came out of nowhere."

Ezra moved toward Maeve, a large crease forming between his eyebrows. "Are you okay? Did he do anything to you?"

Only things that she would not speak of with him.

She looked into the distance, shaking her head. "Don't worry, I'm fine. I just have no clue what I'm getting myself into." She felt Hagan's eyes on her, she knew she left him with even more questions. Questions that she wanted to answer for him. Things that she had never thought she wanted to tell a male before.

"Just make sure you're being careful, M." Ezra leaned in to speak with her in a low tone. "I just don't want you to get hurt, is all."

She nodded, putting her hand over Ezra's. "I can take care of myself, Ez. I always have. Not without you two, of course. But I've got this. I can handle a cocky male *aimsura*. General, or not."

He eyed her suspiciously, but leaned back on the towel to bask in the sun, seemingly content with her response.

"And in the off chance you do need some back up, if he does try anything stupid with you, I'll be there to rip his cock off." Petra said, her teeth lengthening as she smiled innocently. Always the protector, the huntress.

Her friends, her best friends, her family there to protect her. But she did not want to be protected this time, she wanted to live a little more dangerously.

He had exhilarated her in those few moments, she could only imagine what he could do with more.

She felt more alive. Her heart was pumping, the memory of his touch replaying in her mind a thousand times over. She had been with a number of males before Hagan, on the wild nights out with Petra and a few drinks, but nothing had ever been comparable to him.

He was pure electricity.

Hagan and the large group left the Lake shortly after she left the water, the crowd slowly making their way to the other side of the Lake where she could make out tents and horses in the distance. Ezra, Maeve, and Petra talked and sipped the vibrant cider they acquired from the Inn, relaxing at the shore for the remainder of their day, seeming to forget about the events that had just unfolded.

Once the sun began its descent, and her face was smattered with a few more freckles and a light reddish burn covered her face and shoulders, the trio began the short hike back home, properly buzzed off of the bubbly sweet cider.

CHAPTER 6
THE BEAST

The next day, her mind raced with the memory of him. Hagan thinks she's the most fascinating thing that Blarra's ever seen, but she thinks he's giving her a run for her money. She just simply didn't know how to respond to such a male who exuded power and dominance, but yet a strangely alluring humor. As if he knows all of the secrets.

The day dragged on and she began cleaning up from her previous patient. The frail male nymph had fallen from the roof of a three-story building, breaking his femur in half. This job tired her out, bones could be difficult to mend —especially a femur. The largest, strongest bone in the body took some force to mend perfectly. The customer did tip an extra Bronze, thankful that he could walk without pain out of the Apothecary and back to his job of hard labor.

She was in the mood for a walk to clear her head. Donning some leggings and a loose top, she braided her hair back into a braid and set out of her room and down to the cobblestone street. The night was cool, but not yet the bitter cold that set her breath to ice. Grasping for the reassuring pressure of the small, curved dagger she kept tucked in the waist of her pants, she was ready to venture out to the barely lit streets of Blarra.

Two winters ago, Petra had gifted her the dagger to protect herself. While the dangers were rare in Blarra, she wanted her to be safe. After all, her saber-toothed best friend could not always be near to do so.

She cherished the gift.

She set off, her boots lightly padding against the cobblestones in a nice bouncing rhythm. Walking out in the crisp night air cleared her head. Her head had felt cloudy lately, but her continued rhythm quieted those crowded thoughts as she shifted through a few different alleyways of Blarra, about five blocks away from the Apothecary. She stopped at the edge of an alley, her eyes straining to peer down the narrow walkway.

Hearing the steps first, she twisted around to see what looked like a *bhiastera* in his beast form. A black wolfish creature's yellow eyes gleamed through the darkness at her, his shape barely discernible under the low light. A growl rumbled from the *bhiastera*'s muzzle.

She could barely manage a scream when she reached for her blade and the beast lunged. His weight took her down, scratching and bruising her back on the rough terrain. A sharp pang resounded through her skull as her head knocked against the hard stone. The teeth of the beast sank into her foot, and she screeched, eyes watering in pain.

The creature was pulling her into the alley.

Her hands fumbled around a large rock as he began to pull her into the alley, and she threw it straight for the wolf's head. A sharp metallic scent filled her nostrils. Her ankle was warm with blood from teeth marks she knew had to have mutilated her calf and ankle. The pain turned her vision a bit blurry, but she got to her feet and grabbed her small knife.

Her foot attempted to drag her body out the alley, the scent of her blood making the air acidic, but she heard a swish that she knew all too well from Petra's shifts. She felt a strong hand push her against the alley wall. His strength far outweighed hers. With her battered back against the wall, which cut into the thin fabric of her now torn shirt, she was stuck. His heat suffocated her, the pressure of his body causing bile to rise from her stomach into her throat. Bright yellow eyes cast a soft light on his hard features, an older Fae male. And he was completely naked. His hunched, pale body was brighter than any light in the alleyway. The *bhiastera* gripped her face by her chin, rough fingers wrapping around her cheeks. His mouth turned up in a sneer. The male's eyes were still that too-bright yellow, and they focused on her as if she were a lamb chop. His breath reeked of whiskey, as he breathed so close to her face that their noses almost touched.

He yanked her chin up to him. "Don't act like you don't want this. I can smell how much you want it."

She grunted, attempting to rip her jaw from his grasp. "You must be confusing that with the smell of vomit. I'm sure you get that a lot."

He pressed his filthy, bare body into hers, crushing her deeper into the stone wall.

"Shut your mouth, filthy whore." Spit rained down on her face.

She tried to scream, but he held his large hand over her mouth, claws coming out just slightly to prick the delicate skin of her cheeks. She decided to heed that warning and not leave with gashes down her face.

This would not break her.

In her short life, she met females who had suffered much, much worse. This society did not bode well for females who did not have power or strength.

Petra wouldn't want her to make that excuse. Females have their own power. She'd tell her to fight until the very end, until there was absolutely nothing to be done and defeat was inevitable. Even then.

She did not want to give up.

Anger flooded through her. This male thought that because she is smaller than him, weaker than him, that he could take what he wanted from her. She felt her blood heat, and she began thinking of what it would feel like to break his bones as he pushed his mouth against hers, tongue thrashing against her closed mouth.

As hard as she could, she pressed her lips together to not allow his drunken mouth access. His scent was becoming abhorrent.

A loud snap echoed down the alley.

The male shrieked, falling to his knees before her. She looked around for who could have caused this male to fall in front of her, but saw nothing in the dim alleyway. Instinct taking over, she punched him in the face as Petra had taught her. In his daze, he wailed, eyes scrunched shut. "Who are you?"

Her eyes scanned over his legs, which were twisted in unnatural directions. They weren't just broken, they were destroyed. She shook her head slowly, backing away from the man's disgusting, contorted body. Vomit found its way up her throat, and she heaved beside him. She threw up the contents of her stomach, the thought of his skin touching her and the aftertaste of his drunken kiss still fresh on her.

Footsteps resounded down the darker part of the alley, as she began trying to run the other way. A familiar scent wafted toward her, and she quickly looked back toward the smell. Though it had not rained for days, the scent of fresh rain wafted toward her.

Hagan.

His power felt like static clinging to her sweat-dampened clothes as he sauntered toward the male. His presence stopped her in her tracks, her eyes didn't leave his large silhouette as the *bhiastera* still writhed in pain between them.

Hagan's eyes flitted from the *bhiastera* to her. "You did this?"

Her breath lodged in her throat. She managed to choke out a short response. "I-I don't know, he just crumpled after he..."

Neon green eyes lit the alleyway. Pulses of his essence pressed into her skin, his restrained power begging to be used. Hagan looked down at the mangled body of the *bhiastera*.

He cocked his head. "What is your name, soldier?"

Her eyes discerned the silver pin Hagan wore on his dark blue Second Kingdom lapel. The male looked up into those terrifyingly beautiful green eyes and answered shakily.

"Remus, alpha legion, sir." His eyes widened in recognition as he looked at his superior.

Hagan met her gaze, his eyes softening. "Would you please heal this male, Maeve?"

Her mouth fell to the ground. She was bleeding from her leg, could barely stand, and he was asking her to heal him. The *bhiastera* who attacked her.

Hagan must be out of his fucking mind.

CHAPTER 7
THE OFFER

Through the shakes and pain, what she felt most was anger. "Now why the fuck would I do that?"

Hagan sighed, maintaining his stoic demeanor. "Because the Second Kingdom Brigade General asks you to, trust me." His eyes flashed, he was serious.

Oddly, despite her gut screaming *No!* she felt it was right to listen to him. She limped to the male, and struggled to bend down to his now restrained body. Hagan shifted to hold the male down against the hard ground.

Remus winced as she dropped down to examine his legs, broken in at least four places on each leg. She looked dangerously at Hagan, disgusted with what she was about to do. Through the pain, she focused, a warm light glowing from her as she mended the bones. Sweat beaded on her forehead, her last bits of energy leaving through her fingertips. She had never heard a male scream so loudly— and so much like a female. Her patients never felt this much pain, but this male did.

Maybe she wanted him to.

After a few moments of extreme focus, she finished and examined the male's now straight legs. They were fixed, but not perfect. He would still walk with much pain.

Dragging him against the rough ground, Hagan grunted. "Get up."

His body further eclipsed over the sweating, squirming male before him. Remus scrambled to his feet, yelping in pain. Hagan looked to her, with almost pitying eyes, "Thank you."

A sour taste sat on her tongue. She did not want his pity.

He shifted his glowing eyes back at the male, landing on his yellow stare. Power unleashed like waves throughout the alleyway, the heaviness pressing her against the wall. She was unable to move, watching Hagan's eyes burn bright. He looked down on the male, who was at least a head shorter, and grabbed his arm. The other hand flew to his throat. Hagan took a deep breath, grinding his jaw. "You can now go find a hole large enough inside one of the bricks of these buildings for your miniscule cock to fit, and fuck it until your pathetic manhood bleeds. Once that happens, you will continue fucking the hole and never finding pleasure but remaining aroused. You will continue this until you die of natural causes or whatever creature the Forge puts in your path to eat your repulsive, feeble body. Go." It was as if melancholy music flowed through his mouth and forced Remus to dance to its rhythm for centuries. His melody was both illustrative and horrifying.

She had never watched a *cleasiera* take the mind of another, but it was strangely beautiful. His words were truly music, a lullaby for the thoughts.

Her body felt so weak.

Vision blurring, her strength finally gave out as her roughened back slid down the alley wall. The last thing she saw through her lashes before falling into dark oblivion were those green eyes rushing toward in an attempt to break her fall.

→» →» «← «←

As she wrenched open her eyelids from the deep slumber, she noticed she was in her own large, cozy bed covered in her thick, feather-filled duvet. She wore an oversized tunic, which she distinctly remembered not wearing last night. After rubbing some of the grains of sleep from her puffy eyes, she heard a deep male voice from the kitchen. It was not Ezra's.

She immediately sprung up, and looked at herself in the mirror. She looked rough. Grey splotches painted her under eyes, and her bi-colored eyes were puffy and red. Her auburn hair was frizzed up and in tangles. She needed a bath, desperately.

Head aching, she rubbed at the sore spot that she had fallen, looking for blood. In her distress, she mostly healed the more severely injured parts of her own body. Her thoughts were slow, but despite the traumatic events of the previous night, she could not stop thinking of who changed her clothes and saw her bare tits and underwear.

Smiths be damned if it wasn't Petra who undressed her.

Rubbing her head, her feet lazily glided from her bedroom and straight into the bathroom where she washed up. The remnants of her scrapes and bruises ached at the warm water and soap, but they had already started to heal beautifully from her Gift. The major gash from the teeth of her perpetrator had closed, but coagulated blood and open skin burned. She gritted her teeth while washing the blood and dirt from the area, which caused her a slight limp still.

Muffled conversation from the kitchen reached her ears, and she was pretty sure those voices belonged to Petra and Hagan. When she walked out in her silken robe, they both looked at her cautiously. Hagan must have stayed the night, but where? Her thoughts immediately turned a few shades darker. A soft smile reached his lips, sympathy turning his eyes a soft sea green. He and Petra stood at the counter, both their eyes trained on her movement.

Petra rushed up to where she stood and hugged her, questions flowing out of her. "Are you okay? Did that motherfucker touch you?"

Petra pulled her back and examined her head to toe. She was reminded of Hagan's presence as he said softly, "He didn't really get the time to."

Raising a thick eyebrow at her, his surprisingly soft gaze examined her face and body for injury once over.

"What does that mean?" Petra asked, looking into her swollen eyes. The morning light danced against them as she went to sit down on the leather couch and tell her what they had experienced. She and Hagan, together.

She sighed. "So I think I broke the guy's legs." Petra's wide stare did not leave her face as sat down in the adjacent chair.

"What?"

She continued, her voice a bit shaky. "He had me against a wall while I was on my walk… and I just did it. He was a *bhiastera*, clearly drunk. I think he would've raped me if…" and looked at Hagan for reassurance.

He was staring intensely at her and nodded. A small message that he wanted her to sway the truth a bit, and not mention the murder he may have committed.

"I was just going to run from him, but then General Hagan showed up. He arrested the guy and he'll be facing the rest of his life in a faraway prison." She said slowly, making sure to keep her voice even and believable. Her gaze shifted from Petra to Hagan and noticed a small smile pass over his full lips. The emotion in his soft gaze made her blush, and turned his face even more handsome, it was pride.

Petra was speechless. "I would've ripped him to shreds… Smiths be damned. A drunk *bhiastera* beta loser. I wish you would have saved him for me." She said pointedly toward Hagan. Maeve rose from the couch and walked to get herself some coffee from the hot pot. Petra immediately shot up to tend to her. Ripping the mug from her hands, Petra poured her a cup of coffee, tossing a splash of milk in with it.

She met her icy blue eyes. "I'm actually good though. Things could have gone a lot worse, very quickly. I guess I can protect myself more than I thought."

Her small shoulders shrugged. She turned around to face Hagan, who was now standing just across the counter from her. His deep green eyes seeped into hers. Inhaling the rich aroma of her coffee with milk, her eyes closed and mind drifted.

Sharp lines and green eyes looked up at her in an unfamiliar room. The room was lined with floor-to-ceiling windows that donned deep red velvet curtains, and he was wearing extremely fine clothes that had to be much more expensive than a General could afford. Those eyes looked up at her lovingly, and he took a light sip of the coffee. That familiar warm buzzing crawled over her skin at his Smith-blessed face. The fine coffee he sipped smelled like nothing she had ever smelled. Sweet, but spicy.

Her eyes eased open, widening at the sight of him standing in her small, barely decorated home. He cocked his head, squinting his eyes at her lapse in concentration.

He must have decided she was okay. "Well, I'm glad you're doing fine. No one deserves to be used like that, and pathetic dickless males like him deserve to be punished. I'll be taking my leave now, I have some duties to attend to." His brief smirk and kind eyes left a warm, fuzzy feeling deep in her chest. He grabbed his coat from the couch. She was relieved, he must have slept there. With a wave, he said goodbye and strode out without another word.

Petra groaned. "For a male, he is nice to look at."

She laughed softly. "He is something."

→» →» «← «←

The following days seemed to drag on. While she had not seen or heard anything of Hagan in the days past, her thoughts were consumed by him.

What he did for her the night of her attack, and the morning after, left something with her. A curiosity that she needed to explore with him, and with herself. As if something awakened in her that was completely new. Not just in him, but in herself as well. She had never used her Gift to hurt before, and he was unphased at what she had done. If anything, he seemed as if he was proud of her.

He was ridiculously handsome, with an air of class to him that she had never witnessed from those in Blarra. His arrogance was rather difficult at times as well, but she supposed with such power he was allowed to be an ass about it… sometimes. His power was obviously far greater than hers, and though they had played their short game together she doubted she would see him again. A General with two Gifts, something she could only attribute to being Born, would not be interested in anything more than a tryst with someone of her minor power.

Her wounds were completely healed— something she could thank her lesser power for— and on Thursday she gathered the courage to take a walk on the main road after she closed the Apothecary early. The day had a chill to it, and she was glad she was wearing her large wool sweater and knitted scarf. She peeked into the Inn, smelling the intoxicating scent of roasted meats and rich cheeses. Warmth invited her inside, the large hearth had a roaring fire that lit the space.

Through the delicious food smells, she caught sight of a tall male with a dark brown head of hair sitting at one of the tables. He turned to meet her eyes, somehow sensing her presence. He rose from his seat and went to the counter, ordering some toasted bread, dried meats, and a few fine cheeses served with grapes on the side. Hagan clearly got enough for three or so to eat.

She strode toward him confidently and reached him at the counter while he was waiting for his platter. He paid the female a Gold, she noticed, which was still far too much for the large amount of food he ordered.

"I think we need to talk." She said to Hagan firmly, unwavering.

Hagan received his tray and looked at her. She swore she saw a hint of fear in his eyes. Fear of her? That couldn't be right. He's the one who told a guy to fuck rocks for the rest of his life.

However, she presumed her new ability to break bones may cause him some unease. They walked together to his table, and sat down to face each other. She took the liberty of filling her plate from his ridiculously large amount of food and filled her glass from the bottle of deep red wine he had on the table prior. She looked up at him expectantly. He appeared completely unphased by her presence as he also filled his plate and glass.

"Well? Are you going to explain anything that happened the other night?" Her eyes searched his, which now looked at her intensely.

She shivered.

Hagan took a long drink from his wine and whispered. "Yes, I was Born and was given two different Gifts. Yes, I made that guy suffer. Yes, he deserved it. No, the Brigade does not know that I am also a *cleasiera*, other than a few close confidantes. And you will not tell anyone of what happened the other night. I appreciate your discretion the other day to your roommate, and I would really appreciate it if you kept it to yourself. I'd like to only be the General who earned his place here, not a Born."

His eyes did not leave hers as he said every word with the utmost seriousness. A smirk found his lips. "Are we good?"

She just stared at him, and she let the smallest flirty gaze peek through. "Absolutely. I just wish I could've done what you did myself." She smiled happily, showing all of her teeth.

Hagan's eyes darkened, and she felt his power surge a bit in frustration. "Did you feel the sentence was just?"

His tone made her face warm. "Yes. The guy fucking deserved everything he was given. I'm just glad I could wash his disgusting scent off of me and out of my bed. Thanks for changing my clothes by the way. I hope you enjoyed the show." She purred the last few words.

Hagan's body tensed.

Loosening up after a moment, he let out a low laugh. "You have quite the wicked mouth, I haven't heard a female speak like that in quite a long time. Except your roommate, that is." His laugh continued, a deep chuckle from his chest.

She countered; her eyebrows raised in amusement. "Oh believe me, Petra is much, much, worse. In the best way."

He laughed in agreement. That laugh reverberated through her, a sound that she hoped to hear more. His face turned more serious. "I have a proposition for you, Maeve."

She looked at him curiously, her head cocking a bit to the side. He grinned, showing his marvelous for the smallest second. He had her full attention. She nodded, urging him to continue as

57

she popped a grape in her mouth.

Hagan's gaze drifted to her mouth, then slowly back up to her eyes.

"I want you to join my Brigade as a Healer."

She nearly choked on the grape.

CHAPTER 8
The General

Her mind was going a million different directions. They sat there in silence, her astonishment rendering her voice useless. How could she even think of joining the Brigade? Her life— and those who she considered family —were in Blarra. Ezra and Petra were the best friends she had ever known, especially Petra, who had felt like a necessity in figuring out this strange world.

Did she really want to stay in Blarra forever? She knew that she could do so much more if given the chance, and she had seen so little of the realm. Moving to the Second Kingdom and becoming a healer in one of the King's armies was considered a major privilege that she could not take lightly.

After staring at the table for a long moment, she looked up at Hagan. She noticed a look in his eyes that caused her cheeks to heat. He looked at her like she was the only one in the room, every fiber of his being focused on her answer. She eyed him for a moment, trying to imagine what her life would be like under his employ.

She finally found her words. "So, what would this entail? Payment? Length of Service? Citizenship to the Second Kingdom? I don't really know what else to ask to be honest with you, but I feel like I need more information before just jumping into this." Her eyes were a bit wide with embarrassment, she had never been offered such a thing. This felt like the right thing to do, negotiate.

He looked at her in that familiar thoughtful way, as if reading her mind. "Obviously you're not forced to agree. You would heal the soldiers when they were seriously hurt. Your rank would be a Sergeant, answering to me." He smirked slightly, eyes flashing humorously, and continued. "The length of service is up to you. If you don't feel fulfilled, you can quit whenever you like and we replace you, of course. Good *helbrederas* are pretty hard to find, and even harder to recruit. Especially one as... talented as you are. Luckily for you, it gives you many benefits. Speaking of that, the pay will be at least ten times what you currently bring in, your own estate in the Second Kingdom, and your own horse."

Her eyes returned to the table; she idly pushed a grape around on her plate. That was certainly a lot of things to be given for serving as a healer.

She nodded. "I mean I would need a few weeks to prepare, sell the shop, and what about... what about my friends? Ezra and Petra?"

Hagan frowned. "You're worried about your roommates and your little Apothecary here in Blarra when I offer to change your life? Of course you are." He shook his head, smiling softly.

She cocked her head at him. What does that mean?

Instead of blurting out her inner thoughts, she spoke a different truth. "Yes, I feel a bit responsible for them. They're like my family. I know you must know what it's like to have a family. Being Born and all."

Eyes glazing over in sadness, she realized how much it had meant to her to have built her small 'family' in Blarra.

Hagan shook his head. "Look, I get it. You have a life here. But you admitted yourself that you are not content, that you want more. Why not take the opportunity? As for the family thing, I am a firm believer that blood does not define who your family is. Even those of us who have families aren't perfect." His emerald gaze drifted to a spot behind her. "However, I thought of Petra in the case that you do join us."

Hagan took a sip of wine, clearing his throat. "She would be extremely valuable as a soldier in the *bhiastera* legion, and there just so happens to be a spot open after the other night's events." His mouth stretched into a sinful grin, setting her cheeks and ears aflame.

"I have seen her saber-toothed form, and she could be quite lethal on the battlefield against smaller *bhiasteras* like the wolfish, and definitely to the rebels. As for her personality, I admire her hunger. We need that sort of energy in the Brigade." He nodded, speaking much more like a General now. All business.

She did not much appreciate the distasteful way he spoke of *ganeras*, or as he called them rebels, but at the same time was not surprised that he thought so low of them, considering his great power would set any other Fae in shadow.

She furrowed her eyebrows. "And Ezra?"

Hagan frowned deeply, his eyes lighting up in an envious green hue. He almost looked like he was jealous of Ezra, and of what he meant to her. She shook her head and continued her stare at Hagan, waiting for him to respond.

He sighed. "That *nadura* boy that is clearly pining after you, the one who follows you around this tiny village like a starving animal, would not be of much use to us. He does not appear at all battle-trained and we don't stay in one place long enough for him to be our personal gardener." Venom coated his last words, causing her to roll her eyes. Irritation creased his features. Her eyebrows rose. "Wow, you're really convincing me with the asshole act. You may be a fancy, handsome, powerful General with lots of influence but your Smith Complex is going to be a problem for me. I don't do well under poor management." Pride erupted in her chest, she enjoyed challenging him like this.

Hagan smiled broadly. "Handsome, huh?" He grinned from ear to ear, head tilted up in an over-confident manner. His tongue scraped his teeth in an irresistible swipe, bringing out his deep smile lines and setting her teeth on edge. She could not stop thinking about how ridiculously handsome he was, his effortless way of charming her.

Her dry eyes blinked and saw Hagan under her, and she felt his hands on her generous hips as she straddled him on a lavish four-post bed adorned with private white curtains that tumbled around them. He was warm beneath her, and more importantly she felt his rock-hard length resting between her legs. She felt the heat of it pulsing against her for the briefest second. His chest was laid bare before her, all deep lines and angles, and his green eyes looked at her hungrily as he smiled.

The same smile that she saw when she opened her eyes. Her eyes softened slightly. Her imagination of this male was beginning to scare her, she was way too wound up to even be around him.

She could not help but giggle. "Don't get too cocky there, your highness." Hagan's eyes turned a shade lighter.

Her smile grew. "I'll think about it, ok? I need a day to think. Then a week to join the Brigade officially, if that is what I choose." Pushing down the feeling she got when these daydreams caught her off guard, she was proud of how she handled this. She stood, gulped down the remainder of her wine, grabbed another grape off the barely touched platter, and walked past him to the exit of the Inn. He watched her walk away, hips swishing generously. She felt his eyes watching her leave.

She had to talk to Petra. She could not talk to Ezra, that task would have to wait until she was sure what she wanted. The Apothecary and her small life was enough for her. Part of her did always think she could do more, and she always wanted to meet and heal more than the occasional townie. She reached the Apothecary, barely noticing her monotonous movements until she reached the swirling black staircase. When she went upstairs, she heard Petra in her room.

She strode toward her door and knocked, Petra opened up almost immediately and told her to come in.

She plopped down on Petra's unmade bed. "I need to talk to you." Joining her, Petra leaned over.

"What's going on?" Petra fixed an icy stare on Maeve.

Not sparing much detail, she told Petra what Hagan had asked of her, including the part about Petra coming with. It was difficult for Petra not to interrupt, the questions growing in her deep, sky blue stare, but she listened intently.

She looked at Petra expectantly. Petra was really thinking about this, the gears in her mind turning and calculating.

"I know this is going to sound crazy. I have always wanted to travel the kingdoms, and lately, I've been feeling like I really need a challenge. Hunting isn't as fun as it sounds, and this offer sounds pretty great to me. It would be a huge change, but I think if we do it together we could really make a life for ourselves in the Second Kingdom. Ignisiem is vast, and personally I feel that I have only seen a facet of it." Sincerity turned Petra's eyes a darker, calmer blue.

Well, that was unexpected.

She stuttered. "I-I'll be honest, I didn't expect you to accept so quickly."

Petra put her hands on hers and squeezed tightly.

Her eyes looked lovingly at Maeve. "You're too good for Blarra, Maeve. I think maybe I might be too, and we should all move on to greater things eventually, right? I mean honestly, what's stopping us from doing this?" Petra squinted her eyes, reading every emotion off of her face.

"I know you're worried about Ezra, but he took care of himself before and maybe this is an opportunity to get over you." Petra looked up suddenly, hearing a sound. "Someone's at the door."

A crisp knock resounded on the main door of the upstairs.

They both stood suddenly, and Petra growled. "Did you lock the Apothecary?"

It was strange for someone to knock on our interior door, as they would have had to pick the lock of the Apothecary to reach it.

"Yeah, of course."

Petra stalked toward the door, and she watched from a bit farther back. They were dead quiet as Petra put her ear to the door and listened. She whipped open the door, her claws extended, and there was nothing. Bending down for something, Petra picked it up and turned to her.

Petra smirked. "Second Kingdom seal." Maeve snatched it up, ripped it open, and went to sit on the couch. The letter read:

Maeve,

Before you so dramatically walked off on me, I was going to tell you something else. The Crown will take care of selling the Apothecary, and make sure it goes to a worthy buyer. They can even make sure the buyer is a helbredera, *as you wish.*

You do not require any belongings other than what you can fit in a bag, The Second Kingdom will pay for everything you may need in your transition.

We depart at 7:00 in the morning in three day's time. I hope that you'll be there.

I await your decision at the Inn, Room #2.

Regards,
Hagan

She dropped the letter to her lap, and Petra snatched it from her and read it out loud.

"Well shit, we better tell Ezra." Petra said, teeth clenched.

Her eyes roamed around the apartment that they lived in for eight years together. "I don't know if I'm ready for this! Three days to completely change my life that I built with you guys. It just seems like we're being a bit hasty."

Petra laughed. "The Forge gives us one life, nothing more and nothing less to do with what we choose. When else will you or I get an opportunity like this? There's so much more world to see, and I think we can both be trained to harness our Gifts even more than we already do. Let's not waste it."

She smiled softly, staring at the letter still clutched in Petra's grasp. "You're right. This is what part of me has always wanted. The more adventurous part, that is. I feel like I've reached my full potential here, which I suppose isn't saying much."

"You still have so much to learn; you are so young. Now's the time. We may lose Ezra, but he will move on eventually. It will be good for him to be rid of you anyways, maybe he can finally focus on doing better in his life, too."

She looked at Maeve, her ice blue eyes sparkling in excitement. She shook her head, Petra was right.

"Fuck it," She said bluntly, returning Petra's excited gaze and letting a smile meet her lips.

A lopsided, sarcastic smile found Petra's full lips. "So… a yes?"

She nodded in confirmation, her eyes twinkling in both delight and fear. They embraced and heard Ezra walking up the stairs. A silent agreement passed between them; they would tell Ezra the next day.

The following day, Petra and Maeve both made it a point to get up and bathe early to prepare for their departure and tell Ezra everything. Their decision to leave affected him too since he lived with them, worked with them, and had almost no one but them. She walked out to the kitchen first, and Ezra was beginning to boil some water for coffee. The sun was hitting his dark curls in a way that made them reflect copper. He turned around to face her, and he smiled broadly.

"Mornin' Maeve."

The gaze she returned was not as happy.

"What's wrong?" he asked, eyebrows furrowed as Petra walked out to meet them.

She sighed. "We have some things to tell you, Ezra. You may want to sit."

He made it very difficult. They sat down at the counter and she explained to him that they were leaving to join the General and they were going to join the Brigade, leaving in two days time.

Petra cut in at parts, but she finally finished by saying, "He only recruited me and Petra, so you will have to stay here. I'm so sorry for springing this on you at the last minute."

She shook her head, looking toward Petra for reassurance.

Ezra just looked at the ground, waiting what felt like ages

before saying a word. His face was like stone.

He snarled, "So you fucking this guy now or something, Maeve? That's great. Go be with the rich and powerful General and leave me here, alone."

Petra growled in warning. "You don't own her, Ezra."

Maeve cut in. "So, you guys are just going to talk about me like I'm not here, huh? This is not something I took lightly. You are like family to me Ezra, the most like family that any of us could wish for, but I want to do more than run this fucking A-"

Ezra interjected, his voice rising to a volume that she had never heard from him before. "Smith damn it Maeve, I don't want to be your family!"

She had never seen him lose his temper.

Weeds had started sprouting up and through the windows, signaling his loss of restraint on his Gift.

He continued, "I just thought that maybe one day you would come around, we could try and start a *real* family."

A piece of her broke, clean in half. He knew that's the thing she always wanted. Just not with him.

Petra was ready to pounce on Ezra, claws extending.

She flashed her reassuring eyes toward the feline predator, she knew that this needed to be handled by herself.

"Ezra… I'm sorry. I am so sorry for not returning your feelings. It has eaten me up for years. It's time for me to move on. As for what you said about Hagan… I'll lay with whoever I want. No one owns me. Whether it be him or any other tall and handsome soldiers that catch my eye, I am free to do as I please. Which includes becoming the *helbredera* for the 22nd Brigade."

Tears stung in the ducts of her eyes, but her voice did not waver.

Ezra's anger had subsided, but tears began to pool in his hazel eyes. "I'm sorry."

He hopped up and strode toward the door and out of the Apothecary. Petra and Maeve sat in silence, and she brushed away the one tear that had almost found its way down to her lips.

An echo of humor laced Petra's voice. "That went well."

CHAPTER 9
THE POWER

The following two days before they joined the Brigade were a whirlwind. Petra and Maeve were rushing to pack up their entire lives, which turned out to be more than they expected.

All of the loose ends were tightened, except for the two most important things. Ezra had been staying with a friend, who he planned to stay with once she and Petra had left Blarra. He had avoided her at every occasion, forgoing his duties at the Apothecary and staying out in the Gardens of Blarra. She didn't blame him, just wished things were different between them.

There was another thing. She needed to respond to the letter on the night before, and she had complete intentions of doing it face to face.

Icy winds attacked her exposed cheeks as she headed to the Inn. She went straight to the staircase and to the top floor to search for Room #2. When she walked up to the door, and saw the small silver plaque that read *2*, she stopped.

She let out a huge sigh of nervous breath and knocked at the door. Bright green eyes met hers as he opened the wooden door, which creaked at the movement.

Hagan was wearing casual clothes, a light tunic accompanied by loose fitting pants that slung around his hips effortlessly. Her eyes wandered to the exposed V that led down and down to places undiscovered.

"Can I come in?" She still stood in the hall, awkwardly shifting her weight between her two feet.

Hagan nodded and moved over to make room for her to walk into his small room. There was a large bed in the corner, with an oil lamp sitting on the side table. On the other side of the room was a quaint fireplace, which crackled merrily into the chilled air. The heat from it made the room comfortably warm and spread the rich smell of smoking wood throughout the small space. After she admired the flames licking at the logs in the fireplace, Hagan walked over to her with a glass of wine he had gotten from the small table and chairs that sat at the far corner of the room.

"Thank you." She looked up at him, smiling politely.

In this proximity he seemed much larger.

Hagan nodded and looked her over, a few messy locks of hair falling over his forehead. "I assume you have an answer for me? In the final hour, I see."

A smile tugged at the side of his mouth.

She leaned against the mantle, letting the fire warm her and give her confidence. Her eyes met his, the amber one enhanced by the dancing flames.

Wanting to exude confidence, she straightened her shoulders. "We have decided to join you." Sipping the wine, she tasted a hint of fresh strawberries.

His eyes softened with relief. His posture relaxed significantly.

Her smile felt a bit silly. "I did have one question, though."

She bit her lower lip and Hagan nodded, eyes on her mouth.

"Why me?" Her eyes slid to his unmade bed, and back to his disheveled mess of hair atop his head.

Hagan let out a chuckle, rubbing his eyes in the process. The sound musically went in one ear and danced through her skull before exiting the other.

She raised an eyebrow. "Well?"

Hagan closed the distance between them, the green of his irises turning almost neon in the fire's flickering light. "You need to stop doubting yourself. There is a great power inside you, and I can see it in your work. Not just that, I feel it when you let those walls down. Power." His breath was sweet, and nearly close enough to her face that she wanted to reach out and taste his mouth. "You have just reached the tip of your potential. But you will see. With me, us." He explained, correcting himself.

She breathed in the smoky scent of the fireplace, backing away to take him in. His magnificent figure was easily discernible through his almost see-through tunic. His eyes were on her, and humor played across his angled face. He thought she was powerful, and his gaze made her feel as such. Her body reacted to his words, warmth pooling inside her, and her mind drifted to the bed only a few feet away. She tousled her auburn hair that was burning bright red from the hearth's flame, collected herself, and attempted keeping her tone even.

"Well, for whatever reason, I am glad. I think this change will be the best thing for my future, and for me." She smiled shyly.

"I hope so." He said, the crackling of the logs beginning to fill the silence between them.

"Bright and early, General." She said, taking a long sip of the wine and lifting her hand in a haphazard salute.

He reached out his hand, grasping her arm at the wrist. She did the same to him, the handshake came naturally. She had seen him do it with others, it was a sign of respect. "Good night, Sergeant." The strength of his hand pricked excitement in the hairs standing up on her skin.

Her eyes met his. "Maeve, just always call me Maeve and maybe this will feel less mad. Goodnight, your highness."

Lips tugging at the corner of her mouth, she handed him the glass of wine back.

She breathed deeply. His scent of fresh rainwater and wine made her steps falter as she strode to the door.

Hagan set down both glasses on the mantle and walked her to the door. He held it open, and she turned to him as she stepped out of the hall.

"See you in the morning, Maeve," he breathed, giving her

the most beautiful, sleepy smile that made her cheeks turn a soft pink as she nodded and walked downstairs and out to sleep in her bed for the last time.

CHAPTER 10
THE VINES

Naturally, she only got a few hours of sleep. She did not remember much from being a Forged youngling, but she recalled sleepless nights of excitement before a big day, like her birthday. Calling it that sounds silly, as no youngling in the First Village was truly Born, but the adult Fae who took care of the new Forged younglings did not seem to care about the difference.

The first village, Geneza, did not have many luxuries. However, her keeper— a *ganera* female with kind brown eyes— would always scrounge up what she could to give the younglings treats to celebrate the day they were brought by the Messengers. They called her Lady El, short for Eliza. As far back as she knew, she had been caring for younglings for hundreds of years as it seemed to be her true Smith's given purpose.

Messengers were rarely spotted, only delivering new Forged in the darkness of night. Those who may have caught a glance recall them as shadows that come as quickly as they leave. No one truly knows where they come from, where the Smiths forge the dwellers of Ignisiem. Some believed them to watch from the sky, others thought they were far underground, but no one had ever encountered a Smith, let alone the Forge.

She bathed in her copper claw-foot tub for the final time. The hot water awakened her bones and prepared her for the long journey ahead. It was important for her to make a good impression on the other soldiers, even if she wasn't expected to fight like them. Attempting to look like a higher-ranking Fae, she donned a bit of makeup and put her hair in a long auburn braid down her back for travel. She wasn't sure what to wear, but she landed on black leggings, a thick tunic, a cloak, and her old leather boots. Hagan did say she would be provided with what she needed. Hopefully that included some new clothes.

She walked out and heard Petra digging around her room. They both agreed to donate their belongings they did not need to the Inn, the owner agreed to give out their things to those in greater need throughout Blarra. By six, they were both ready and headed down with their bags in tow. There was still no sign of Ezra, even his room was emptied out.

With the autumn breeze cooling their cheeks and the smells of dew-covered earth growing with every step, Petra and Maeve walked down the cobblestone path to their new lives.

They chattered anxiously as they walked the distance to the Lake. Passing the town garden, they caught no sight of Ezra. It was still quite early, so none of the common townsfolk had yet ventured out to the cobblestone street. Mornings in Blarra were always her favorite time; there was something calm about a deserted, small town.

A tinge of sadness plagued her busy mind. "I really hate to leave things with Ezra like this," she said quietly, side-eyeing Petra as they walked.

Anger brimmed in Petra's icy stare. "The immature bastard didn't have any right to talk to you like that. He deserves whatever sorrow he is feeling. You weren't his to lose."

She sighed. "He loved me, Petra. He loves us. We are family, or as close to it as the Forged can get." The rocks shrouding the Lake came into view. They heard the faintest sound of a large group beyond the rocky outcropping.

Petra nodded slowly. "I know, it does sadden me, but none of it matters now. We have each other. You are my best friend and

I refuse to leave your side. No matter where we end up."

She smiled, but then heard quick steps behind them as they reached the rocks.

"Maeve!" Ezra yelled; his voice hoarse from running.

She and Petra whirled around as Ezra reached them. Petra growled in warning, and her canines began to lengthen, sharp at the ends.

Ezra caught his breath and looked warily at Petra. "Listen, I know I don't deserve to tell you anything. If I didn't do it, I'd regret it forever. I love you Maeve. I have loved you ever since the first day I met you. I want you to stay here with me. I want us to be together."

His hazel stare brimmed with desperation. He grasped her hands. "Please."

She shook her head, unable to speak. His grasp was tighter than she would have preferred, and she had never seen this shade of desperation in his eyes.

A smell of fresh dirt filled her nostrils. Slight wispy noises rose to her ears, the sound of quickly sprouting plants. She felt vines from the rocks encircling her ankles.

Looking from Ezra to the vines, a strange mix of anger and fear flooded within her. "What do you expect me to do with that Ezra? I made it very clear that I only wanted to be friends, and you couldn't handle that. I'm sorry, I don't love you like that. Like how you claim to love me." She struggled against the vines, but they just grew tighter around her ankles and crawled up her calves. "Now release me. Don't do this."

Petra walked forward, claws coming out of her nails. "If you don't let her go I'm going to rip out your throat, Ezra. Family or not. You get one chance."

Thunder erupted in the now darkened sky. Wisps of her hair stood on end, and a tickle danced down her spine. Power surged around them, and Ezra stumbled back in horror when he spotted him. Hagan jumped down from the rocks that separated them from the Lake. She could have sworn the ground shook beneath her when he landed.

His expression looked lethal, lightning beginning to erupt

73

against his green irises as he stepped forward and spoke. "Do we have a problem, *nadura?*"

He scanned the scene, his eyes landing on the vines now up to her thighs. Panic settled in as she wriggled against them, but they would not budge. Ezra's eyes stayed on Hagan; he was still. Ezra spoke to her, but his eyes were still on Hagan. "You're really going to go with this guy? This isn't you."

She clenched her fists, feeling her Gift pushing against her skin. "Let me go, Ezra. I don't want to hurt you."

Ezra's eyes snapped to Petra, who was now shifting into her saber-toothed form.

His voice began to shake. "You wouldn't hurt me. I know you love me back."

Lightning erupted three feet away from Ezra. Hagan strode the remaining few feet forward and stood dangerously close to Ezra, looking down as he had a head on Ezra.

"Leave now, *nadura* boy." Thunder erupted in the sky above, storm clouds gathering at a rapid rate. Hagan's eyes began to glow a devious color of green, and the earth beneath Ezra started to shake.

Hagan's voice boomed over the crack of the thunder. "If it were up to me, you would be a burnt crisp of a male. Since it is not, you get one chance to release her, or I will shake the ground beneath you until you fall into its deep, fiery depths. Choose wisely, boy."

Maeve winced, the vines growing ever tighter. "I've got this, Hagan."

Ezra's gaze stayed on Maeve, and he laughed. "The good guy never fucking wins, does he? After all I've done for you."

Ezra shrieked in pain.

Her eyes were pooling with tears, but her hands began to glow. He had stepped close enough, and she grasped his hand with an unyielding force. In her frustration, she shattered his phalanges. She knew they would heal easily, almost any *helbredera* could heal fingers with ease.

His vines faltered just below the tops of her thighs. Ezra shrieked again from the pain she caused. He released his vines' grip, tripping back and away from her Gift's range. The skin on her palms glowed faintly with a minimal use of power.

He sank to the uneven ground, tears running from his eyes.

Surprise bubbled in her, she never thought she'd be able to have such control of her Gift, or harness it to hurt so easily. But now she had done it twice, both times when she was put under pressure. She shivered. "I did warn you."

Hagan glared down at Ezra. "Go, *nadura* boy. She is a Sergeant of the 22nd Brigade now. If you even dare to think in her direction again, I will personally end your miserable existence. Is that clear?"

Her eyes flitted to Hagan, a new anger brewing in them, then looked back to her attacker and friend. "Go, Ezra. We don't want any harm to come to you."

Petra returned that with a hiss, the dark fur of her saber-toothed form shifting a blue tint in the sun's first rays. Maeve could only assume she did not agree.

Ezra stood, cradling his hand. His voice was broken. "Bye, Maeve. I wish things could be different." He ran off back to the village, his stagger embarrassingly clumsy.

Hagan summoned a lightning bolt five feet ahead of Ezra, an extremely dangerous warning.

Her anger boiled over. "What's your fucking problem?"

He looked at her in shock, feigning innocence. "Just lighting the way for him."

She could have sworn Petra let out a small growl that mimicked a laugh.

CHAPTER 11
THE SERGEANT

Dark storm clouds retreated from the sky, her muscles strained as she made the climb over the rocks to reach the shore of Blarra's dark blue Lake. Petra glided effortlessly in her stunning saber-toothed form. Her large paws grasped each crevice with expert dexterity, her ice blue eyes brighter than ever. Her teeth were long and sharpened, they were her most dangerous weapon. In her saber-toothed form, she could tear through the body of another with the right motivation.

When she looked toward the other side of the dark blue lake, she saw all eyes were on her. There were about two hundred Fae standing before her when she made it to the camp, some only for a moment while running errands before the departure.

They seemed to be oddly color-coated by stripes on their coat sleeves, or even scraps of fabric around their heads. She could tell who the *bhiasteras* were in their bloodthirsty reds, some in their wolfish or hawkish forms. She couldn't help but think of her part in the killing of one of their comrades. Not that the bastard didn't deserve it.

There was a small group of females accompanied by one male who bore purple stripes, they were all impossibly attractive. She was not sure, but she assumed they were *cleasieras* because one group couldn't possibly be perceived as that good looking unless tricked to. That was an interesting way to make a good first impression, with lies. A group of about nine or ten were chattering outside of their tent, which was decorated with varying shades of blue on the entrance. The *aimsuras* wore light blue bands and sunny attitudes. That explained the nicer than usual weather.

Most of the group wore beige or brown. A few of them were heavily muscled and lifted large sacks of supplies, the brown must represent the *treaniera*. The cream colored, about eighty of the soldiers, must be *ganera* —who had no power except for their wills and Smith-given grit.

The colors were used to divide, to segregate all the different Fae with Gifts and without Gifts. It was intentional, and it was clear those here enforced the hierarchy of power with something as simple as uniform color.

After scanning the group and smiling awkwardly at them, she and Petra strode through the crowd to find a pale-yellow tent that was being taken down by some of the *ganera*. They reached this central area while others were working to get the tents down and packed onto the horses. They stopped and Hagan turned to her. "This is the *helbredera*'s tent, you will have everything you need in here to heal. We do have another *helbredera*, somewhere around here. She cannot do many of the things you are able to, due to her breeding, but she has served us well nonetheless." He looked down on the ground as if looking for a small animal.

She nodded; the space was more than adequate for a few soldiers at a time.

Two males walked up to flank Hagan, and she could only assume they were also Sergeants. They both bore small, silver pins on their lapels. One had a bright red ruby adorned, in the shape of a teardrop. The other was a deep purple stone, presumably amethyst, that was oddly shaped like an eye.

She introduced herself to a gorgeous male named Mikael. His light blonde hair was styled to perfection and his ivory skin did not have one single blemish. He gazed at her in curiosity, and something a bit darker.

He bore a purple stripe to match his brooch, and his voice was surprisingly deep. "We are excited to have you join us, Maeve." He kissed her hand, his sea-blue eyes glittering with questions.

Despite his best efforts, she was not in the least charmed by him. "Nice to meet you, Mikael. Thank you."

The other Sergeant, who had deep ebony-toned skin and a scar that tore across his full lips took her hand in a firm handshake. His golden eyes looked down fondly upon her, he had to be over six feet tall. His stripe was the deep red tone, matching the blood-likened brooch he bore.

"Good day, Maeve. We are blessed to receive such a Gifted *helbredera*, or at least that's how the General here swings it." He smiled, his straight white teeth shining.

She noted his large, pointed canines.

"I am the Sergeant of the *bhiastera*, but you can call me Elias." He was an exquisite looking male with broad shoulders, a strong jawline, and the type of gaze that warmed your heart. If she were being honest, the three males that stood before her were better looking than any male she had ever seen in Blarra.

She gave him a kind smile. "I do hope I can live up to your expectations, Elias." With a warm smile, he switched his gaze to Petra, who was standing there in her beast form.

"Who is this extraordinary feline friend of yours?" His golden eyes glittered.

Petra transformed right before their eyes into her stunning Fae form. In the standard Petra fashion, she was completely naked. Maeve's eyes widened, and she heard Hagan and Mikael chuckle. Elias cocked his head, and a dazzling smile appeared, accompanied by deep smile lines. Even more charming.

"I'm Petra. I hate to tell you, Elias. I won't be your beta bitch. And don't get any ideas, Sergeant. You are far from my type." If it weren't Petra speaking to Elias, it would be comical. However, it was Petra, so she imagined Elias was in for a rude awakening to think that she wouldn't make his life a nightmare.

A smirk found Petra's lips, and she walked, hips swaying and plump chest bouncing, into the *bhiastera* tent. *Bhiasteras* were no stranger to nudity, but Petra's physique was pretty impressive. Meeting someone for the first time in the nude was not customary for anyone. Elias crossed his arms, shaking his head.

A deep growl came from him. "We'll see about that, sweetheart." He turned back to Maeve, and shrugged.

Her face had turned scarlett. "I'm sorry about her."

Surrounded by the three males, she felt vulnerable. She corrected her posture, not wanting to seem unconfident.

Hagan smirked at Elias. "They came as a pair, sorry my friend."

Elias laughed, and it was sound of merriment that immediately caused her to smile. "Ah, it is no trouble. You know I like a challenge."

He winked at her, and he and Mikael walked away toward their respective groups. She was relieved, because between the three of them, the overload of masculine energy nearly overwhelmed her.

Her awareness shifted to Hagan. Her mouth curled into a frown. "The way you behaved earlier was extremely unnecessary. You could have killed Ezra."

Hagan looked around, his eyes wary. "Let's talk about this in private."

She rolled her eyes and followed him as he walked to a dark blue tent that must belong to him. He waved away his two *treaniera* guards who were about to tear down the tent and walked inside.

She whipped around to face him. "You could have killed him."

Hagan seemed to be towering over her in this low-ceiling tent. "He needed to know his place. He was a threat to you. I will not stand by and allow that sort of behavior towards my Sergeant."

She raised her eyebrows and her voice, "It was none of your business, and trust me, I had it under control. And don't play it off like you were protecting your liability. You wouldn't have done the same for Elias or Mikael. You did it because you don't think I can defend myself."

Heat spread across her face when Hagan's eyes found hers, his head tilting down to meet her height. "You really have no idea, do you? You think pathetic low-powered peasants like him should even associate with someone like you? He was completely out of line, and if it were up to me, he would have gotten much more than a few broken fingers."

His Gifts chilled the air around her. "As for Mikael and Elias, the difference is they would have never let it go that far. Mikael would have crippled that boy's mind the moment he tried to ensnare him with those silly little vines. While you simply stood there and tried to talk it out."

Suppressed anger brimmed to the surface.

"I'll have you know that before you showed up in Blarra I was a peasant too. And I'm not going to apologize for not using violence against one of my best friends. I don't just go around maiming others because I can. I am a healer before anything else." Without a second glance, she marched from the tent.

She heard him huff a swift "Fuck" as she pushed open the entrance of the tent and marched toward the yellow tent that now belonged to her.

CHAPTER 12
THE NYMPH

A tiny female with a pale-yellow stripe on her sleeve was fiddling with her long hair outside of the tent. She had to be two heads shorter than Maeve, the smallest living thing in the camp. The small female looked up at her anxiously, her shy voice ringing like a songbird. "Oh, hello... Sergeant." Her petite shoulders sagged a bit when she spoke her title.

She smiled sweetly at the short female. "No, you do not need to call me that. I hardly feel like a Sergeant myself. You and I are equals, we're just *helbrederas*. Nothing more." She continued. "You can just call me Maeve. What is your name?"

The female's lavender eyes widened; her small face could barely fit the doll-like stare as it was, but widening them made her look even more ethereal. She had dark eyelashes that blinked slowly up at Maeve, and the palest skin she had ever seen, almost translucent. Maeve noticed her semi-pointed ears, and her blue-black waist length hair braided loosely behind her back.

Her appearance was odd, but also beautiful. Her features could not be that of Fae. The female spoke softly. "Clover, my name is Clover. If you're wondering about my ears, my mother was a garden-nymph."

This surprised her, as she had barely ever heard the term

mother used in everyday life. To have a mother was a privilege, but considering the way Clover said mother, she could only assume she was no longer alive. Then again, the nymphs were not Forged by the Smiths, but existed on these lands eons before. They were born of nature, whether that be of the land or the sea. They were a piece of the realm.

She stammered. "Oh, I didn't mean to offend you. I have not met many nymphs. You are quite beautiful; I love your hair."

Clover giggled, a small rosy blush forming on her cheeks. "Oh! Thank you. Do not worry about offense, Miss Maeve. Curiosity is a Gift of its own, though I know you were granted a great Gift from the Forge. I am delighted to learn from you."

Clover looked up at her dreamily and stared into her eyes. Her lavender-hued irises had a wisdom behind them, and she wondered just how old Clover must be considering her bloodline. Since their energy was derived from nature, the nymphs could live for as long as land or sea continues to exist. Adding in the Fae blood must limit her life somewhat, but not by much.

A soft smile appeared on Clover's mouth, which was so small compared to her opalescent eyes. "You have the most intriguing eyes, Miss Maeve. It was a wonder to have met you."

With a slight bow of her head, she took her leave toward a small dark brown pony that held her belongings. Clover was a bit strange, but then what did she know about nymph culture? Clover was nothing but polite, even if her servant's attitude caused Maeve great unease.

Maeve roamed through the camp; many Fae were packing up but stopped to meet her. She met a few approachable *aimsuras*, as well as the unnaturally gorgeous *cleasieras* who always spoke like they were flirting with her. Many rugged *ganeras* introduced themselves with stiff bows. She quickly put a stop to such behavior and asked them about their lives. They showed her the scars they received from years of battle and rigorous training as a Second Kingdom soldier and spoke of the horrors of war.

One handsome caramel-skinned *ganera* showed a deep scar over his abdomen that should have been lethal. Parts of his skin were unrecognizable and healed sloppily. He would be considered quite attractive if it weren't for the shredded bits of skin and flesh that still protruded from his stomach. She learned his name was Conor.

Conor spoke of the battle with a distant stare. "Me and two fellow warriors fought the largest bearish *bhiastera* we had ever seen in battle. They fought with great bravery, but I am the only one who came out alive."

She frowned at the sorrow in his warm voice. "I am so sorry." Her Gift tingled her fingertips, a spark of something that surfaced from a duty that was Gifted to her along with her healing abilities. She wanted to help, or at least try. "Do you have a moment from your work?"

Conor nodded, and he followed her into one of the remaining tents that had not yet been taken down.

Her voice soothing, she instructed him. "Please lift up your shirt. I want to see if I can help you." Conor seemed to trust her immediately, and did as she asked, his eyes wide in wonderment.

Curiosity took over as she examined the damage. At least, she wanted to try and repair some of the destroyed tissue. Back at the Apothecary, she would only perform this difficult task to those whose faces would be affected by their vicious scarring. In Conor's case, it was only his abdomen, but her Gift urged her to heal the ragged skin. Not just the physical healing, but the mental healing of getting one's body back. She approached him and lifted her hands toward his stomach. Focus scrunched her eyebrows together and squeezed her eyes shut. Light sprung from her hands, and the familiar tingling sensation spread to the tips of her fingers as she traced across the ravaged abdomen. The light grew stronger, and the tissues began to regenerate around Conor's diagonally torn stomach.

He winced but looked down at her hands in shock. "H-How are you doing that? I barely feel it!" He watched as her hands slowly moved around the scar, and the skin and tissues around the scar merged to reveal his toned stomach.

His smile widened, amazement spreading across his handsome face as he revealed charmingly crooked teeth.

The tent opened, both she and Conor were surprised at the intrusion. She was too focused to notice who was standing there, but she couldn't break concentration. She finished up, sweat starting to drip down her back as she whipped her head around. Her amber eye glowed with the intensity of a new star as she looked at Mikael, the *cleasiera* Sergeant.

"Well, I can say with utmost confidence that I have never seen that before." His eyes were uncharacteristically wide with shock, and a smirk grew upon his plumped lips.

Conor looked down at his still exposed stomach and pulled in a sharp breath. The scar was now simply a long pink line that spanned from oblique to oblique. Not perfect, but a few thousand times better than it looked before.

Conor stepped back, and twisted around fully, trying out the new abdomen. "You fixed my pain. Smiths bless you, Sergeant." She spotted tears in his eyes as he went to shake her hand. She smiled and returned the handshake. "Just Maeve will do, and may the Smiths bless you as well, Conor."

Confusion furrowed Mikael's brow. "Good. Please return to packing duties, *ganera*. Sergeant, may I have a word with you?"

Conor bowed again to her, then Mikael, and jogged out to join the other working soldiers.

"I must confess. Our General did not give you enough credit, Maeve." He said her name like a new flavor of honey dripped from his soft pink lips. Mikael approached her.

Wiping the beads of sweat from her brow, she replied. "He didn't deserve to live with that pain and restraint, especially as a reminder of a *bhiastera* killing his friends, and almost him as well. So, I helped him. It took a fair amount of my energy, but I believe it was worth it." Her lips curved in a soft smile, and she tilted her eyes up to Mikael, who was only about four inches taller than her.

"Why would you choose to exert so much energy on a *ganera*?" Mikael asked, the last word acidic.

Her cheeks heated, her teeth biting her lip. "I do not see him as just a *ganera*. His existence is just as valuable as yours or mine. I don't give a fuck that the Smiths did not make him with a Gift.

He has many Gifts, just not those that this society deems worth anything."

He cocked his head, his perfect smile growing into a full grin. "Very well, then." He licked his lips, eyes trained on her. "A powerful, kind female like you is hard to come by. Hagan better keep you close."

She returned his sensual tone, mockingly. "Oh, don't worry. I am not his to keep close." The oceans of Mikael's eyes writhed, a smooth brow raised. She really could not help but make fun of him, he was a tad ridiculous.

A laugh bubbled from her; she shook her head. "See you later, Mikael."

As she exited the tent, one of the last ones still erect, she caught sight of a silvery mane. It's sheen reminded her of the color of the moon. The horse was black, the midnight hue contrasting against the shiny mane. A *ganera* walked the horse over to her. "Welcome, Sergeant. I am Ingrid. The General instructed me to give you one of our best horses. She is a fine steed, especially for beginner riders." The female *ganera* bowed, then set to prepare the saddle and bags for their departure.

Thanking Ingrid and grabbing the reins, her gaze shifted to Petra talking to other *bhiasteras*, including Elias, who had just finished packing his golden horse for the journey.

Before anything else, she hoped to clear the air about the punishment of their comrade. She wondered if they knew the extent of his sentence.

Petra smiled as she walked up. "Hey girl, are you ready to head out?"

She nodded to Petra and the small group of *bhiasteras*. "I think so."

A beautiful blonde female *bhiastera* spoke. "You did the right thing, you know." Maeve shook her head in confusion, her stare flitting from the female's dark brown eyes to Petra.

"I told them about the other night with the wolfish that tried to have his way with you. I also told them about your badassery and him getting the punishment he deserved. They hold no bad blood with you, apparently it wasn't the first time for the male. I knew you'd be worried about it, so I talked with them."

She was mildly stunned. The blonde stepped to her, shook her hand, and smiled softly at her. "He tried the same shit with me. I'm just glad you put him in his place."

Maeve lowered her voice. "I am truly sorry to hear that."

The blonde smiled, her dark brown eyes lowering in understanding.

A large, pale male spoke. "You really broke his legs?"

She looked around awkwardly and nodded. She received a few nods and many smiles from the group. As strange as it felt to have pride in herself, she did, and it was confirmed by the group of *bhiasteras*. Petra grabbed her hand, pulling her away.

"You guys can ask about the dirty details later." The group laughed. They were a bit more sadistic than she was expecting, but knowing Petra, she should not have been at all surprised.

"What do you think of all this? The others love me already, naturally." Petra said to Maeve, her smile almost reaching her ears.

That came as no surprise to her, as Petra has always been the social one.

She smiled, but it did not reach her ears. "Naturally. You'll be the Alpha of the pack in no time, I am sure of it."

She looked down, her eyes wary. Her body still felt a bit drained from the scar she healed earlier. She may have pushed a little hard, and needed time to recover.

Petra smiled sympathetically. "Do not worry, Maeve. I can feel your tenseness, and I know you're nervous about all of this. Just remember this." She grabbed the other hand, pulling Maeve to face her completely.

"You are just coming into your Gift. I have an easy eighty years on you, you know. Confidence comes in time, and I think you're just starting. You are incredible, you're going to kill. You have gotten more powerful every day that I have known you."

Petra's reassurance warmed her heart, breathing a new energy into her bones. "Well, to not kill would be ideal."

Petra scoffed, understanding her mix of words. "Ah, you know what I mean."

As they laughed together, happiness bloomed through her,

this new adventure in her life was just beginning and she planned to make the most of it.

CHAPTER 13
THE DAHLIA

The 22nd Brigade were packed in a group of about one-hundred and fifty horses, divided into groups of twenty each. Hagan and his Sergeants, now including Maeve, rode at the front of the group. They rode organized in rows by type of power, the *ganeras* taking up the rear both on foot and atop horses. Hagan slowed his large, white horse so that he was in step with her.

He looked over at her, curiosity alight in his vibrant gaze. "You are pretty good at this for someone who has never owned a horse."

She smirked. "Yeah, pretty good for a peasant."

Hagan sighed, then kept his voice low. "You know I do not think that of you. I am sorry if you thought that I meant that. You are so much more."

Confusion scrunched her face. "That's just it, Hagan. I am proud of where I come from. I am not angry because you think I am a peasant; I am angry because of the way you and your fellow Nobles think of the less privileged." A sigh left her lips. "I know that many think that way where you come from, but I do not. I refuse to treat others as if they are below me."

He nodded, his eyes staring thoughtfully into the wooded brush around them.

"I understand, I am sorry. It may not be much of an excuse, but I was raised to think this way. Where I come from, power is everything. It is just the way things are." He smiled, charming her. "I should have known you'd cause a stir. Many are speaking about the way in which you helped that *ganera* male. I'm sure he is thankful. You did what most *helbrederas* deem impossible."

He raised his eyebrows at her, and she smirked.

"Conor is good, he deserves to have his body back. Even the most skilled swordsman is going to struggle against razor sharp teeth and claws." She shook her head in disgust. "The least I can do is make his existence a little less terrible."

His eyes softened. "A little? You changed that male's life. He is indebted to you."

A soft smile found her lips. "I love to help these folk, to hear their stories. Not because I want any recognition, I don't want that at all. I simply want to help those who are suffering, in any way that I can."

He shook his head, a smile growing across his usually serious features. "I do believe you will do just that, Maeve. I am glad you're here."

Her heart skipped a beat, the rhythm of it faster than her horse's hooves against the soft ground.

→»→»«-«-

They rode until twilight cast its shadows upon the surrounding trees. There was a creek flowing through the loosely wooded forest, its water trickling lightly amongst the sounds of horse hooves and boots. The Brigade would sleep in a quick camp for the night, fires and bedrolls for the soldiers, and a mid-size tent for the Sergeants and General to share. Some *ganeras* quickly put up the tent, and the *bhiasteras* returned with some rabbit for dinner. The modest camp lit up with life in what felt like seconds.

She decided to sit with Clover, who warmed herself by the fire. Plopping down beside her, she smiled and grabbed a few slices of the roasted rabbit that was turning on the spit.

Clover turned her luminescent face to her. "How was the ride, milady?" Her light, enchanting voice rang through the hustle and bustle of the camp.

She gave the small female a kind smile. "Maeve, please. It was good! My ass is super sore though."

She shifted her weight to sit on one hip.

Clover let out a delightful, quiet giggle. "You are quite funny, Maeve."

Her long, inky lashes batted, and she looked down at the flower she was holding. Sickly, brown petals turned to a blossoming red dahlia in seconds.

Maeve gasped.

Clover looked up at her, her tiny smile beaming. "I am blessed with this Gift as well, from the garden nymph side of my family. My mother lived four-hundred years ago, before her death at my birth." Her face went sullen, her skin dulling to a slight grey. "She was a nymph, a powerful one. One of the Fae took her to his bed, despite her wishes. Her body could not handle me, being half-Fae, you see." Maeve covered her mouth, subduing her shock, and listened while her eyes glistened with fresh tears.

"I was told she looked like me, but her skin was the shade of ivy. She was the Guardian of the Greenhouse of a long-forgotten Nymph Kingdom that now belongs to the Third Kingdom. I am quite proud of her, and of the power she passed on to me."

Clover beamed with pride, but a shadow of sadness pierced her stare as she stroked the blood-colored petals of the dahlia.

"I'm excited to learn from you too, Princess of Flowers. I am sorry for what you suffered, even if it was before your birth."

Clover smiled softly and handed her the flower. She tucked it behind her ear and finished the strips of cooked rabbit she had been nibbling on. "I'm going to get some rest, you should too. Thank you, Clover."

She rose from her spot by the fire, and grabbed her bag from her horse who was tied to a near tree. She threw one of her blankets over her horse, who she decided to call 'Callistus'. She remembered seeing the word in an astronomy book when she lived in Geneza and thought it was fitting for a horse that would nearly disappear under the stars of the night sky.

She brushed Callistus' silvery mane. "Sleep well, Callistus."

With a soft nudge from the horse, she smiled and headed for the tent.

She took a calming breath before walking into the tent, knowing she was walking into a male's den. Holding open the curtains at the front, she stepped in to see a quaint tent with four corners, one for each of them. Mikael was writing in his journal but looked up and gave her a sly smile. Elias was changing his shirt for the night, and she spotted heavily muscled chest and abs that were highlighted by the flickering lamp beside him.

He pulled the new shirt onto his head and said, "Well, hello there Maeve. How did the mount serve you?"

She smiled. "Callistus was lovely, she is a beautiful horse."

Elias' golden eyes glimmered in the lamplight, and he nodded, a hint of curiosity in the tilt of his head.

Maeve nodded to them both and retreated to her corner, she noticed a lamp of her own along with a few other new belongings. A bedroll was laid out for her, with a few new articles of clothing. She noticed a warm fleece tunic, some dark brown leather pants, a few pairs of leggings, a thick velvety cloak, and some warm socks. A new set of black leather boots awaited her, and a thick jacket with a pale-yellow stripe on the right arm. She managed to cool her excitement to try on those leather pants and look at her bottom in a mirror.

Hagan swaggered into the tent just a moment later and settled himself into the adjacent corner to her.

His eyes flitted to hers as she was examining her new wardrobe. "Are the clothes to your liking?"

She nodded. "Yes, thank you."

He eyed her and the clothes and changed into his night clothes. He pulled his layers off, exposing tan muscled arms that made her eyes do a double take. She averted her glance as he forewent his leather pants for fleece ones.

Mikael caught her glances. "No need to worry Maeve, there's no shame here. We're all in this Brigade, we're bound to see each other naked eventually. At least, I certainly hope so."

He flashed a stunning smile, and his eyes scanned her up and down.

Hagan glared at him and interjected. "If you're not comfortable changing in front of us, we can get you your own separate tent."

She looked between the three males, thinking that her response could define how they viewed her as a part of the Brigade.

Petra would have shown dominance in a situation like this. She decided she was not going to allow a few males to scare her. Despite her flaws and insecurities, she was pretty confident in her own skin. If this were a test of her grit, she was going to pass with flying colors.

Her shoulders rose in an innocent shrug. "I'm not afraid of a little skin."

She turned her back to them, and pulled off her sweater, exposing a bare back underneath. Her brown-pink nipples peaked in the slight chill, but the air around her warmed as she felt their eyes on her defined back. Quickly finding her fleece sweater, she threw it over top and grabbed her new wool leggings. Without hesitation, she inched out of her old leggings, exposing her bare ass for all eyes to see.

She sensed the male arousal wafting in the air. It was an intoxicating feeling, but she did not mind the attention. Smiling at herself, she squeezed her round ass into her new thick leggings. Once she managed to yank the waist of the leggings over her hips, not forgetting to jump and indulge herself in a jiggle, she sat down and turned toward the males who now pretended like they didn't catch every move she made. Elias specifically seemed to struggle to keep his gaze on the tunic he was folding with the utmost care.

She untangled her braid to let out her long, auburn waves and looked the three of them over. Her hair was a jumble of messy strands that she tumbled to one side, exposing her long neck and defined collarbone.

Mikael licked his full lips and shook his head warily, "Anyone want a drink?" whilst pulling out a bottle of golden liquid that looked like it would make her head pound in the morning.

CHAPTER 14
THE SCENT

Hagan had his eyes on her, thunder clouds darkening his green irises. She scooted over to Elias's side, Hagan watching her intently. Mikael and Hagan joined them, sitting in a relaxed circle passing the bottle around for a few swigs.

"So, Maeve darling, what on earth was a thing like you doing in that dreadful pit of a town?" Mikael asked, his deep voice thick with disdain.

Elias scoffed, shooting a strong look of distaste toward Mikael.

She squinted her eyes, thinking about all the ways she could break the pretty little bones in his perfect face. When she focused on him, she noticed a crook in his nose, as if she were seeing it for the first time. *Cleasieras* were often known for their vanity and wanted to make others think they looked flawless at all times. "I don't know Mikael, maybe I am just used to ugly things. Speaking of, why do you try to hide that dreadfully crooked nose of yours? I mean really, it's not that bad."

Mid-sip, Elias huffed a rough laugh, swallowing the swig of spirits before bursting into a full fit of laughter. Hagan's laugh was the loudest, his joy sending shivers down the back of her neck. They all smiled broadly, besides Mikael, who took the bottle from Elias and drank deeply.

With a scowl, Mikael responded. "You must have quite the sharp mind to see such things. Regrettably, I am impressed."

She grinned wider; dominance achieved.

Changing the subject, Elias turned to Maeve. "So, how old are you Maeve? You have clearly harnessed your Gift to a high level of skill, which can take some decades to accomplish."

She pondered this, her cheeks turning a bit pink in embarrassment. "I was Forged twenty-five years ago."

Mikael's eyes widened, but Hagan and Elias just looked at her contemplatively.

"Very interesting, that is quite impressive." Elias said, his smile warm.

Mikael was nodding, his brow furrowed in frustration. Hagan cut in, raising the bottle of spirits. "Cheers to our new healer, Maeve *Helbredera*." She laughed, amused by them using the ancient marking of someone based upon their status, but she watched as each male before her took a swift gulp of the liquid in her honor. When she finally received the bottle, blushing in drunken merriment, she took a deep drink which resulted in a fit of coughs. Laughing it off, she wanted to clear the air with Mikael after her quick-witted attempt to shame him.

After grabbing her canteen of water and refreshing in cleansing the taste of alcohol from her mouth, she asked Mikael. "So, Mikael. How did you come to serve the Second Kingdom? Your accent is not like Hagan's, I noticed."

Mikael smiled, excited to talk about himself. "Now that is a rather intriguing story." He brushed his hair back, leaning into a dominating lounge across the tent floor. "I grew up in the Fifth Kingdom, I was Forged about one-hundred and seventy years ago now. Like you, the beginning years of my life were spent in a home for the younglings, near the Port of Smiths. The difference is, I began causing… mischief when I was very young." A wicked gleam hinted in his blue gaze as his eyes roamed the group with emphasis. "I began controlling the minds of my housemates at the age of three. It started when an older boy of a few years took my lunch from me, eating it to fill his fat belly while mine remained growling and empty." A muscle in his sharp jaw ticked. "So, one day I made him starve himself skinny. Every day, I would simply tell him not to eat and so he would not." A dangerous smile returned to his lips, but then he shrugged, "Of course, they caught me eventually. By then the boy's ribs were showing and his face was severely shrunken in, so perhaps I took it too far."

He laughed, straightening his posture.

She was listening intently, the intrigue of this seemingly mad male keeping her on every word as he spoke. When he stopped, she immediately spoke up.

"So, they kicked you out at three? How was it possible for you to survive that?" Her voice was anxious, anticipation building to hear more of his story.

He bit his lip and looked her dead in the eyes as he continued. "I do like your curiosity, Maeve. Do not worry, I lived a wonderful life growing up. Fifth Kingdom, in the nice part of one of the towns by the water that were lined with black sand beaches. I was not stuck on the streets; I did not ever have to beg for a thing after that. In fact, once word went around to the Fifth Kingdom nobles who travelled to and from the village I grew up in, a wealthy family decided to take me in as if I were their Born." He smiled reminiscently. "Or it was at first. Those who I called Mother and Father were low-powered *cleasieras* who amassed quite the wealth in their dealings. They mostly dealt in the type of trickery you hear of in the back corners of the grisliest taverns. Once I was brought to the family, they could control any outcome. I was a great investment to them." He sighed, as if he were boring himself.

Maeve's eyes widened, she needed to know what sort of things *cleasieras* did behind closed doors. Their Gift was so interesting, and easily could turn evil with the right motivation. She'd also like to know more about the Fifth Kingdom, which existed at the other end of Ignisiem, surrounded by the Aeriös Ocean. With a glance to Elias, who was listening like he knew the story already, she understood that she shouldn't push him to learn more just yet. She shelved questions about Queen Flora for a later conversation. It's not like Mikael didn't like to talk about himself.

They chatted after that, all attempting to lighten the mood as they slipped into the later hours of the night. Elias made her laugh endlessly with a story about how he was recruited, and Hagan sat and smiled at his friend as he regaled the group.

"I did not know what I got myself into, fucking with a high-powered *aimsura's* betrothed. But, hey, it got me the job, so here I am forty or so years later." Elias' laugh roared, the spirits clearly taking effect. More stories were shared, and the four of them drank into the night speaking of war stories and noble drama that they had experienced in their much longer lives. She chimed in at times, related to a subject or reacted to stories, when necessary, but she was just fascinated by these males' exciting lives. She found herself craving some of that adventure.

It took some liquid courage, but she became more and more at ease with the male tension and the power that surged through the tent. She grew comfortable around them and embraced the comradery with her fellow Sergeants as well as the stolen glances between her and Hagan. However, nothing she had heard had given her any inclination that Mikael or Elias knew Hagan was Born.

She could not be the only one who knows unless they didn't say anything because they thought she didn't know. That was possible.

Hagan finally broke in, glancing between the three Sergeants. "We should get some rest gents, and lady…" bowing his head drunkenly at her.

She smiled and bid goodnight to the group of males, scooting back over to the comfort of her cot. They each blew out their respective lamps and crawled into bed. Outside of the tent, it was silent besides the grumbling of a few remaining soldiers. The fires were still roaring, kept up by the night guards who surveyed the camp for threats. She listened to the crackling of logs on a fire and the males in her tent breathing heavily as she drifted to much-needed sleep.

She looked out of a large window that overlooked a picturesque mountain scape. The snow-capped majesties filled the horizon, the range going as far back as she could see. Wind whipped a few pieces of her hair over her face, and the smell of fresh water drifted by with it. Hearing the sound of rushing water, she looked down over the ledge to notice that there was an immaculate waterfall below the balcony in which she stood at the apex of.

Warmth spread across her lower back, and she looked to her right to see Hagan, wearing some loose night clothes. His pants were slung dangerously low over his hip bones that pointed down invitingly. He looked into her eyes deeply and leaned in to grab her face in his large, strong hands. The static hum from his fingers made her cheeks tingle, the feeling slithered down her body. She let out a soft exhale.

Hagan looked endlessly into her eyes, hunger growing in his stare. He leaned in a bit closer until their lips were an inch from touching, and she gave in to the desire that was dying to be released from her body. The fresh rain and hickory scent of him made her shiver, and she knew he could sense her arousal pooling between her legs. She closed her eyes, giving into those desires. She felt the warmth of his breath at her lips, and she parted her lips slightly. Inviting him to taste.

She woke with a start, feeling sweat beads falling from her forehead and an aching in her groin. That aching belonged to him. Maeve quickly recovered herself, shaking off the incredible scene that played out in her head just seconds ago. She looked around and noticed that Hagan and Elias had already left the tent, but Mikael remained.

He was reading a book, but looked up at the sound of rustling, and smiled seductively. "I do hope that delightful dream was about me. Your scent is exquisite."

She bit her lip and eyed him suspiciously. "In your dreams, Sergeant."

Playful waves swam across his eyes. "Apparently in your dreams, Sergeant." Mikael purred that last word, using it in the most inappropriate way possible.

She scoffed and shook her head. She began packing away her things, rolling up her cot. With her belongings attached to Callistus, she trotted in place. She was excited to get moving. Callistus nuzzled her face, and she watched as Petra strode up to her.

"How was the orgy?"

Maeve's eyes widened, and Petra roared in laughter.

"Shut the fuck up, Petra!" Her cheeks were reddening in embarrassment.

"Just fucking with you, I'm sorry. But... if that ever does happen you must fill me in on every detail." Petra said, biting her lip to stop from laughing.

Maeve and Petra giggled together, and she watched as Petra returned to her *bhiastera* legion, who were all mostly in their beast forms. A certain sadness fell over her, her conversation with Petra was short-lived.

She went back into the tent to double-check she had everything and found Hagan alone, packing his things up. She was pleasantly surprised that he didn't get a *ganera* to handle that work for him.

Maybe it wouldn't hurt to play with him a bit. "You're holding up the Brigade, your highness."

He looked at her, a smirk finding his lips. "Good thing I have you here to help me procrastinate further."

He stood up and faced her. She suddenly felt just how alone they were in the tent.

Hagan breathed in a long breath, his face turning to stone. "You need to learn how to control your scent. The males sharing a tent with you will be put in a frenzy if you keep having dirty little dreams like that."

Hagan let out the subtlest ripple of power, and his pupils dilated enough for her to notice.

She took in a sharp breath. "Maybe you and the other males should learn to control yourselves in the presence of a sexually-liberated female." She took extra effort to control the tone of her voice. She did not want to reveal anything to him.

Hagan raised his thick eyebrows, and the green of his eyes turned intensely bright.

He inched toward her, and she backed up against the edge of the tent. The room shrunk significantly as he pressed toward her, his body just inches from hers now. She looked up at him, attempting to shield her face in an unyielding expression.

A warm sensation spread from her navel to the rest of her body as she looked into the illuminated green eyes glaring down upon her.

She cocked an eyebrow up at him, and his voice became hoarse. "You drove me wild with that intoxicating scent hours before you woke up. I couldn't stand it. You were sleeping so soundly, so quietly. But I could feel the heat of your mind racing, I could taste your arousal. I couldn't stand it. I can't handle it. I don't know what you dreamt of, but I hope it was worth me losing a few hours of sleep. Your power is directly related to your feelings. When we're so close like this, it feels..." He shook his head.

Desperation flashed across his eyes, and his tongue swiped over his full lips.

Her eyes widened, and she tried to control her power's presence, noticing her growing arousal as he leaned down to meet her gaze.

She now noticed the dark shadows under his eyes.

His body was so close to hers she felt every inch of heat seep into her body. Her mouth was dry.

He unleashed his restrained Gift upon her, and she noted the smell of him. It was almost exactly as she smelled it in her dream. Smoky hickory and fresh rainwater.

Only those with a sense of power can feel these scents he mentioned. For some it was an inkling, for others it was like being overpowered by a harsh wind. Hagan's was more like a storm.

Hagan must have heard something, because he immediately spun around and continued packing his things.

She stood there still, shivering. Without his warmth surrounding her, she felt a bit chilled. Pushing her hair to one side, she watched Elias walk in to grab his remaining things from the tent.

"The *bhiasteras* are ready to go, General." Elias' golden eyes flitted between her and Hagan suspiciously.

The three of them took their remaining belongings and trudged out to mount their horses. *Ganeras* immediately went to work to disassemble their tent. She unlatched Callistus from the tree and trotted around the perimeter of the camp. Callistus was the most mild-tempered horse she had ever ridden. Her experience with horses was indeed limited, but she found leading the horse came almost as natural as healing.

She spotted Petra and a few other *bhiasteras*, foregoing horses for their beast forms. A large hawkish form perched on a tree overhead while a few wolfish stalked around. Petra stood with a fellow saber-tooth with grey eyes and snow-white fur. On her other side was a blonde wolfish with deep, piercingly dark eyes. They all stood in calm, sitting positions on their haunches as they tilted their heads and sniffed into the air around them.

The lines began to form, and the General went to the front to speak to the group. Heads from every group shot in his direction while all other sounds ceased, to listen to his words.

"Word has come from the King. We will be making the trek back to Court to replenish and rest. In a few days, we will be meeting a small army of the Freed Fae to take back our King's lands. Once we have finished, we shall return to court to enjoy ourselves." She was impressed at his ability to command the crowd, hearing whoops and hollers around her. The soldiers were proud to serve their General and fight the King's cause. Even the *ganeras*, who seemed to have accepted their lower rank given to them by society and the crown.

Then, they were off.

She trotted up to the front, which was beginning to feel like a more natural place for her to ride with the Brigade. They headed East, toward the border of the Republic of Freed Fae. Beyond the Dorcha Mountains, there is another way of life, a different type of ruler. He was a *ganera* who was one of the first to rebel against the Five Fae Kingdoms and their classism. From what she remembered of recent Fae history, there was a Rebellion, driven by the divide between Gifted Fae and non-Gifted Fae. Their Leader, who does not take a title, is said to not rule, or govern those who live there. He takes no subjects and makes little rules or regulations. He simply represents them.

Many of the Fae not blessed with power decided to gather and challenge the Kings in every Kingdom. It started small, with a few strikes or rebellions in villages. Then, the flame of the rebellion grew much stronger, so much so that it was affecting all Five Kingdoms.

While she found the effort respectful, and not without a valid cause, part of her thought it may not have been worth it at the cost. Many deaths occured, and of mainly the Freed Fae who had little or no power to properly defend themselves. Especially against the Born, who would want the rebellion least of all, to secure their status. After the First Kingdom Queen caught word of the genocide of the *ganeras*, she asked her husband, the Mind King, to stop the war. She did not see fit to spill precious blood. In her wise, historic words, "The Smiths would not be pleased, the Forge burns hot enough as it is."

Many of the other Kingdoms agreed with her sentiment, while some were coerced into agreeing to the creation of the Divide. This line divided the kingdoms from the mountainous wilderness that the Kings Gifted to the *ganeras*, to fortify as they wished. The land that is riddled with unheard of monsters and old, dark power; the place that they were supposed to make their sanctuary.

Those Non-Gifted Fae as well as others like the nymphs were resourceful enough to build in the trees and have a community of treehouses to inhabit. This guarded the *ganeras* from many threats, but not all. The way of life in that treacherous terrain was hard, but the Freed Fae saw it as better than being servants and laborers for the classist Kingdoms. She did not comprehend the feeling, because even lesser Gifted *helbrederas* are well-respected in society and could make a decent living off minimal power. *Ganeras* were forced to be laborers, cooks, and forms of entertainment for the higher-powered Fae or the Kingdoms.

She had never seen the world in this light, having grown up in Geneza. Lady El was a *ganera*, and she held her Keeper in the highest of regard. That may be how they think in some of the higher courts of the Kingdoms, and she was now working for the King of the Second Kingdom, but she refused to fall in line when it came to how she treated others. She will bow if she must, but she will not allow others to bow before her.

A KINGDOM OF MISCHIEF & MEMORIES

CHAPTER 15
THE FIRE

They travelled quietly, only the sounds of hooves stomping on the cool, leaf-covered ground. The *bhiasteras* lurked around, ahead, and behind the group on quicker feet to ensure their safe travel. She spotted Petra's saber-toothed form a few times coming to report to Elias on the surrounding terrain and if there were dangers. Well, she didn't really report, but she let the three of the Sergeants and General know. Maeve stayed a bit farther away from Hagan and stayed by Elias in the formation. She needed to keep a bit of space from him since their last encounter.

The long ride caused her mind to drift. Every time she caught Hagan's masculine scent her mouth would dry up. Watching his muscled back shift through his fitted tunic made her think of his strength that had her pressed against the tent a few hours ago. If she wasn't careful, she would think about how that conversation would've continued had Elias not walked in. She realized she was biting her lip, nearly drawing blood.

Elias sniffed, side-eyeing her curiously. He raised his eyebrows, lifting a hand to scratch his nose in signal. The fact that her Gift was directly linked to how her power is sensed in the air, mainly scent, was becoming quite the hassle.

They stopped when the evening light began to fade deep in the woods, the autumn foliage nearly obscuring the night sky with hues of orange and red. The ground crunched underneath their feet, hooves, and paws as they ventured to find a spot in the vast pockets of large tree trunks and boulders. Large trees soared high into the sky; their trunks as large as two horses in some places. One side of the area was obscured by rocks, leading up a small, slowly trickling waterfall that was painted in the hues of fallen leaves.

Only settling in for the night, the Brigade did not bother with tents or formalities. She was pleasantly surprised the General did not need a tent to sleep in every night or force the *ganeras* to put one up for him. Even though he could.

Fires erupted in a few spots of the campground, carefully assembled with large rock barriers around them to shield from the highly flammable leaf-covered ground. Settling her bag and bed roll near the trunk of a large tree, a fire beginning to glow bright only a few feet away, she felt at ease. This place had a sense of ancient magic, a power that comes from existing for an unfathomably long time. It soothed her, almost bringing her power to its surface in a comforting embrace.

Once most of the camp had settled in, the darkness and noise were only interrupted by the luminescence that the camp fires cast upon the wood. Until she heard a holler from across the camp. Leaving the comfort of her spot, she walked toward the sounds, which grew louder the closer she got.

Through the brush, the brightest bonfire she had ever seen blanketed the clearing in orange-yellow light. They had set the fire at the base of the rocks, and black smears began to form from the dark smoke that followed the flames' lick. Black char shot up the surrounding boulders.

A space had been cleared near the center, adjacent to the blazing fire. The fire was the least surprising thing she saw, as a massive brown bear strode to the center of the space. He pulled back, standing at his full height in front of the fire as the light flickered off him like copper. His eyes are what caught her attention most. They were the same glittering gold as Elias', just brighter in his *bhiastera* form. The shadow he left in front of him left a menacing mark on the leafy ground. Other *bhiasteras* circled the shadow.

Elias let out a deep, rumbling growl as he fell back on all four feet. His eyes glittered in the firelight as he watched the legion of *bhiasteras*, waiting for one of them to challenge him.

A shadow-like figure stepped up to him, her feline form was small in comparison to the presence of the bearish form. Black fur kept her looking stealthy, but the ice-blue gaze and long, sharp teeth looked equally as menacing. Petra.

Beginning to step forward in protest, a firm hand grabbed her shoulder to keep her in place. "What the—" She breathed, turning to see the long, pale fingers of Mikael clutching her.

As she shook him off, he let out a soft laugh. "Let them play, love. If anything really bad happens you'll be safely over here to patch them up. They are training, learning from each other."

"But Elias will destroy her. Do you see how huge he is?" She asked, watching his long black lashes slowly blink from her to the two *bhiasteras*.

He cracked a smile, teeth bright white even in near darkness. "Have faith in your friend, Maeve darling. She is fierce."

She nodded, accepting her fate of watching Petra and Elias rip each other apart. She had never seen Petra's beast form in real action, but she was about to.

Petra paced back and forth, her saber-toothed form like liquid smoke against the brightness of the flames ahead. Elias stood in place, his eyes watching her as she slinked from side-to-side. She let out a low growl.

With a slight flicker of her feline ear, she lunged in attack. Her quickness proved to give her an advantage against the two tons of muscle and fur that was Elias. Missing him, she landed with grace on a rock to his left, only just avoiding the flames that threatened up the rocks. As soon as she landed, she was in the air once more. A streak of blackness soared through the air and landed on Elias' large, furry back. Her claws were on him, careful to hold onto him without ripping open his skin entirely.

A deep bark of pain came from Elias, but he stood his ground, attempting to shake the feline off his back. He chomped backward at her, trying to connect with flesh as he struggled to get her feline form off him. With a growl, he stood abruptly, surprising her enough to cause her to lose her grip. She fell onto her back, but quickly recovered herself and stood on her four limbs. She hissed.

He faced her, and he stomped his feet in a challenge. He charged, his bearish form barreling toward her. Again, speed was her ally. She dodged him, but not before receiving a swipe of his claws against her long ribcage. Petra let out a loud yelp.

Gasps and growls came from the crowd, and Maeve had not noticed how close to the action she had drifted. She now stood near the front of the crowd, watching in mild horror as her best friend bled from her side. She noted a sandy-colored wolfish standing to her right, watching the scene with extreme focus.

Petra limped away quickly, attempting to shield the one side from further harm. Shaking off, her inky black fur shimmered in the low light. She licked her chops, a dangerous glare present in her crystal-clear gaze.

Elias sauntered away in victory; his massive head held high as he gave Petra his back. An act that proved to be a mistake.

She pounced, the muscles working, and managed to pull Elias down with her. He let out a high-pitched yelp, a sound that was a strange mix of surprise and pain as they rolled around in the leaves and dirt. Petra's blood was still leaking from her flesh wound, but she acted as if she didn't feel it. Once they finally came to a halt, Petra was on top of him, her long fangs nearly piercing the skin of his neck.

She stayed there and halted just before the lethal blow.

Elias let out a low growl, and his glowing golden eyes rolled in annoyance. She may not have known much about *bhiastera* training, but she was almost sure that Petra won this match.

"Ah, wonderful. See Maeve? I told you!" Mikael cheered, clapping his hands with the crowd as applause erupted from the Brigade. "I must go collect my winnings. I love an underdog, or cat." He smiled sneakily and walked away.

Petra and Elias stayed in that position, as if giving time for everyone to remember. They both just stopped fighting, in respect and acknowledgement of who was the clear winner. It was the simplest form of respect. If only all wars were fought like that, and the Forge would not have to burn so brightly with death.

She stood there, clapping softly and aimlessly as she watched Petra hop from him and limp toward her and the blonde *bhiastera* beside her. The wolfish trotted up to meet her, she nosed and licked the wounds she had gotten in training. Petra nuzzled the wolfish intimately, lovingly. She felt their affection, like a heartbeat coming from only one body. Something that affected their bodies and health, which was why she could feel it. A soft smile found her lips.

A shadow flickered in her peripheral, in front of the fire, and a commanding voice brought her attention to the center. "Ah, Sergeant. You let the warrior get your back. Until you know their blood no longer runs warm, you wait to give them your back." Hagan let out a hearty laugh, something only created at the expense of his best friend. He patted Elias' bear form on the shoulder, which sat above Hagan's hip. Speaking louder, he addressed the entire Brigade. "Get some sleep, you lot." He cracked a smile, and her breath caught in her throat. He was a vision of grace and grit, the fire glowing off of his muscled, tan skin against his cream tunic. The crinkles of his eyes and the wideness of his grin made her skin prickle.

His smile did not belong to General Hagan. She was looking at someone that thrilled her even more than him.

Petra and the blonde *bhiastera* had stalked off somewhere, and she made a note to go see her for healing. She walked with purpose to Hagan and Elias, his bearish form now sitting back in a casual position. Like this, he looked cute. Endearing, even. The blood on his claws promptly reminded her that he was much more than a big, furry bear.

Hagan's eyes flitted to hers, and he smirked. She eyed him speculatively, then looked into the gold eyes staring up at her.

"Elias?" She asked, even though she knew the answer. He leaned his head down, nudging his nose against her hip. A flicker of amusement hinted in his stare.

She smiled down at him, feeling Hagan's eyes on her. "Is it proper to scratch you behind the ear?" She asked, and Elias let out a loud huff before nudging his ear underneath her hand. His fur was coarse, like a woolen blanket. She scratched him, and he let out a growl that almost sounded like a cat's purr. She could not help but laugh as she looked up to see Hagan staring impatiently at Elias. Giving her one more nudge with his shoulder, he looked wryly at Hagan before he stalked off. Presumably to get dressed.

"I'm assuming you've never met a bearish before, based solely upon the stunned look on your face." Hagan presumed, closing the short distance between them.

She nodded. "They're kind of incredible." Her lips turned up, and she looked into his gaze before quickly looking into the bonfire. After their encounter that morning, his closeness only made her shiver.

"I apologize for the way I acted this morning." He said, inching toward her. He stiffened, as if realizing something. "You're cold." He said, and the air warmed around her within seconds. "There." He muttered, then continued. "If I can be honest with you, it has been a long time since I have shared a tent with a female, it may have gotten the best of me."

"Thank you," She managed, confusion creased her brows. She had rather enjoyed the moment they shared, even if it made her feel bold. "Why would sleeping in a tent with a female affect you?" She wondered, surprising herself by saying it aloud. He had to attract females, not just for his Gift, but for his ridiculously good looks.

He cocked a brow, his eyes studying her as he thought. "I guess you could say it's been a long time since I've done that."

She wondered how he was involved before, who with, and how it ended. She decided to keep that curiosity to herself, part of her knowing she would not like whatever answer he gave her.

"I should go find Petra and Elias, they both got pretty torn up." She said, giving him a soft smirk before walking to find them.

"Goodnight, Maeve." He said, the not-General Hagan smile peeking through.

She turned back, and a soft blush covered her cheeks. "Night, Hagan." When she turned to leave, her heart began to beat incessantly.

→→ →→ ←← ←←

Petra was easy to find. After walking a short distance, she heard a loud, "Fuck!" resound in the woods to her right. She walked to the curse, knowing it came from Petra's historically bad mouth.

"Hold still!" She heard another female say impatiently. Another fire's light came into view, and she watched as two female figures sat close on their bedrolls near it. Petra layed half on her side, her torso and breasts exposed to the night air. A sheen of sweat coated her dark skin, her nose scrunched in pain as the other female attempted to treat the wound on her ribs.

She remembered her from their brief interaction but had not gotten her name. Her pale, golden hair fell down her back, exposing a strong jawline and deep, dark brown eyes. At that moment, her dark brows were furrowed in concentration. "I'm trying to clean it up, Petra. Could you please stop squirming?" The female said, and Maeve let out a chuckle that announced her presence.

"Do you want some help with that?" Maeve asked as she walked toward them.

Lyra spoke, looking up to meet her stare with kind eyes. "Thank you, Maeve. I cannot stand her complaints any longer." She smiled, revealing a smile with a small gap between her front teeth. Her beauty was authentic, wild. She realized instantly that she was the *bhiastera* that stood beside her, and that Petra had been so intimate with.

"Maeve, please come fix this." Petra requested, wincing as she sat up.

"Of course," she said, and leaned down to examine the wound. The claws had gone against the lines of her ribcage, leaving three streaks of blood and flesh open.

"I don't know if you know, Maeve. But this is Lyra." Petra said. She kept her gaze away from Maeve, to avoid looking at the wound.

She smiled at Lyra, who looked worried. "Nice to meet you, Lyra. You already cleaned her up pretty well, I'm just going to seal her up. She'll hardly feel it." Barely touching the end of the gouge, her fingers glowed above the skin. The fibers began merging, and the flesh tucked neatly into the skin that regenerated in seconds. She made quick work of the claw marks. Petra felt nothing except for a warmth around the area, she made sure of that as she sealed up the last of the bloodied skin.

"Keep a scar, please." Petra grunted, "I'll need something to remind him."

Maeve let out a soft laugh through her concentration, her face lit with the healing light of her hands. When she was finished, all that remained after her fingers left Petra's skin was a whisper of a scar under her breast.

Petra sighed, stretching her arm over her head to loosen the new muscle. Lyra watched with a focused curiosity, her eyes landing on Maeve's.

"When they said a powerful *helbredera* was joining the Brigade, I did not expect someone who could do that. It looked effortless." She watched Maeve intently, clearly interested in her Gift.

"Well, thank you. But it was not without effort, believe me. That exhausted me." She laughed, and Petra hugged her around the shoulder.

Petra released her. "Thank you, M. You're always fixing me up."

Maeve shrugged. "You're always getting into fights. Well done, by the way." She watched Petra throw a loose tunic over her bare torso as Lyra cleaned up the bloody rags.

Petra chuckled. "It was pretty marvelous. I won't lie though; I was not confident that I would win when I stepped up to him.

He is the largest bearish I have ever seen." She shook her head and glanced at Lyra.

Lyra nodded. "Most of the bearish stay in the Fourth Kingdom. The Hybrid King has an entire legion of them at his disposal. Completely unstoppable."

She hoped silently that the Second Kingdom was in the Hybrid King's good graces.

CHAPTER 16
THE LAKE

The Brigade travelled for two more days before settling for a longer rest by a beautiful, aquamarine lake set deep in the forest. They also stopped here to do some hunting— fruit, leftover bread and dried meats did get a bit tiring after a few days. Of the *bhiasteras*, all but Elias went to hunt for the night's dinner. The sun had not quite set, and the colors played off the bright blue lake in a spectrum of hues. There were dense trees that surrounded the lake, and small pebbled shores surrounded the receding water.

Hyper-aware of the grime that had layered her during travel, she knew she could really use a bath. She knew it would be cold at this time of year, but it would be well worth it to wash three days of travel from her exhausted body.

Petra was off hunting, so she was going to bear this alone. She made sure to pack a few bars of her lavender soap, she always indulged when it came to scent. Something about lavender soothed her worries and enlightened her senses. There were more tents for this camp, but some groups did not bother with a tent for a two-day stay. The Sergeants' and General's tent was up, and she ducked inside to gather the things she needed for her bath. She missed her copper claw-foot tub, but the crystal-clear lake wouldn't be a bad substitute. Other than the freezing cold water.

Hagan, Mikael, and Elias were still patrolling and giving orders around the camp, so it was as good as any time to sneak away. Clover seemed to manage herself pretty well without her constant leadership. That was not the type of Sergeant she wanted to be. She carried a small piece of her soap and one of her blankets she would use to escape the cold of the water.

The forest was thick, and she snuck through about three-hundred yards of forest before finding the small outcropping she was eyeing on their way in. There was a small, pebbled shore that met water that had darkened to a royal blue from the setting sun. Before leaving the safety of the trees, she scanned the area for any sign of Fae and listened intently for footsteps when she decided to make her move.

She untied her cloak, pulled her tunic over her head, knocked off her boots, and peeled off her leggings. She unraveled her loose waves and walked into the waist-high water. Her body stilled except for her feet moving against the soft, yet bumpy ground. It was some of the coldest water she had ever been in, besides the time she and Petra went skinny-dipping at the Lake in Blarra in Winter. They may have shared a bottle of wine beforehand.

Her breathing was labored as she tried to adjust to the temperature. The water had the freshness of fresh-melted glacier ice, which it may have come from at one point. They were only a day's journey from the border, so the icy mountains were close. If the sun hadn't been setting, this water could have been nearly transparent as it was clearly undisturbed. She held her nose, breathed in a sharp breath, and dunked her head in the ice-cold water. The feeling was almost cathartic, she felt acutely aware when she rose to the surface. Using the broken-off piece of her soap, she scrubbed herself from head to toe. Once the soap was fully dissolved, the water began to feel oddly warm. At first, she thought maybe she had just gotten used to the cold, but then she heard his footsteps.

She was facing the direction of the deeper parts of the lake, but when she caught the sound of boots on pebbles, she yanked her head around to see Hagan standing there. He was watching her bathe.

"Lavender, your favorite scent," he said just loud enough for her to hear.

His green eyes glowed in the almost-darkness as he willed the water around her to warm.

She was shivering. "H-How did you know that?"

The water was now steaming around her, and despite his intrusion she welcomed the hot water. She sank to her knees in the water, luxuriating in the feel of it as the soap fully dissolved off her skin and into the water. He was heating her up in more ways than just the water.

Hagan was still standing there. It was nearly dark, so she knew what had to happen next. She decided to turn around, still sunken low enough to cover most of herself.

Her eyes met Hagan's. While she couldn't remember a time where she felt so vulnerable, she also felt a level of comfort and confidence in his presence that eased her.

His eyes roamed up and down her body as she rose from out of the water, his voice became gruff. "Anyone could have found you here. I caught the scent of lavender in the wind and knew it was you." A dark humor danced in his eyes.

"Are you going to continue to smell all of my things to know exactly where I am?" She cocked an eyebrow.

Despite his intrusion, she was glad it was him and not a stranger.

His eyes were molten. "I haven't been able to get your *scents* out of my fucking head, Maeve. The lavender is just obvious in a tent full of barely washed males."

His voice was tense, and he picked up the blanket she had planned to dry off with. "I'll be here with your blanket when you're ready to get out of the water. Sorry if it starts to get cold again, I just *cannot* manage to keep it warm any longer."

Knowing just how Gifted he was, she doubted that to be true. She laughed. "Your sense of humor is rather dark, General."

The right side of his lips tipped up.

She shook her head. "Fuck it." She murmured to herself. She rose from the quickly cooling water to find the breeze caressing her with icy fingers. Taking in a sharp breath, she closed her eyes briefly to get accustomed to the cold air.

Her eyes opened to a pool that expanded in front of her. Hagan was sipping a glass of deep red wine when he turned to cast his eyes upon her. She hopped up to sit on the edge of the dreamy pool under the stars. The dark blues and purples of the speckled sky reflected off the near-still water. She spotted two thick, luxurious towels folded by the pool's edge. She smiled, a giggle bubbling from deep within her chest as he swam to the infinity pool's edge that opened to a vast mountain range, watching her walk farther away and giggle like a youngling.

Hagan shook his head at her, his eyes flashing dangerously.

She slowly backed up, smiling. "I'll be over here when you're ready for your towel."

Practically shaking with laughter, she backed away with her own towel wrapped tightly around her. Hagan seemed to enjoy this challenge. Smiling, he hopped out of the water, and she bit her lip.

Hagan seemed to have no qualms with revealing himself to her. His chest was so exquisitely carved with lean muscle. He was clearly a warrior, bearing a few battle scars and the elegant muscles that came from handling a sword. Water dripped off him and invited her eyes down his defined hips, down to his unbelievable length.

Her eyes widened, he appeared to be more than ready for anything that followed. She did not foresee herself wearing this towel for long. He was rock hard, and his eyes were focused directly on her. She licked her lips, a deep exhale escaping from her parted mouth.

Her eyes fluttered open to see Hagan examining her naked body as she stood in the waist deep water of the mountain forest's lake. She was bare to the night, facing him with the water barely lapping at her thighs while he stood there fully clothed.

Victim to the icy wind, her pink nipples elongated to their most extreme point. Quickly covering up with her arms, she hunched out of the freezing water. She shivered, keeping her eyes on him, and walking up to the shore like he was just doing in her mind. Her imagination was getting extremely intrusive, but by the Forge if she didn't enjoy it. Nevertheless, these daydreams were getting out of control, he was her General for Smith's sake. "I thought you weren't afraid of a little skin!" He teased. "I'm not, but I am afraid of freezing to death." She countered, and the air around her immediately warmed, as if he were wrapping a warm blanket around her.

Squeezing her arms around herself harder to luxuriate in the warmth, she padded up to Hagan, who could not keep his eyes off of her. She reached out her hand for her blanket. Hagan's breathing became ragged.

He looked at her in the exact way he was looking at her in her mind just seconds ago. As if he knew of her filthy thoughts of him. As far as she knew he couldn't read minds, but then again him holding that power wouldn't surprise her either. She snatched the blanket from him as his eyes twinkled with dark amusement. Turning around to put on her warm clothes, she felt heat on her cheeks.

Squeezing warmth into her bones, she pulled her arms tightly around herself. She looked up at Hagan curiously. "I was wondering something."

He looked down, a concentrated determination scrunching his thick eyebrows together. "All right."

She breathed in deeply. "Do you think I will be expected to fight with the Brigade? Say, if things go awry."

His eyes widened; she had clearly surprised him. "Why would you fight? Do you want that?"

"Well, I am just not sure how it works. I am capable of fighting, we saw that in Blarra, and with Ezra." She turned her eyes downward, watching the water ripple at the shore of the Lake. "I just don't want to lose their respect by not fighting. I don't want to hurt anyone, I don't like it."

He took a step closer, a consoling hand going to her face. His fingers were surprisingly warm, and she leaned into him. He whispered. "Lose their respect? You must know you are powerful, Maeve. You may not be sure of it but reversing the healing process is no simple feat. Taking away the pain of others is not something the everyday *helbredera* can accomplish. You offer so much more than a warrior; you offer a second chance for every one of these soldiers. Respect does not need to be earned by you. Respect is your Smiths given right."

She stilled, looking into his dark emerald gaze. She did not realize that he had been taking notes of the things she'd done, and she could see his heart swelling with pride for her. "I will earn their respect regardless. But thank you." She smiled, stepping away from the heat of the moment.

He smiled back, his casual charm making her ache. "You do that. They will worship you for it, I'm sure."

"I suppose I have a lot to catch up on when it comes to Brigade life, and soon Kingdom life." She pondered.

"You have no idea." He whispered.

A sharp break of a branch resounded near them, and Hagan's face immediately turned to stone. "We should be getting back, before our absence is noted." His voice seemed strained, like he was regretting ending this trist.

She turned to face him, and the visions of his body plagued her mind. Brushing his arm as she passed, the air around them warmed, static buzzing between their exposed skin.

Hagan's eyes were luminescent in the dimming light. He looked down at her as she passed. "Wouldn't want to be seen with your female Sergeant alone, your highness. Wouldn't want to tarnish your reputation, now, would we?"

Her eyes flashed with humor, but a small undertone of truth came with that statement.

He rolled his eyes, but his tone turned serious. "Let's just go."

CHAPTER 17
THE BONE KING

Maeve and Hagan returned to the camp, and she scampered away into their shared tent. There she found Mikael and Elias looking over a map and discussing the Brigade's next moves. They both eyed her suspiciously when she walked in.

Mikael's aqua gaze flashed with delight. "Darling, you smell lovely. You must invite me the next time you go for a night time swim." He smiled with sparkly white teeth.

She rolled her eyes. "You're not my type, Mikael. Just a little too pretty."

Elias stifled a laugh.

"You'd be welcome to join, Elias." She winked at the *bhiastera*.

Mikael stuck out his lip and pouted. His eyes still twinkled with amusement.

Elias chuckled, but they all stiffened a bit when Hagan walked in. "I see the three of you are getting along splendidly." He passed her without a glance.

His indifference pained her more than it should have, she cursed herself for creating these visions of him in her mind. As well as spilling her thoughts carelessly when she was alone with him. She sighed. "What's the plan? As you all know, I am new at this whole war thing."

Elias snorted, and Hagan shot him a silencing look.

Looking down, she saw a beautifully drawn map that outlined the Divide, which separated the Five Fae Kingdoms from the Republic of Freed Fae. While they were allowed the domain of the mountains and beyond, the foothills were still considered the Second Kingdom's land. The King of the Second Kingdom, also called the King of Thunder, is said to be an extremely powerful *aimsura* who was unyielding when it came to maintaining his lands and protecting his citizens. Especially the ones who are Gifted.

Elias explained, pointing toward the foothills of the mountains on the map. "There have been *ganera* armies of the Freed Fae camping along these foothills, occupying the King's land. Luckily, there is a dense forest here—" he pointed toward the dark crisscrossed lines that opened up to the foothills. "—a few deer have told me that they are hunting in these woods, but only in the early morning."

She looked up at Elias, astonished. She had never met a *bhiastera* who could speak with other animals. She had only heard legends, but only the most Gifted *bhiastera* Fae could converse with animals. *The deer told him.* She was jealous of that Gift. Elias winked at her, like he knew what she was thinking, and he knew it was amazing too.

Hagan examined the map and picked up one of the figurines that represented the Freed Fae. She looked to him as he twirled the figurine between long fingers with great dexterity.

Hagan looked around. "So, we strike at night. We push them back into their own lands. If they stay behind the border, there is no reason for them to be harmed."

He pushed the other figurines onto the drawn mountains.

Mikael looked to Elias. "My *cleasieras* will be in the trees here—" He gestured toward the tree line parallel to the foothills. "—we should still be in range to obstruct a few minds of the Freed Fae from there."

His smile was beautifully lethal.

Hagan ordered. "Make sure you save some energy for after the fight. We want to make sure the Freed Fae don't ever want to visit this land again."

Mikael nodded; an understanding struck between them.

Her brows furrowed, a certain unease settling over her at their words. "What does that mean? You're going to trick them into never coming back?"

She almost immediately regretted it when the three of them looked at her. She stiffened, and the air turned a few degrees colder in the tent.

Hagan's eyes hardened as they met hers. "It's better this way. The King will not show mercy to the Freed Fae if any are caught invading his lands a second time. Burning that fact into their minds will only help them. It is the law for them to live past the Divide."

His head tilted upward, and she felt the male's gaze in her bones.

The months were getting colder, surely the Freed Fae were just coming to the foothills to be in warmer conditions. She could not imagine a group of *ganeras* camping at the border would cause any harm in a Kingdom as vast as the Second. "It just seems like a harsh response to something so minor as camping on the King's land."

Elias glanced kindly at her. "It takes some getting used to, trust me. This is mercy compared to what the King of Thunder would prefer us to do. If it were up to him, we would kill them all in minutes." He touched her arm lightly, reassuringly. "At least in this case we give them a chance to surrender, but upon attack we will defend the Second Kingdom land. It is our duty."

She did not feel this pull of duty to the King of Thunder, her duty lied with the living. Her duty was to heal, to avoid the deaths of others at any cost. To use her power to keep the Forge's flame from burning too brightly. To ensure balance. With that power came her own personal duties. Her duty was also to the Brigade and wanted to help those in it.

Her concern properly squashed, they went over the remainder of the plans.

Elias continued. "Maeve, you and the other *helbredera* will be stationed here."

He then pointed toward a random part of the woods, far behind where the *cleasieras* will be perched in their trees. "We will need you and her ready for some nasty injuries. The Freed Fae are usually somewhat battle-trained, and they possess many skilled archers that have taken us by surprise before. We'd prefer to come out of this with zero deaths."

As if she didn't already feel anxious about this.

Hagan cocked his head at her, sensing the anxiety that scrunched the lines of her face. She looked up at him, and her anxiety eased as her eyes met his.

"With power like yours, you will have no problem meeting that mark."

Her eyes brightened the slightest bit.

"Good. We're in an understanding. For tonight, let us enjoy the feast. Tomorrow, we begin preparations."

The three Sergeants nodded, and they all walked out of the tent to join the Brigade.

Camp was alight with many roaring fires, which laid a warm glow on the Fae surrounding them. Smells of roasting meats filled the air. She took it all in, walking through the camp by herself. Sitting down on an empty log, she warmed herself by the fire. She immediately recognized the *ganera* who sat opposite her, it was the male she had healed just the other day. He looked up to greet her, and his honey-colored eyes glowed in the fire's light.

She smiled. "Hello, Conor. How's the stomach?"

Conor still looked at her as if she were some Queen, adding a slight bow in his greeting.

He smiled up at her. "It feels better than ever. I can now wield a sword with ease, and all the pain is gone. Thank you, again." He rubbed his stomach.

Her glee was palpable. "It was my pleasure."

She warmed herself for a moment by Conor's fire, then continued strolling through the camp that glowed with life. Her eyes darted to a dark corner, and she blushed when she caught two Fae entangled in a dark corner by one of the *aimsura* tents. Two male Fae, one bearing a red *bhiastera* armband, and the other with a blue *aimsura* band. They did not notice her, and she quickly shooed herself away to give them some privacy.

She aimed toward the *bhiastera* tent, looking for Petra. Her unit was relaxing by their large fire, chatting animatedly when Petra spotted her from across the campfire.

Petra's ice-blue eyes lit up, and she jumped from her spot. She dragged Maeve over to the log that she was sitting on with the blonde *bhiastera* she met earlier. "Lyra was just thrilling us with a story about the Bone King."

Petra raised her eyebrows dramatically as she took a swig from a bottle of wine.

Maeve inclined her head toward Lyra, the blonde *bhiastera*. "The Bone King?"

Lyra nodded. "The Bone King is the ruler of the Third Kingdom. Many call him by that name because his favorite torture technique is breaking bones of those who have wronged him."

Maeve's eyes widened, and her mouth felt dry. "I-I had never heard of him… he sounds awful. He's a *helbredera* then?"

Petra handed her the wine, and she took a deep swig from it.

A few of the group nodded, acknowledging her question with a solid yes. She felt an odd twinge of guilt, one of her kind only used his Gift to hurt.

Lyra's dark brown eyes turned almost black. "He is awful. As I was saying before, a good friend of mine, Remi, was captured by a Third Kingdom unit. To be fair, he was caught stealing from the King's stores of aged whiskey. His other form was a wolf, which he thought would aid him in being sneaky."

Lyra paused, taking a sip of the passed-around wine.

Maeve listened intently.

Lyra continued, looking around the group. "After he was imprisoned for a few days, the Bone King came to see him. See, the King did not take well to thievery. Especially from him."

Lyra's face paled. "Once the Bone King was done with him, each hand's bones had been shattered so many times that Remi couldn't use his hands again. Even shifting became nearly impossible, as his paws would no longer carry him."

Lyra looked down at the bottle of wine, a shadow of sadness crossing her face. Maeve put her hand on Lyra's shoulder in reassurance. A veil of silence covered the group for a moment.

She sighed. "I am so sorry for your loss, Lyra. It pains me to know that any *helbredera* could become such a monster."

Lyra looked up and smiled softly at her. "It was in the past. Anyways, enough about him. How are you faring, Sergeant?"

She smirked, a soft blush finding her cheeks. "Maeve. You all can just call me Maeve. I think it's silly to call me a Sergeant when I do not even fight." She made sure to look everyone in the eyes, she knew it as a sign of respect to *bhiasteras*.

A sense of comfort fell over the group, and a few of the *bhiasteras* smiled at that.

"You are a warrior all the same, Maeve. I know that you will fight to keep us all in one piece, to your last drop of energy." Lyra said. Maeve knew that she liked this duty-bound female, who happened to give her the reassurance she needed before her first 'battle'.

The night went on, and she chatted and drank with Petra's unit until the night was so dark, she could see every star that lit the speckled sky.

Finally, she left the group, giving Petra a stronger-than-necessary hug. Petra almost broke her ribs in return. Wobbling from their side of the camp, she looked around at all of the remaining Fae that were asleep under the stars. Many of the fires were out, but enough light came from the still-burning fires that she could find her way back to her shared tent.

She made it to the tent, hiccupping from the wine. Taking a sobering breath of fresh forest air, she stepped into the tent.

The view was almost comical. Maeve took in the view of the three mighty males that usually overwhelmed her, sleeping like babies in their separate cots. She especially watched Hagan, whose face was almost unrecognizable. He was completely relaxed, and the slightest hint of a smile played on his lips as he slept in peace. This was quite contrary from the usual intense General mask he donned most of the time. It was more like the version he liked to show her when they were alone. Smiling to herself, she tip-toed to her cot, as well as she could manage given how much wine she'd had. She plopped down on her cot and fell straight to sleep.

She looked into the eyes of a stunning female. Maeve could sense that she was much older than her, probably by a few hundred years by the way she carried herself. Her eyes were a beautiful, bright, sage green. Freckles dotted her porcelain skin, and she looked at Maeve with admiration.

She felt a grin on her face.

The female's mahogany brown hair was ornately wrapped into a braided bun that topped her head, showing off her long, defined neck and sharp collarbones.

She wore a deep emerald dress that clung to her shoulders, showing off her petite figure. Drifting her eyes up, she noticed a crown made of carved bone that was set on top of her head. Small, delicately carved bone wrapped around bright red rubies that were the color of fresh blood.

For some reason, this fact that the female was clearly wearing bones did not scare her. The energy from this female was nothing but warm and comforting.

The female's lips parted, and she spoke in a delicate, musical voice. "You look stunning, darling. We're just missing one thing."

She looked down and noticed the female holding an ivory-colored brooch, a large blood ruby glittering in the center of the bone casing. Smiling from ear to ear, she reached to grab the brooch from the female.

Maeve's eyes eased open into the morning light that filled the tent. She heard stirring of the camp and groaning from the males that shared the tent with her. A deep yawn resounded from her, and she wiped the grains of sleep from her eyes.

She looked around and saw the males around her laying in their cots. Elias was snacking on some leftover meat, scanning a map in his lap. Mikael held a mirror up and looked at himself in disgust.

He saw her looking, and grimaced. "Too much whiskey."

Maeve smiled and looked over to see Hagan examining her. "Where did you go off to last night?"

Her mind immediately went to their encounter at the lake

while she was bathing. Her cheeks heated slightly. "Here and there. Petra and the other *bhiasteras* make for interesting company. They have some stories to tell."

Hagan raised an eyebrow, and Mikael took his gaze off himself to listen to the conversation. "And what kind of stories did they share with you?" His emerald eyes examined her intently.

She furrowed her eyebrows at the three of them who were now waiting for her response. "Lyra was telling us about the King of the Third Kingdom. Apparently, they call him the Bone King... because he likes to break people's bones as torture. A *helbredera* King who only hurts. Her friend was so fucked up after stealing from the King, and then being interrogated by him that his hands, his claws, could never be used again."

Hagan stared at her intensely.

She read so many emotions on his face. Anger? Sadness? Fear? The room suddenly felt two shades darker than it had been before. "Do you know why he gives such brutal punishment? I feel like the other Kingdoms could intervene." She regretted her question immediately, realizing she was treading into dangerous waters.

Hagan coughed, then made his voice low. "What the Bone King does in his Kingdom is of his business, it is not of our concern."

She broke her gaze with Hagan to glance at Mikael, who explained. "The Bone King is one of our King's allies. He can be quite cruel to those with more delicate sensibilities."

She rolled her eyes.

With a smirk, he continued. "There have been rumors of his broken mind, that an illness of the brain has been veiling his senses for two or three decades now. At least as long ago as his Queen's passing."

She had heard of the tragic death of the *Cleasiera* Queen shortly after she herself was Forged. It was all the inhabitants of Geneza talked about because it was such a conspiracy. She was beloved and respected, for she was one of the most Gifted *cleasieras* on record.

Hagan snapped his head to the side to stare at Mikael.

"Careful, Mikael." His eyes glowed with fury, a soft snarl in his words.

"Be careful about what? She needs to know about the ins and outs of the Five Kingdoms. I'm not going to hide it from her, she is a soldier of the Brigade just as I am." Her eyes darted between them, looking confused.

"The Fae in the village of Geneza said there was a fire in her bed chambers, too many candles lit as she was sleeping. An incredible tragedy that swept over all Five Fae Kingdoms, one of their beloved Queens who had lived for nearly six-hundred years, gone so quickly. Many were especially sad, because she was never granted the Gift to sire an heir to the Third Kingdom." She said, now questioning the truth of those rumors.

Mikael's eyes tensed, feeling Hagan's pressure.

He still pursued. "There are whispers within the Second Kingdom Court. Some are saying that the death was intentional. That the Bone King was upset at something the Queen did."

Elias and Hagan stiffened.

The green in Hagan's eyes was close to neon, and the room cooled. A threat. "That is sufficient, Mikael. In any case, those who do think such things are speaking of treason against an ally of the King. A rich, powerful ally that supplies weapons to half of the Second Kingdom army." His voice was low, but the three Sergeants were sure to hear every word.

Hagan's Gift surged through the tent, and Maeve heard a vicious wind ruffle the tent and camp outside.

Maeve, Mikael, and Elias nodded to Hagan in understanding. Though he could have a flair for the dramatic, something about his power gave her goosebumps.

"Good. Let's prepare for the trek then. We will travel overnight, closing in on the *ganera* camp around midnight. Then, we attack and leave the area within the day to return to Court." Hagan was wearing his unwavering General mask.

She saw past that mask, there were clearly things Hagan was hiding. Before this was all over, she would make sure to learn his secrets. At least, she would try. She nodded in agreement, and quickly packed her things to head to the pale-yellow tent.

CHAPTER 18
THE GANERAS

Clover was idly packing at the pale-yellow tent, which was also where her cot and belongings lived. The inside of the tent had multiple small cots spread throughout, no one occupying them at that moment. Clover and Maeve both had a small station to work, both with two corresponding baskets of healing supplies.

Maeve spoke up when she saw Clover's lavender eyes meet hers, not meaning to intrude on her. "Good morning, Clover. I'm sorry I haven't come here sooner; I was just getting acquainted with everything"

Clover looked at her kindly, her pale skin near glowing in the mid-morning light. "Not to worry, Miss Maeve. I manage well enough on my own."

She helped Clover and a few *ganeras* pack up the tent and healing supplies, strapping some to Callistus since she had the extra room. The scent of trampled mud and extinguished fires filled her nostrils, a smell that she was beginning to appreciate. It signalled new journeys, new adventures.

Most of the camp was back to normal, save for a few burnt scraps leftover from the fires of the previous night. Mud caked their boots, and the squishing of hooves against the terrain alerted the Brigade was soon to ride out. The *bhiasteras* went ahead, scouting for any dangers.

She made sure to wave off Petra when she passed. Her saber-toothed form growled in delight and sprinted forward to join the rest of the pack. How something could be so dangerous yet so beautiful, she did not know. Petra's black fur reflected blue in the morning's light, a shadow dancing through the trees. She smiled to herself and walked with Callistus up to the front where Mikael and Hagan stood. They were both talking to other soldiers.

Elias walked up next to her, looking up to her as he patted Callistus on the head. "How are you?" He asked her, keeping his voice low.

Callistus pushed him off, nearly knocking him in the skull with her long snout. "Woah, horse. What's your problem?" He asked, his eyes gilded over, and his dark brows furrowed deeply.

She held tight to the reins and leaned down to calm the horse. Callistus grunted, then let out a faint whinny as she stood up straight to stare Elias down. His dark skin was glistening, a bead of sweat forming from communicating with Callistus.

"Oh, is that what you think? Well, I'll have you know I am the predator here. Top of the food chain. So, I won't take disrespect from a horse." Elias explained to Callistus, his anger brewing.

Callistus simply tilted her head into the air, looking down on him in disdain. She let out a soft neigh. She then snorted and averted her gaze in the other direction.

"Your horse is a real cunt." Elias stated, his language surprising her.

"Would you please explain to me what just happened?" She asked in desperation. Before he could answer, her mind cleared to find the answer. He could talk to animals. He had an argument with her horse. He called Callistus a cunt.

She stifled her laughter, watching as Elias fumed beneath her. His eyes cooled to a softer gold.

"Time to go." He said and stalked off into the woods.

She wanted nothing more than to be able to read his mind, to know what Callistus said to him to make him so annoyed. She bit back a smile. She patted her horse lovingly, a new bond formed between them.

Hagan dismissed a *treaniera* female and motioned for Maeve to join him at the front. His eyes examined her. "Are you ready for your first battle, Sergeant?"

She nodded. "I am. Something about this feels so familiar. Like I'm meant to be here. And I'm not one to question fate."

Hagan furrowed his eyebrows at her and gave her a rare smile. "Good."

They both set their gaze forward as they began their trek to the foothills.

They rode constantly, only stopping once to water the horses until the light faded behind the distant mountain tops. She let her mind drift as they trotted in silence, some of the hawkish *bhiastera* flying overhead and cawing amongst the tops of the surrounding trees. The wind grew icy, signaling her that they were farther north into the Second Kingdom, near the foothills of the Mountains of Dorcha.

She pulled a blanket over herself as they rode to block against the bitter chill. Hagan stole glances at her, a smirk on his mouth and a sparkle in his eye. Each fleeting glance heated her blood, causing her heart to stammer against its rhythmic beats. His striking face was slowly becoming the thing she pictured most, and her vivid visions didn't help her ignore it.

So unique, yet so familiar. As if she knew him in a past life. Her visions of him were the hardest part. Her imagination was running in directions she was not yet ready to explore. As for his standing on the subject, she was even more unclear.

She noticed the Brigade slowing down and remembered that the Brigade would be walking by foot the last mile or so to avoid unnecessary noise or detection. Though the *ganera* warriors did not have Gifts from the Forge, they still had guards and precautions to defend against intruders.

Night had fully cloaked them in darkness, and the *bhiasteras* made their appearance once again. Everything was clear to set up a small camp and begin the ambush. She looked East and saw smoke pluming into the air. The *ganera* camp.

The camp slowly prepared for battle. The more Gifted soldiers were idle, sitting atop sleeping bags or talking in hushed voices amongst themselves. Warriors of the *ganera* and *treaniera* groups sharpened weapons, archers readied themselves with full quivers, all while she and Clover set up their clean blankets and bandages while waiting for the first of the wounded to seek their aid. The Brigade was ready.

A wolfish *bhiastera* howled into the star speckled sky, and a shiver ran down her spine. Though she was too far back in the woods to see the battle, the sounds told her enough. Screams filled the air toward the Freed Fae camp, and she heard the clashing of metal against metal that would surely mean bloodshed. Growls followed by screams of terror echoed in her ears. Storm clouds ruptured over the Freed Fae camp. Lightning struck the camp a few times, and the high-pitched screams lit up brighter than the deadly white streaks in the sky.

Her eyes burned, and she glanced down at Clover. Clover was looking forward, eyes unfocused and dreamy. A defense mechanism against the unsavory, to ignore it. She was trying to drown out the sounds of their Brigade destroying the group of Freed Fae.

Curiosity taking over, and no soldiers to be healed yet, she set off with her small dagger and a lightly packed bag of healing supplies to see what was going on beyond the veil of tall trees. The edge of the wood was farther than she thought, and her calves burnt at the incline at which the ground went. She was determined to see things for herself, to know what happened before the wounded sat on her table. She needed to understand, at least a little better. It felt wrong to be a bystander when there were such horrendous sounds echoing beyond the tree line.

After the incline subsided, she moved as stealthily as she could manage. Not quite a *bhiastera*, but she thought she was doing well as no one had noticed her yet. Quickly and quietly, she stepped through the brush near the front of the tree line. As promised, she noted Mikael perched in a branch above looking out toward the scene at the foothills of the Mountains. His usually subdued blue eyes were glowing bright, his Gift at work. He sat lazily upon a thick branch; legs reclined as he worked. One mind at a time. Ahead, she could see *ganeras* dressed in shabby clothing walking unbothered toward the border. They walked in stiff motions, seemingly unaware of the chaos around them. He was helping them.

She smiled to herself, glad to see a softer side to Mikael.

Still going unnoticed, she squatted behind a large bush to watch the battle unfold. Part of her wished she had not. The encampment was already destroyed, the lightning strikes had clearly decimated what was there. All that remained were splotches of blackened earth, with a few tents smoking and burnt.

Many *ganeras* had retreated. She watched as they were scrambling up the foothills with the only belongings they could carry. Many of them seemed thin and emaciated as they struggled up the treacherous terrain to the even greater dangers beyond.

Warriors clashed swords, a *treaniera* soldier quickly overpowered one of the opposing Freed Fae, whose throat was slit without another thought of surrender. Blood spilled recklessly across the small battlefield. Bile surfaced in her throat as she watched the unnecessary massacre.

The Freed Fae had a rather large number of soldiers, but it did not matter. Wolfish and hawkish *bhiasteras* ripped through them with ease, leaving writhing bodies on the ground. Despite the circumstances, the Brigade's *ganeras* were fighting with a high level of intensity, slashing, and killing Fae of their own kind.

Blood mixed with mud; screams mingled with begs for mercy. She could not let this happen; the Forge would burn much brighter than it should. Too much blood, too many deaths. The scene before her was a disgrace to the Smiths and to the Forge. To ruin the life that the Smiths had so carefully created, to allow the Forge to burn so brightly. She could not allow it. First and foremost, her duty was to maintain life. Instinct took over, and a strange courage blossomed deep within her. A duty.

She strode out to the clearing, nothing but a bag of bandages and a small dagger hidden beneath her cloak, she made her way to one of the writhing bodies that had been torn apart by a wolfish *bhiastera* just seconds before.

The Freed Fae lay there in agony, unable to move her arms or legs. She was pale, the blood beginning to pool around her. Her breaths were heavy, but the female was breathing. Her light brown eyes met Maeve's, fear widening them. Her face was ashen, the flames of life being blown out.

"I am not going to hurt you." She whispered, bending down into the muddy ground to assess the damage. "I am a *helbredera*, all I want to do is fix you while I can."

The female was crying, tears running down her freckled face. "I-It hurts. Muh leg." She looked downward, pointing toward her right leg. With a glance, she knew the artery had been severed, a large claw mark tore open the flesh from her hip bone around to her knee. To her side sat the sword she must have swung, that would have clattered away and out of her reach when she was struck down by the sharp claws of a wolfish.

Breathing deeply, attempting to get fresh air in her lungs, she was met with nothing but the scent of blood and dirt. While the smell churned her stomach, it also made her mind focus, it helped her to be able to ignore the sounds of battle around her. Many still fought around them, but a few had begun watching Maeve and the dying *ganera*.

"May I?" She asked, reaching toward the lethal gash.

The female grunted, and she could only take that as cautious consent.

Trembling, she lightly touched the area around the gash, which was still gushing with blood. A dangerous amount of blood that would mean death if not treated immediately. She took no time to notice the onlookers, nor to do anything but act.

The warm, familiar tingling manifested in her fingertips. A soft light came from them, making the dark red blood turn bright crimson. She started at the artery, just a whisper of a touch on the sensitive area. The fibers began merging, and a sigh was released from the female as it closed up and stopped hemorrhaging blood.

A strange vibrating began at the base of her skull, and she took the quickest glance up to notice bright blue eyes staring at her from the tree line.

Mikael did not look pleased.

She returned to her work, too concerned with this female's

wellbeing to be concerned with anyone, especially him.

Speaking with a delicate tone, she informed the female. "The worst is over. Now I just have to stitch up the skin here." Her touch sprang to life again, slowly willing the fibers of her muscles and skin to bind together anew. Much of the fighting had subsided, she only heard faraway entanglements near the other side of the foothills.

Finally, the gash was sealed. A sliver of light pink skin remained, but the scar would be minimal. The female was watching her with confusion as Maeve sat back on her knees, surveying her work.

The female reached to touch her thigh, amazement lightening her features.

"Tank yuh, I tought fur a segund der I was goin' tuh take muh last breath." Her accent was thick, but charming.

Maeve smiled, but quickly replaced it with a firm line when she noticed the dark shadow looming over her shoulder.

"You need to go back to your station, Sergeant." Hagan's voice was thick, his breath heavy from battle. She stood, facing Hagan head on. "Now." He said, his eyes glowing neon and his mouth set in a stern line.

For the first time, she was afraid of him. The female beside her stood too, testing her weight on her healed leg. Her eyes were roaming around the group, everyone now standing around watching, seemingly having forgotten about the battle that was meant to be occurring.

"You will not hurt her." Maeve said defiantly, her voice shaking.

His eyes flashed bright, eyebrows raising in surprise. "I will not." He promised.

"And you will stop this killing?" She asked in a breath, only allowing him to hear.

"I will." He muttered; his voice nearly indistinguishable as their gazes locked. His thick brows were riddled with dirt, the tan skin shiny with exertion. The veins in his neck were swollen, a reaction probably due to his impatience.

Satisfied with his answer, she gathered her things. The female bowed to her, her face a mix of confusion and fear. She inclined her head to the *ganera*, turning to head toward the treeline.

A large brown mass appeared in her peripheral vision, and before she turned, she could feel the heat of two tons of muscle against her. The bear's breathing was ragged, Elias had run on four legs to come to her. She looked down at him and reached out her hand to scratch behind his ears. If the life of a rebel weren't dripping from his mouth, she would have found him adorable.

Elias' jowls were covered in blood, dripping on the already damp ground. His usually golden-hued eyes were pools of liquid gold, the glow of them so intense from the magnitude of his power. He appeared unscathed as he sauntered up to her hip and pushed against it, nearly knocking her over.

He whined, eyes appearing impatient.

"He wants you to get on him, he intends to take you back to camp where it is safe." Hagan explained, his voice stiff.

The fighting had ceased, the Freed Fae had unofficially surrendered. However, the Fae around them watched the scene unfold between a Bear, a Healer, and a General. She did not know what to say, but her anger and confusion managed to form a few words. "I can walk."

Elias huffed, a low growl forming in his heaving chest. His glowing stare pleaded with her. Hagan simply stood there, the fire of his anger growing with every second as he appeared to lose his grip on the situation. He had to put on his facade as the audience watched intently.

Fine. But only because she thought it would be great fun.

Giving in, she hopped onto Elias' hulking back and tightened her legs around him. She leaned heavily upon him, his warmth a relief in the chill around her and the shiver that had begun to form deep in her bones. He shook once, presumably to check she was holding on tight enough, and began trotting off from whence she came.

Passing Mikael, who was staring at her incredulously, she listened as Hagan addressed the remaining soldiers on both sides. "No more blood needs to be shed today. As for the rest of the rebels, know this: The King of Thunder does—" His words faded from earshot. He had put on a mask, the mask of a General, as he spoke and as he commanded her to stop healing that female. At least the fun of riding a bear— Elias —kept her mildly distracted.

She enjoyed it more than she wanted to admit, a peacefulness coming to her as the awakening icy winds pinched her cheeks and cleared her thoughts. His pace was even, careful, so as not to throw her off. The colors of the forest whirled past them, and sooner than she thought, they were back at the camp. He slowed, the muscles underneath her hands working to stop moving. He stopped, tilting his head back to see her.

"Oh, uh—right. Thank you, Elias." She said awkwardly, a surprising grace in her descent to the ground beside him. He turned back at her and turned his head up to meet her gaze. His eyes were intense, as if he wished she could read his mind. Like he had so much to tell her that he could not utter in this form, or even in this time. He did not shift or speak. Not that she would have understood what he growled or huffed anyway.

He turned to leave, and she gave him a soft smile before turning her back as well.

She walked the short distance to the healing tent, Clover gawking at her like she had just sprouted a second head. She gave her a look of dismissal, like her going to the battlefield was not insane, and sat in one of the cots. Now she waited to heal the ones who had already hurt so many, had killed so many. Scowling at the dirt, she felt a strong obligation to run back and heal every *ganera* that lay on the ground in their own blood. She knew she couldn't. Not only could she not manage to heal them all in time, but she also knew if she went against orders there could be grave consequences that even Hagan could not intervene in.

CHAPTER 19
THE REBEL

There was plenty of work to do. A surprising number of soldiers were injured, and she watched as Clover was hard at work on a female with an arrow sticking from her shoulder. Carefully, she snipped off the flimsy wood of the arrow at the shaft and slowly pulled it from her skin. The female, who wore a stripe of *aimsura* blue, yelped in pain.

She rushed over, dropping her bag at the foot of the cot, and light sprung from her fingertips as soon as she touched the pierced skin. The *aimsura* sighed, relief settling her features. Blood was pouring from the hole in her shoulder, but Maeve made quick work of it, sealing the muscle fibers and skin until nothing but a light pinkish brown dot remained.

"By the Smiths." Clover whispered, dropping the bloody rags she was holding and stepping back to examine the now healed *aimsura*, her face stretched with astonishment.

Maeve smiled, she moved on to the other soldiers amongst the cots. "Clover, focus on the small wounds, I can take the more severe ones."

Clover nodded; her eyes still wide from witnessing Maeve's display of power.

The tent was near bursting with those in need of healing, but the labor kept her mind at ease from worrying about the consequences of her actions just moments ago.

She worked quickly, her power surging through their small healing tent. She healed a slashed shoulder, which was cut right at the tendon. Blood spattered on her apron, but she concentrated and closed the wound with ease.

Clover cleaned a large *treaniera* male up, and Maeve went to work on closing the wound completely.

She was in her element, healing soldiers one after the other. Clover followed all orders and took on soldiers who had smaller injuries with ease.

Her memories burned with what she had seen. It was not a battle; it was a massacre. Some of the *ganeras* were armed with no more than a knife, yet the 22nd Brigade had the arsenal to take down hundreds. Her heart ached for the ones who were killed, who were simply defending themselves, but she could not feel that pain right now. Now, she had to do her job.

Clover was healing a female with a few smaller sword slices on the arm, and Maeve had begun healing a gouge down the back of a *bhiastera* female when she looked up to see the General returning from battle.

They strode toward the center of the camp.

Her amber eye was glowing and turned to liquid fire as she pushed her Gift further and healed the female with a quick sweep down the back. The muscle and skin fibers quickly bent to her will, fusing together with ease within the timespan of a blink. The female jumped in surprise and whipped her head around to see her back. A thin, minor scar replaced that of the bleeding gash that was present seconds before.

"W-Woah. How did I not feel that? It usually hurts like a bitch. Thank you."

The *bhiastera* female got up, stretching her back in exploration. She scurried away from Maeve with a bow, she spoke with her eyes wide. "Thank you."

Maeve bowed back, smiling.

She wiped her hands on her apron and brushed the sweat from her brow. Gulping down some water, she noted her growing exhaustion from the extensive use of her Gift. There was only ever one time where she had worked this hard in her life, a memory that had haunted her and changed her life forever. When she was around the age of thirteen, an explosion tore apart her first home. By this time, she had mostly outgrown the dwellings that housed most of the new Forged. Lightning struck there, and the youngling home burst into vicious flames. She was out with a few teenaged Fae shopping for groceries when she heard the crack, but then she saw the smoke. The group ran to the dwelling, where many younglings resided. A group of lower-powered *aimsuras* gathered to quickly drown the dwelling in rain, but not before many were hurt. Keepers, some with younglings swinging from their arms, ran from the destroyed building. Older younglings quickly ran out too, and the injuries were vast. At the time, she had not yet shown any inclination of being Gifted of the Forge. Or so she thought.

She remembered her only thoughts at the time: *Help them.* The fire was quickly diminished, and all were accounted for besides one. Lady El.

When a group of *treaniera* retrieved her from the destroyed building, she was covered in major burns. She was immobile, the pain evidently knocking her unconscious. Maeve went to sit beside her, the female who raised her. Without real thought, she tried to touch her. Tears welling in her eyes, she felt true fear for the first time. She refused to lose her. At that moment, her Gift presented itself. Lady El, who she had started to just call Eliza, lived.

From that day, Maeve was a *helbredera.*

She walked toward the center of the camp, where she noticed Mikael standing above ten prisoners, a wicked gleam in his sea-blue stare. The Fae in the Brigade surrounded them, watching carefully.

Whispers began when Maeve walked up to meet her comrades, no doubt speaking of what she had done on the battlefield.

She pushed through to the center, joining Mikael, whose gaze remained on the prisoners. He was keeping them in check. He looked completely different than he did up in the tree. When others were watching, he wanted to appear powerful and unyielding. She had caught a glimpse of something much different.

Finally, the crowd parted for their General.

She took in a sharp breath when she saw him. His face was splattered with blood, and his power made the space feel like it was vibrating. His green eyes were the brightest she had ever seen them. He just bore his eyes into hers, as she felt her own power glow around her in response to his. His tunic was coated with sweat, and she noted a nasty gash that tore open the fabric, revealing parts of his golden rippling chest.

Finally, Elias sauntered over in his bearish form. He joined her to the side, throwing her a golden glance of warning.

Her eyes darted between the three of them, unease settling in her as she thought of the bloodied Freed Fae and the consequences of serving the King of Thunder.

Mikael gazed at the group; head cocked in concentration. "On your knees." He purred.

His eyes were twinkling in wicked delight. The small fire that was in the center of the camp allowed a soft light to shine up at her, allowing only the main features of the prisoners to be visible. They consisted of males and females, all shabbily dressed. All clearly in good shape, they were warriors. She glanced between them, one by one. They all shared a look of unaware daze. From what she could tell, Mikael was keeping them in a sort of trance. Keeping them complacent.

A red-haired female looked up at her, eyes lacking any emotion. A gash plunged across her face, from the side of her cheek to her bloody lips.

Don't do it. Maeve thought to herself, despite every nerve ending in her body protesting. She had already gone too far in the eyes of the King of Thunder, and she could easily lose her position or worse if she defied him again. Unfamiliar with the King's punishment methods, she could only imagine.

She stepped toward the female, who would have been lovely if not for this gash that would plague her face forever. As if her

Gift controlled her, she needed to heal this female more than she needed to protect herself.

She crouched down. "I'm going to fix this for you. Okay?" The female's brown eyes seemed to clear ever so slightly, and she nodded. The air turned icy around her. It appeared his highness did not approve.

She summoned her energy and slowly closed the gash. Prisoner or not, she did not want her to have to feel this pain now or in the future. For *ganera* females, who could not easily find work, sometimes a pretty face could get them far enough in life that they could survive.

Focusing, she closed her eyes. She felt a threatening shove against her power, as if someone was squeezing her temples with their palms.

A presence loomed over her. Mikael, who had his head cocked while his bright blue stare was directed at her. His dark, defined eyebrows were furrowed in confusion. She watched the sweat bead on his forehead. The *ganera* squirmed in discomfort, the healing must be hurting her.

Taking in a cool breath, she pushed a step further, and the female's face eased with comfort. She made quick work of the gash, and opened her eyes to see the female, cleared-eyed, staring back at her in astonishment. Gasps erupted from the crowd around them as she pulled back her glowing hands to reveal a renewed face. Her mouth was wide open, Mikael's grasp no longer clouded the female's mind.

She reached up to touch her own face, when she made an odd guttural noise in surprise. Something between a cry and a wheeze. "Thank you, Milady." She noted the lack of accent in this female, she could have easily come from Blarra.

Maeve examined the *ganera* female's restored face. "Just a teeny tiny scar. No one needs to know." She smiled down upon her as she stood shakily. Her body felt like it would collapse. She returned to stand beside Elias' bear form, his fur brushed up against her gently. His boulder of a head turned to her, golden eyes shimmering in admiration. At least that's what she thought it was.

At this point, being near him was the only place she felt safe. She had an odd connection with him. Something completely platonic, but a strong understanding between them. A friendship.

Everyone stared at her, and she caught the glint of glossy black of Petra in saber-toothed form to her other side. Her ears were alert, she was protecting her.

Without looking, she could feel that Hagan was close to erupting with fury.

Maeve had openly healed the enemy, twice.

CHAPTER 20
THE BATHTUB

Whispers scattered across the group, almost the entire Brigade now watching the scene that had unfolded before them all. Thunder struck in the sky, and Hagan stepped forward.

"Silence." General Hagan snarled.

Mikael smiled, glaring down at the prisoners as he spoke. His voice was like silk that unfurled from his full lips. "Listen to my words. You do not want to cross on to these lands again. This is the King of Thunder's domain. You will return to your own lands and you will warn your fellow Freed Fae of what may befall them if they cross the Divide. Consider this mercy."

His glowing stare bore into each of the prisoners, and they each nodded in understanding.

The complacency forced upon the prisoners made her wince. Every bone in her body screamed against their treatment, but she did no more. At least they weren't going to be killed.

He focused on the red-haired *ganera*, crouching down to her level. She shuddered, fear peeking through the emotionless daze. His fingers brushed her chin, and jerked her face to his. "What is your name, darling?"

Her eyes cleared, Mikael loosening his hold on her. "Olivia, sir."

"Olivia. I have a special task just for you. Will you do this for me?" A cruel smile parted his lips, aware that there was no choice in the matter.

She nodded, her chest rising and falling heavily.

"Ah, so kind of you Olivia. Now, I need you to get an audience with your so-called Leader. With your pretty new face, I need you to deliver a message to him, from the King of Thunder."

He leaned in, whispering. Maeve strained her ears to listen.

"Tell him that if the Freed Fae set a toe over the border into the Second Kingdom again, the King of Thunder will not yield. He will destroy each and every one of you."

He stood abruptly, pulling a handkerchief from his pocket. He blotted at the few beads of sweat on his forehead, taking his time as he kept each of the Freed Fae's minds in a cage. With a disgusted sneer on his face, he rubbed at his hands, specifically the one that had touched Olivia's face. He returned his stare to the ten prisoners and uttered a final command.

"Go." His hand gestured toward the foothills, discarding the handkerchief on the ground at Olivia's feet.

All the prisoners rose, and the crowd parted in the direction of the *ganeras'* destroyed camp.

The General addressed the Brigade, his voice booming in the night. "Well done, soldiers. I wish we had time to celebrate. We must journey back to our Kingdom's Court, where we will regroup and ready ourselves for the journey ahead. We will be taking leave for the Celebration of the Blood Moon. Take a few hours now to wash up and rest, prepare for our departure. We will walk through the night, and the trip will be five long days. You have all served your King well."

The crowd of soldiers cheered as a few howls echoed into the dark night. She had loved the Blood Moon Celebration, ever since Geneza. The whole point was to honor the lives of the dead, but it usually turned into drunken merriment and bountiful feasts. When she died, she would want to be honored that way too.

The crowd dispersed, some hoping to get a nap in or to wash

the blood from their battle-bloodied bodies. She spotted Petra, now dressed and in her Fae body. Red streaked her chin, likely one of the opposing soldier's blood. Petra had always lived for a good kill.

Peering warily in Hagan's direction, she saw him cleaning the blood off him in one of the water stations she and Clover had set up. He wiped his face, then his eyes met hers. They darted from her to the *helbredera* tent.

Fuck. She had almost let herself forget about what she had done, twice. This was not going to be good.

Hagan strode into the healer tent. "Clover, could I have the tent?"

The small female looked up at him and gulped. Her high-pitched voice all but screeched, "Yes, General." She skittered out without another word.

Maeve walked into the tent, closing the opening behind her. It felt even smaller when it was just the two of them. The room shrunk and he closed the distance between them. She stood her ground, even if her exhaustion wanted to take her to one of the cots. His scent surrounded her, riddled with the stench of sweat and blood.

His voice was rough. "What in the Forged Fuck were you thinking?"

She took a deep breath. "I promised to heal those in need, which is what I have done. I refuse to apologize for my actions when I know in my heart that they are right. The *ganeras* were outnumbered and out-Gifted by far too much. It was a massacre."

His lips turned up. "They were disobeying the law, Maeve. We had to intervene."

"You did not have to kill so many. They were defenseless."

"Defenseless? Do you see this?" He gestured to his bloody chest. "If a broadsword is swung in your direction, I would hope to the Smiths you would fight back."

She had not thought of it that way. While she did not want death, it is possible that the Freed Fae's hate of the Second Kingdom caused them to react in a violent manner. Even if they were given the chance to surrender.

"Okay, but if I can save a life, I will do so. It is my duty. I'm glad I got there when I did, or I fear far more blood would have been spilled for no reason."

Hagan shook his head, but his eyes softened as he looked into hers. "Your kindness is not what I am angry about. Whether your heart is in the right place or not, you cannot put on shows like that, healing our enemies. The King of Thunder would not tolerate such mercy. Next time, this must be done in private." He grabbed her hand, and he whispered, "One of the things I admire most about you is your kindness, but we just cannot put it on display when the eyes of the King are upon us. If he senses weakness, he will eliminate it. We cannot risk such a thing reaching his benevolent ears."

She breathed in, a sudden burst of energy flowing through her as he held her hand and she took in the full presence of a warrior. She looked up, and his eyes were looking down at her, heavy with something she couldn't place.

The tension between them was almost too much, their powers dancing and twirling around each other in the small space.

"As you wish, your highness." She smirked, her head tilting up toward him. "At least I'm not in trouble." A laugh skittered across her lips.

His green eyes twinkled despite his previous anger, and she switched her gaze to his chest. "You should let me heal that."

She stepped back to motion toward one of the cots.

He rolled his eyes but decided against arguing with her. "Are you sure you're not too tired for this? You healed many today, so you must have exerted a lot of energy." He sat down on the cot.

She shook her head, a soft smile on her lips. "I am fine. Remove your top, your eminence. It's disgusting."

He smirked, and he removed his tunic, which peeled off of him to reveal his muscled torso. She managed to keep a completely straight face, pushing down the urge to trace those exceptional abs with her finger. She kneeled to clean the wound, and a few tendrils that had loosened from her makeshift bun fell onto his bare chest.

He sucked in a breath at the light touch and swallowed. "You did a fine job today, the others are talking of your significant contributions. Especially how you managed to heal them all without them feeling any pain. I assume none of them have witnessed this Gift in a *helbredera*."

She glanced up to meet his gaze under thick lashes. "And you have?" She was curious, because before joining the Brigade no one had ever commented on it when she worked in Blarra or lived in Geneza.

He nodded. "Once." He paused, as if a certain memory had popped into his head. "Have you ever wondered why you can do that?" A wince broke from him as she patted the wound.

She shrugged. "I think I just always figured some other healers could do it. The Smiths were pretty generous to me when I was Forged. I suppose I got lucky." She smiled, looking into his subdued green gaze.

They looked back at her intensely. He opened his mouth to speak, but a sigh parted his lips.

Returning to her work, she began sealing the wound.

Hagan stared at her as she worked, and she tried to ignore what his stare was doing to the coils in her stomach. She finished healing the wound, and stood.

When she wobbled, Hagan was up in a second. He balanced her, but her eyes felt heavy. "I'm fine, I just…"

The room went black. The last thing she felt was his warmth, and the strong arms picking her up from the ground.

Snow covered the mountains outside the large, black-framed arched window. The sky was splattered with purple and blue swirls of night, and stars smiled down upon the mountain range underneath. She was soaking in a tub that was sunken into the ground, large enough to fit five of her. Lavender swirled through the air, and relaxation eased over her body as she breathed in the soothing scent. She sank deeper into the tub, as an alluring male voice spoke.

"What a view."

Her glance drifted from the window to Hagan, shirtless and leaning his hip against the curved bathroom door frame. His eyes were bright with wonder, aided by the numerous lit candles scattered around her bath. His hair was pushed back, revealing his strong brow and powerful jawline. He strode over, a smile playing across his lips. Hagan knelt on the side of the tub where her head was. She tipped her head back to look at his striking face staring down at her. He was even handsome upside down.

"You want to join me?" She asked, her lips parted as she gazed up at him. He smiled, his eyes crinkling the smallest bit at the end. His hands moved into the water, and his grip tightened on her tense shoulders. Her body hummed with his touch, but she tipped her head forward and groaned. His fingers expertly rubbed the sore muscles of her shoulders in the steaming water of the bath. His Gift warmed his hands and the water around them to deepen the massage. It felt incredible, and she let him continue for a few minutes before tipping her head back to meet his eyes again. They had turned a shade darker, desire bubbling in them.

She bit her lip, and he leaned in closer. "I worship you."

She closed her eyes, feeling a torturous ache deep within her.

The familiar tinge of blood that filled the air of the healers tent plagued her senses. Clover squeaked, noticing she had woken up. Those round eyes appeared over her face, and Maeve smiled with only her lips. "How are you feeling, Miss Maeve?"

Maeve groaned. "I'm alright." She was about to be better, if she wouldn't have woken up from that delicious dream. Her mind still raced; she could've sworn she felt those strong hands on her shoulders still.

She rose, shoo-ing Clover from fretting over her. Her eyes searched the tent and outside of the curtained opening. An evening glow settled upon the camp as soldiers hustled back and forth preparing for the next leg of the journey.

She shook her head, clearing the fuzz from her brain. "I am okay now, thank you Clover."

The small female returned a toothy smile.

She straightened. "Let's get things ready, it looks like the Brigade is preparing to leave soon." When she glanced at Clover, she noticed dark circles shadowing her lily-white skin. She hadn't rested while Maeve was out.

The Brigade was ready to move out, sounds of huffing horses

and the movement of soldiers surrounded her. Soldiers chatted about what they would be doing for the Blood Moon Celebration and how they wished to sleep in their own beds. Apparently, many of the soldiers were granted estates that were in surrounding villages of the Crown for their service. The grandest celebration was at the Second Kingdom castle, if one could manage to get an invitation. She walked up to Callistus, offering her an apple and looking into her endless midnight eyes. "You ready for the long ride, girl?" the horse neighed happily, and she smiled and mounted her.

CHAPTER 21
THE WHISKEY

The days were long as they traveled at a steady pace toward the North. The soldiers were tired, but they persevered each day, only to get a few hours of sleep at night. She was not used to living on three hours of sleep a day, so on the fourth day she was a dead Fae walking. Thankfully, Callistus was strong and rode as hard as was necessary. Hagan finally announced to the Brigade that they would be stopping at an Inn in the upcoming village, Brekka. He wanted them all to rest up and look halfway acceptable for their arrival to the Second Kingdom.

The village was three times as large as Blarra. Similar cobblestones dotted the streets, but they were polished and shown with much more vibrancy than her old home's single main road. The colorful buildings surrounding the street on both ends boomed with life, and the inhabitants beamed at the 22nd Brigade with pride as they walked toward the Inn.

Hagan, Elias, Mikael, and Maeve stopped at a bright yellow building, which was about ten stories tall. It had to have one hundred or more rooms in it. The Innkeeper was a small, plump female who smiled from ear to ear when she walked out to meet Hagan. Her dress was bright red, and her lips matched. Her warm, golden eyes peered between the group, and landed on

Maeve. She gave her an even happier smile. Hagan handed the female what appeared to be a large sac of Golds. Nausea settled in, that amount of money would have fed all of Blarra for at least a year.

"We require all of your vacant rooms for the night, but I do understand some soldiers will have to bunk together." Hagan stated, more of an order than a request.

"Well of course, General. The horses can be stored in our stables behind the Inn, and we'll make sure we get hot meals going for all of you." Her smile was so warm, and she waved out a few *ganera* Fae to help tend to the horses and bags. The four of them ambled into the Inn, and her mouth watered instantly. Her eyes were heavy, but her stomach was rumbling with hunger.

The Fae who worked at the Inn were already laying out warm bread, fine cheese, and fresh fruits of many kinds on the sprawling mahogany bar.

She looked around, her mouth slightly agape, at the fanciest place she had ever been. Gold gilded the ceiling, and detailed murals covered the walls behind the bar. The Fae who worked there were all dressed in lovely, black uniforms, and their buttons were shiny gold. Wine poured from small fountains at each table, which were surrounded by plush chairs. It was immaculately decorated, it felt like a castle to her.

She had to restrain herself from ravenously digging into the tempting platters of food. The Innkeeper, who she learned was named Rose, personally showed the Sergeants and General to their rooms. They walked down the long hall, doors flanking them on both sides. She noted the ripe stench of four travelers stuffed into a hallway, grimacing at the fact that she was one of them.

Rose handed her a bronze key, and gestured toward room forty-two. "For you, Sergeant." Maeve thanked her, and nodded to Mikael, Elias, and Hagan as they were ushered to their respective rooms.

Opening the door, her eyes widened, *this* was her room. Large windows were covered in dark blue drapes, sweeping the ground which was laid with gorgeous dark hardwood. A large hearth accompanied by two plush chairs were set in the corner, and the fire was already warming the room to a delightful temperature. She walked in, setting her bag down, and turned to see a large bed, draped in thick blue blankets, and covered in pillows. She wanted nothing more but to jump into the welcoming embrace of those pillows. She restrained, walking into the small, adjoined room that held a marvelous tub.

"Fuck yes," She whispered, and immediately began taking off her dirty, travel-worn clothes.

She was in desperate need of a real bath. Maeve turned on the warm water and looked through the shelf's products. She decided on a glass container that held lavender petals floating in a liquid that smelt of soap. Liquid soap was a major luxury compared to the blocks she made from scratch. She poured a generous amount into the tub, since the Crown was paying.

A groan broke from her lips as her sore muscles hit the steaming water. She let her hair out of its braid and held her breath as she sunk into the water. Maeve scrubbed her hair with the soap, and then took the loofah that sat on the side of the tub and lathered the rest of her body until she was utterly satisfied, and her skin was a bit raw.

Grabbing a towel that was set on the small table against the tub, she dried herself thoroughly and wrapped its soft warmth around herself.

She took a glance in the floor-length mirror and noticed a beautiful glow about herself. The sun had given her a few more freckles, and her skin was about three shades darker than it had been when she left Blarra. A knock resounded at the door, and she tucked the towel farther around herself. When she opened the door, golden eyes looked back at her.

A smile appeared on her lips. "Hello, Elias."

He smiled back, but quickly stiffened as he beheld her in only a towel. Her collarbones were pronounced, her exposed skin flawless.

"What can I do for you?"

He raised an eyebrow. "We will be dining in a few minutes; won't you join us?"

Nodding, she looked down at herself. "In a bit."

His eyes roamed down her body, and he inhaled deeply. "Right, well, meet us down there when you're ready. I'm starving." His golden eyes glittered, the innuendo causing her to blush.

She nodded, closing the door to him. Squeezing into some fresh pants and one of her favorite open-shouldered sweaters, she felt the aches in her legs from days of riding. After drying her hair and tossing it to the side, she made her way down to the main floor of the Inn.

Rich smells of roasting meats, some she had never smelled before, devoured her senses as she strode down the steps to the level below. Her body, led by her stomach, made a beeline for the bar, where many of the soldiers began to fill their plates with all of the delights of the Inn's kitchen. A few *ganeras* in line gestured for her to go first, and usually she would have rejected that sort of special treatment, but she was starving.

Cheeses, meats, fruit, and toasted bread filled her plate as high as it would allow. At the end of the sprawling bar, the working Fae were handing out small plates with what appeared to be chocolate cake. A hum of glee reverberated through her as she accepted one, having never tried something so decadent. Her hands were full, and she looked out to all of the tables to find Petra. She scanned the almost full dining room and finally spotted Petra, devouring that same chocolate cake.

There was a large container of a sparkly white wine at the center of the table, and she sat there with Lyra, who smiled up at her as she sat down with her food. The females chatted, each of them devouring the food on their plates.

"After this, I am passing out. Those wolfish boys better not keep us awake in our room." Lyra looked vexingly at Petra, and they laughed.

A twinge of guilt hit her. Petra had to bunk with other soldiers.

Petra nestled her chin in her hands. "So, how have things been going with all of the delicious males you bunk with?" Her eyes flashed, and Lyra leaned in to listen. "I think I'd pick Elias.

I can't even imagine the size of his—"

"I'm going to stop you there." Her shocked face caused the two females to grin.

Lyra giggled, her dark eyes shy and her voice low. "Okay, but you cannot say it hasn't crossed your mind."

She opened her mouth but closed it abruptly. She could not argue with that. They were all attractive males, but her thoughts only dwelled on one.

"Sure, but nothing has happened! Is the whole camp betting on who I'll fuck first or something? I didn't join the Brigade based upon how attractive the males are." She whispered, trying to not attract attention toward herself.

Petra took a sip of wine, her mouth turning up in a smirk. "It's got to be Hagan. You're obsessed with him, have been since you healed him at the Apothecary."

Her cheeks flamed red, trying to think of a reply when the scent of fresh rainwater intruded her nostrils. "Ladies." Hagan crooned, and sat in the seat facing her.

Lyra sat up straight, stiffening. "Good evening, General."

Her eyes settled on Hagan's; she knew he must have heard what Petra said.

"What can we do for you, your highness?" She asked innocently.

Lyra shot her a look of confusion at the nickname that was becoming a habit between her and the General.

Hagan smirked, his eyes heating up. "Just here for the wine." He poured himself a glass from the large decanter and set it beside his plate. He licked his lips to took a sip. He kept his eyes on her the whole time.

Petra cut in, like a sharp knife through the tension. "Mmmmm. Chocolate cake. I haven't had chocolate in decades. You have to try this Maeve!"

Maeve kept her gaze with Hagan as she took a bite of her own chocolate cake. She let the fork rake down her lower lip. Hagan's green eyes were near glowing with hunger.

The cake was delicious, the chocolate icing thick and rich with sweetness.

The side of his mouth lifted, and he looked down to eat. "Dig in, ladies. We'll need the energy for the morning. We leave at dawn." The four of them ate their huge plates of food. The ease of conversation lessened in his presence, but she welcomed the quiet company. She caught Hagan stealing glances, making Petra giggle beside her.

After a bit more chatting and a few glasses of wine, she decided to retire to her big, comfy, blue bed. Hagan had already bid them goodnight, but Petra and Lyra said their goodnights to her as she took a final swig of wine and turned to go upstairs.

She couldn't tell if it were the wine, or the encounter with Hagan that caused it, but her body felt warm and tingly. When she opened the door to her room, she was struck with surprise. His scent washed over her, dripping in fresh rainwater. She tiptoed in, and saw the back of his head sitting in one of the plush seats by her hearth.

Standing by the seat opposite him, her eyes met his emerald gaze as he offered a glass of brown liquid with an outstretched hand.

She scrunched her brows in confusion, understandably surprised by this casual visit. His face was turned into a thoughtful expression, as if contemplating something extremely important.

"Sit," he half-ordered, and she felt obliged to take the glass of whiskey and obey. She looked at him expectantly. He was gazing at the hot flames bouncing around the logs in the hearth. The sound of crackling was the only thing between them for a long moment.

He slowly turned, shifting his gaze to her. "What are your plans for the Blood Moon?" The fire light played across his defined features.

She smirked, leaning back into her chair. She took a sip of the whiskey that pleasured her tongue with hints of honey and vanilla. "Mmm. This is lovely." She tilted her glass toward her lips once more.

"Careful, the good stuff will cloud your inhibitions much quicker than the Inn's wine." His lips curved.

She giggled, the spirits making her voice confident.

"Inhibitions. We wouldn't want those compromised." Her voice was sardonic as she took another sip of the delightful liquid. She licked her lips with an ounce or two extra effort than was necessary.

Hagan smiled, looking at her in that way, as if she were a puzzle.

Her shoulders lifted in a soft shrug. "I have no idea what I'll be doing for Blood Moon. I have to find a place to live when we go to Court, you know."

Hagan shook his head, smiling. "You'll be staying in the castle with the other Sergeants… and myself. You'll have your own chamber, new clothes, and anything else you may desire." His voice turned to a whisper on that last word.

She raised her eyebrows, and laughed. "Well, I guess I can't say no to that. What about the private estate?" Sipping her drink, she watched Hagan looking down at his glass in thought.

"Well, I suppose if you want to stay there, we can have it prepared for you. It is a rather old cottage, so it may need renovation. All expenses covered by the Crown, of course."

She stifled a laugh, taking another sip from her glass. "I lived above an Apothecary with two roommates and one bathroom, and you're concerned about the outdated design of my own private home?"

He chuckled, his eyes crinkling on the sides. "You have a point, we can discuss the logistics later." He hesitated, his smile fading. "I need to tell you something. I haven't been completely honest, but you're going to find out when we go home anyways."

The way he said home puzzled her, especially since they were to share the same home.

She leaned forward. "Well don't keep me waiting, your highness."

He peeked at her with a contemplative side-eye. "It's funny you call me that. As you found out that one night in Blarra, I am Born. I don't flaunt that to the Brigade, besides Elias and Mikael of course, and avoid using my other Gift unless necessary. I do not want to be treated like anything other than a General, so I keep my identity a secret."

His gaze bore deep into hers, lips parting ever so slightly. Her gaze dipped to his lips. Listening intently, she tilted her head to the side, beckoning him to continue.

He sighed. "I'm not just Born, my father is the King of Thunder."

She leaned in further, her mouth wide open. "You're the Prince of the Second Kingdom?"

Failing to hold it back, she let out a laugh. "Your highness, indeed." He was the heir to the Second Kingdom throne. She didn't find herself surprised at this news; it made much more sense. His confidence, his power, and his ridiculous spending habits. He was the Prince.

"I'm glad I could make you laugh, even at my own expense. You have the most beautiful smile." He said softly.

She laughed again, her smile reaching her ears. "Thank you."

He took a sip from his glass and sighed. When he looked into the hearth, she noted a sadness in his eyes and a furrow of his dark brow. The urge to go over and hug him and rush away his sorrow came over her. The part of her that heals wanted to ease his sorrow, and the part of her that feels for him was beginning to want the same. She felt the whiskey form her words, a sudden confidence in her voice. "What's wrong?"

He drifted his eyes up to hers, and his expression was a strange mix of sadness and desire. Longing.

His voice was almost hoarse. "Have you ever wanted something so badly, but it was just out of reach?"

Her mouth went dry, she breathed in deeply, and his scent and power were almost overwhelming her senses. Her thoughts went to the dreams she'd been having, how vivid they felt. How he had made her feel in them. She wanted so badly to feel that again. She stood from her chair and stepped toward Hagan.

His eyes read nothing but intense desperation, but she kept her gaze steady. Hagan watched as she crawled into his lap, her legs straddling him on either side of his thighs. Both of their breaths were ragged, and the heat of him surrounded her. Every part of her body that touched him was alight with desire.

She smiled, lips closed, as she looked down at his face. She succeeded; he no longer looked the least bit sad. His eyes were burning with hunger, while his strong hands found her hips. She closed her eyes, breathing in the musky scent of him. When her eyelids fluttered open, his deep green gaze stared up at her.

She parted her lips, inviting him to taste.

His eyes met hers so deeply that she thought he looked into her soul for what felt like an eternity. He searched her, peeling off every layer to see her. Really see her. He looked strained, like his eyes told her everything she needed to know.

She smiled, touching her fingers to his cheek, taking in every beautiful inch of his tanned face. She wanted this more than anything she's ever desired in her twenty-five years of life.

Licking her lips, she dipped her head down and stopped just an inch away from his. His breathing was heavy, and she could feel him hard against her inner thighs. Hagan's hands moved to her back, pulling her closer, his lips against her ear.

"Are you sure?"

She couldn't take it, she vibrated in pleasure at his breath against her ear. She pulled back and answered by pressing her whiskey coated lips against his.

He groaned, moving his hands to her face as he deepened the kiss. His lips were soft, but firm and commanding against hers. She wrenched his mouth open, needing more. His tongue thrashed against hers, a complex dance that she matched with every movement.

Her mind raced, and she couldn't help but grind against him as they attempted to touch every inch of the other's body.

Hands roamed, and she let out a low moan when his hands trailed down to her ass, and he grabbed at the suppleness of it. The kiss felt natural, as if their mouths were meant to intertwine.

She was wrapped around him, all her senses overwhelmed with him. She reached to pull off his shirt when he stopped her.

He pulled her head back, his hand holding her chin in place as he took in every detail of her face.

She knew her eyes were glowing, pleading with him.

Sadness darkened his gaze once more.

He lifted her off of him with powerful grace, then he stood.

She was placed on her feet in front of him. He backed away quickly, restraining himself from going any further. Her body ached, a chill trembling through her.

"I can't do this. This was a mistake." His voice cracked, the look of longing returning to his features. His lips glistened with the kiss he regretted. His pants strained with arousal, telling her a completely different story.

Maeve objected. "No, this isn't right. You want this, this is the thing that you want so badly. You can have it. I'm right here. Please." She hated begging, the weakness it showed, but she was desperate for more of him.

An ache deep inside her roared, and she knew only more of him would calm it. She stepped toward him, but he forced himself back. His voice wavered. "I'm sorry, Maeve. I should not have done this, it was inappropriate of me."

Before she could object further, he strode out of the room without another word.

Hands shaking, her eyes stared at her door for what felt like hours. She felt his warmth in every place that he touched. Those spots turned cold without him there, and she shook her head.

He rejected her and left her wet with no release. "What the fuck…" she whispered as she looked at the chair that they had just shared.

A male had never had this sort of effect on her. It gave her comfort to imagine him in his own bed, and she hoped he was suffering like she was. Maeve stoked the fire in the hearth, and flung herself onto the bed, surrounding herself with pillows and blankets until she felt like she was in her own cocoon.

She felt the wetness that had pooled in her, and she groaned. It was meant for him if he would have just taken it. Shoving the pillows around, she finally got comfortable and covered herself completely with the blanket. Exhaustion setting in, she drifted off to a dreamless sleep.

→» →» «← «←

Sunshine flowed in through the small gap in the curtains, shining rays of gold across the room. She awoke with a start, hearing a loud knock at her door and a high-pitched voice. "Breakfast!"

Maeve hopped out of bed; she had overslept a bit. She quickly packed what little things she had and looked in the mirror. Her hair was askew but looked good enough when put in a quick half ponytail. She pinched her cheeks to life, wiped her tired eyes, and put on her boots.

Rushing downstairs, she found an exhilarated group of soldiers accompanied by the smell of bacon that invited her to the bar. She sat at one of the barstools, looking around anxiously for Hagan. After last night, she had no idea what was going through his head. One of the *ganeras* put a plate of bacon and various fruits in front of her.

She thanked them, and dug in.

The fruit was so juicy, almost to the point of decadent. The *naduras* of Brekka must have been highly Gifted, to grow fruit of that caliber. She bit into a fresh, ripened peach when Mikael came to sit on the stool beside her. A little closer than she preferred. He took a grape from her plate and smiled with his near perfect features. He had clearly bathed, and he smelled of rich peppermint. His gaze shifted to her exposed collarbone in the sweater.

He purred, "You know, when you're sick of Hagan teasing you, I'll be happy to fulfill your... desires." Maeve squinted her eyes at him, taking a bite of a reddish-green apple.

When she looked to Mikael's left, she noticed Hagan's eyes burning into hers. He was in hearing distance.

Maeve looked back at Mikael and leaned in to close some of the distance between them. Her stare was on those almond-shaped, ocean blue eyes. A curious smile played on his full, pink lips. A soft tickle started from the back of her head down her body, his power stroking hers.

While she felt a bit sick from it, she knew Hagan was watching them intently. Pettiness was not usually in her nature, but she was in the mood for a bit of revenge today.

She giggled, making sure she spoke loud enough for Hagan to hear. "It's like you read my mind. And what would you do if you got the chance?"

Mikael lowered his head, peering at her through long lashes, looking at her as if she were a meal. "Oh, darling. I'm not one to spoil a surprise." He scanned her features, eyes landing on her exposed neck. "But, I would love to see those stunning eyes roll to the back of your head."

She straightened, swallowing to push down the bile rising in her throat. "Well, that is tempting. How would you manage to do that?" He smirked, his overconfidence fueling the game she was playing. He reached out, stroking his thumb on her lower lip. "Many ways. I would absolutely ravish you. I could start by licking your—"

She cleared her throat. "That's enough."

His eyes flashed in delight. He had taken it too far, to a place she was not willing to go with him. And he knew it.

"I win." Mikael whispered, his power buzzing at the back of her skull as a reminder.

He poked out his lip, looking like a youngling. "Please don't use me to make our Hagan jealous, love. It's a bit pathetic."

With a glare at Mikael, she turned to return to her food.

CHAPTER 22
THE KINGDOM

The journey to the Second Kingdom Court was enlightening. Valleys and large estates that sprawled the surrounding villages were nothing short of picturesque. Large mansions and cottages dotted the sprawling lands, only more elegant the longer they rode.

Elias trotted his horse up to hers. "What d'ya think?" His golden eyes were luminescent in the overhead sun.

"Honestly, it's incredible. My only reservation is knowing the citizens of Blarra are living the way they are while all of this —" She gestured to the vast landscape. "—exists. It just doesn't seem quite fair."

Elias nodded, his eyes forward at the trail ahead. "Sometimes I envy the simple villages we visit, like Blarra. Noble life, despite its riches, can be rather exhausting. Sometimes I crave a simpler life." His lips turned up in a soft smirk.

She smiled back, his warmth and kindness filling her with glee. She had made a friend in Elias, instantly. His influence was catching, and she found herself in fine spirits for the remainder of the trip.

Mountains began to blur into the Brigade's line of sight. They were nothing like the treacherous mountains that the Freed Fae called home. The snow-capped majesties jutted into the clouded sky, waterfalls cascading from jagged outcroppings all over the range. As they trotted closer, the Brigade speeding up without order, she was able to take in the sight of the castle. Many of the soldiers branched off down different roughened paths, presumably to their village or estate, before they reached the capitol of the Second Kingdom. Only the most noble lived there, and by the time the castle came into full view, the group had thinned out to her, Hagan, Elias, Mikael, Petra, Lyra, and a handful of others whom she did not know. She did notice that none of the remaining groups bore the beige or brown stripes of the *ganeras* and *treanieras*. Wealth or power were the only things that landed someone in any of the capitals, which were impossible to attain without being Gifted by the Forge.

The castle was like nothing she had ever seen. It's presence was both beautiful and intimidating. Sharp lines decorated the architecture, mixtures of metal and stone slicing into the mountains.

Carved from the mountain itself, the building sat many stories high. The exterior was made of bright, white marble and was obscured with surrounding waterfalls. Black veins broke up the ivory in patterns like lightning. Dozens of black-framed windows and terraces opened to the hills and valleys below. It was a well-thought-out architecture that symboled power. Black and white everything. Every wall and window built into the mountain, a part that had been there for millennium. A display of longevity. As the Brigade approached this outcropping in the tall rocks, a parade of well-dressed Fae celebrated their arrival.

While the buildings were predominately black and white, it was lively. At the base of the King's Mountain, the bottom of the roaring waterfall poured into the running river that edged the city and eventually flowed into the River of the Five to the West. The inhabitants of this wealthy town cheered and threw flowers into the air as they passed. The bright reds and yellows of the flower petals dusted the gray brick of the town's city square.

Smiling faces looked up to her, and she stopped as a youngling's bright blue eyes glittered up at her. Dismounting, she bent down to meet the girl's gaze.

The young Fae smiled. "Your horsey is so pretty."

Maeve's smile lit up, and she picked up the girl and let her pet Callistus' moon-silver mane. The horse's eyes brightened with excitement as she nuzzled her snout against the young one's face. "This is Callistus, she likes you!" As she held the young one, she glanced to her left. Hagan's eyes were on her, and a small smile danced on his lips as he saw her with the youngling.

She gave him a quick glare as the young one was petting Callistus. After his actions the previous night, he could take his kind eyes and shove them up his royal ass.

Maeve set the young one down and glanced up to see matching blue eyes from a tall, blonde female.

"I'm sorry!" She spoke nervously, picking up the youngling. "She's quite the escape artist."

Maeve smiled as she shook her head. "It is not a problem at all, that little girl is a Gift. It was nice to meet you both." Maeve said as she mounted her horse with the other soldiers to continue their trek into the city. The little girl waved frantically in her mother's arms as she walked away, laughing as Elias made a funny face at her.

She had always been good with younglings, in Geneza she had to take care of many and watch them either be adopted or grow up to fend for themselves. While Eliza was as close to a mother as she could have and she was grateful for her, she did wonder why she was never chosen to live with a family of her own.

They approached the town center, the sounds of the waterfall attempting to drown out the sounds of the townsfolk. Petra met Maeve, with Lyra at her side.

"I feel like we haven't talked in ages." Maeve said, dismounting Callistus.

Petra smiled sadly. "I know. We must catch up soon. I'll be staying in town; Lyra has a townhome here. Apparently if you save the General's life you get to live in the capitol." A sly smile pulled at her lips.

She met Lyra's dark eyes. "You saved Hagan's life?"

Lyra smiled, rolling her eyes. "She's making it seem like more than it was. I just took an arrow for him, and I didn't even mean to do it. It was either his head or my ribs. The healing process wasn't too bad." Lyra shrugged humbly.

She scoffed, amazed at Lyra's humility.

With a kiss on the cheek, Petra said goodbye and walked with Lyra to the far side of the town.

A large group of Fae in pristine white uniforms met them at the base of the mountain, the waterfall breaking behind them.

The male *ganera* in the front bowed. "Welcome, General. We will attend to your horses and baggage as you make your way to your quarters."

He lifted his hand toward the castle that was about half of a mountain up. Hagan nodded, thanking the *ganeras*.

Maeve's eyes widened as she looked up the sprawling staircase that was mostly shielded by the waterfall.

Elias noticed her shock. "You don't look too comfortable with the climb."

Maeve didn't know what to say as she was looking at the castle above, her neck craned. She had no idea how she was going to climb all of those stairs.

Elias laughed. "I'm only kidding. There is a lift just behind the waterfall, which is the way we'll be taking."

Hagan came up beside her, gesturing for her to follow.

Behind the waterfall, they came up on a wooden platform attached to a pulley system that led all the way up the mountain, to the base of the palace.

Uncertain, she watched as Hagan and Mikael stepped onto the platform with ease, each of them holding onto the edge. Elias pulled at her hand, beckoning her to join them. Letting trust take over, she relented. She had never been afraid of heights, but she was afraid of falling to her death.

She stepped onto the platform after him, and a call from one of the *ganera* servants signaled for their ascent to begin. With a soft jolt, they were rising in mid-air. Her breathing hitched, and Mikael stifled a laugh behind her.

She whirled around, her stomach turning over as she did. "Do you have something to say?" She yelled over the sounds of the lift.

Mikael shook his head, looking innocent.

"Good." She turned back around to the edge, watching as the capitol grew smaller and smaller beneath her. The landscape sprawled, many hues of green swirling amongst the hills and valleys. She noticed small, yet lovely villages dotting the land and she wondered where her home would be.

The wind brushed her face as they went, caressing her skin until goosebumps began to form. Her knuckles were bright white from holding onto the edge. A slight jerk stopped them once they reached the top, and following the lead of the three males, she stepped out onto the platform of the carved-out piece of mountain, where the palace loomed overhead.

The palace was even grander up close, the front courtyard adorned with manicured lawns and clean lines. The entrance was lined with a curved, black entry. Guards stood at the front of the entry, wearing red stripes across their uniforms to represent *bhiastera*.

The four of them walked toward the entrance, and they were met by a gorgeous female with familiar bright green eyes. Her hair was cut to her collarbones, a sheet of black against sepia skin. The simple tiara on top of her head was matte black, with white opals and purple amethysts clustered in the front. She wore an elegant, long-sleeved dress that fell to her ankles in dark purple and grey sheets, and a fur shawl wrapped around her arms. Fine lines cut into her skin, her age clearly matured past mid-life. Her power felt old, too. The magnitude of it brought tingles to the mind. Hers was not a power that shook everyone in the room, like Hagan's. Hers was a soft caress against the cheek. *Cleasiera.* The female smiled upon them, and the soft crinkles in her eyes told her everything. Hagan's mother.

Pride welled in her upturned eyes. "Son. Welcome back."

They embraced, he squeezed his mother tight before releasing her. The female eyed Mikael and Elias, smiled, and shifted her eyes to Maeve. Her eyes lit up when she looked at her. "Welcome, dear. I am Revna, please make yourself at home here. I do think you'll fall in love."

Maeve smiled and shook her outstretched hand. "Thank you, my Queen. It is a pleasure to meet you, I'm Maeve."

Revna's eyes flashed. "Oh, I know dear. Everyone is talking about a powerful *helbredera* joining our court. We must fit you for some new dresses." Revna grabbed her hand and dragged her into the palace. The males followed, all looking slightly dumbfounded.

The foyer was just as fancy as the outside. A grand staircase had alternating black and white marble steps up to the second floor. The railing swirled out at the base of the stairs, creating an elegant design. The ceiling had to be as tall as a normal three-story building, boasting intricate black beams that went back and forth in a crisscross pattern.

Despite the exuberant elegance of the palace, the furnishings were comfortable. Oversized plush seating was scattered throughout, and luxurious rugs covered areas of the stark white marble floors. No piece was out of place, and no color stood out more than the rest. It was simple. Beautiful.

Revna led her up to the landing of the second floor, where the floors switched to a gorgeous black marble. Her heels clicked as they strode down a long hallway.

"I wanted to make sure you had a view." Revna said, her eyes bright with amusement. She stopped at the end of the hall, where a large hardwood door met them. "These will be your quarters, dear." She turned the matte black knob to Maeve's room.

The bedroom was subtly decorated, but elegant. The oversized four poster bed sat welcoming her from the corner, draped with more large pillows and blankets than she could have possibly asked for. The color scheme was mainly black and white, but with pops of a soft purple.

Lavender.

A small hearth was in the other corner, warming the space to a lovely temperature. A black velvet chaise lounge was set right in front of it on top of a snow-white rabbit fur rug. The arched black frame windows covered the far wall, which led out to a small terrace that overlooked the city below and the rolling hills that followed. The more she looked, the more at home she felt. Revna must have noticed the awe and delight on her face. "The other boys will be down this hall, but I saved the most beautiful room for you."

Maeve smiled and blushed, thanking Revna. "We almost forgot the best part!" Revna grasped her hand and led her to the black archway that led to the luxurious bathroom. The back wall was black marble and centered against it was the largest clawfoot tub Maeve had ever seen. It was midnight black, she imagined it could easily fit Elias in bear form.

Her face lit up, and she noticed a large vanity, toilet, and everything she could dream of in a bathroom. Next to the tub was a small table, which held a glass vase with sprouts of lavender exploding out of it.

She thanked Revna several times, and she could not take the smile off her face. "Welcome home, dear. I'll leave you to explore." She strode out of Maeve's room. Maeve could definitely begin to imagine this becoming her home, even though her dreams seem to be ahead of schedule.

Her belongings had been brought up, but the first thing she wanted to do was lay in that incredible obsidian tub. A faucet that came from the wall immediately ran hot water, and she filled the tub. Atop the vanity, she found a variety of soaps, oils, and salts. She dumped a few different things in until the tub was practically overflowing with bubbles. Slowly dipping into the water, she felt the hot water heal her sore muscles. What felt like hours passed as she bathed, the sky had begun to grow dark.

Maeve dried herself with one of the soft purple towels on the side table. Sitting at the vanity, she rummaged into the drawers. Basic make up was already supplied for her, so she took advantage. She darkened her eyelids with dark brown eyeshadow, causing her bi-colored irises to stand out. After darkening and lifting her lashes, she applied a stunning red lipstick to her lips and her cheeks.

When she was done, she barely recognized herself. She looked like she belonged in this palace. And she sort of loved it.

Striding to the armoire, she was relieved to find some new clothes. A red long-sleeved number caught her eye, and she tried it on. What she thought was a sweater turned out to be a dress that hugged her body with soft fur-like fabric. The dress exposed her shoulders and collarbones and went down to her knees. She found some black skin-tight leggings to put on underneath. A few pairs of shoes were in the closet, and she chose a pair of short shiny black leather boots. Her hair had mostly dried, so she swept it to one side and strutted out of her room. She was absolutely famished and was dying to explore the palace.

While walking down the hall, she met a *ganera* servant who greeted her kindly. The female led her downstairs and to the dining room. A table the length of her old Apothecary filled a grand room, which was accented by a chandelier that had too many candles on it to count. It appeared to be dipped in gold, and the warm lights from its candles made the room glow in rays of amber.

At the long table Mikael, Elias, and Hagan had already sat down. They each wore fine silk tunics, and Maeve was relieved that she dressed to the same caliber as them for dinner. Hagan looked especially noble, his pitch-black tunic accenting every shade of green in his eyes, his tanned skin glowing against the shiny onyx fabric.

The three of them looked up to see her, and she couldn't hold back her bright pink blush. Hagan was subtly gaping at her, his eyes wide as they roamed down her body, stopping briefly to admire her round hips in the fitting sweater dress.

Mikael licked his lips. "Look-y there, from Blarra to Beauty." His comment caused her to roll her eyes and take the seat across from Hagan, which was already set with ornate plates and silverware, a full glass of red wine placed next to her plate.

Hagan's eyes stayed on her, and she felt that irritating excitement he caused her.

She returned his gaze. "I wouldn't have thought you were a mother's boy."

Mikael and Elias roared with laughter. Hagan didn't release his gaze from hers, his eyes only grew darker as a smirk grew on his lips.

A group of uniformed *ganeras* walked in, multiple food trays in tow. She snapped out of the stare, as trays of fine cheeses, fruits, vegetables, breads, and cooked meats filled the table. The smells made her dizzy, her stomach grumbled in protest. Finally, a few bottles of wine were added to the table and poured into their crystal glasses.

An old *ganera* servant spoke to Hagan in a low voice. "The Queen will make her entrance shortly. Welcome back, my Prince."

Hagan inclined his head at the servant. "And the King?" A fire began to burn in his eyes.

"Otherwise engaged, sir." the greying servant answered, a knowing look in his kind, wrinkled eyes as he bowed and left the dining room.

Hagan's face immediately turned to stone. There had to be a story there. Shelving that thought for now, she heard heels clicking in the adjoining hall. They stood for Queen Revna to enter for dinner. Elias immediately went to pull her chair and tuck her into the table, and everyone sat down.

She had never had such a formal dining experience, but the etiquette was simple to pick up on. Revna had dressed down from her previous dress into a sleek black long sleeve dress that was lined with a silver fur at the neckline.

She gazed at them all, nothing but love in her green eyes, Hagan's eyes. "Well, what're you all waiting for? Let's eat!"

They each piled food upon their plates and ate until their stomachs were full to bursting. The three males ate ravenously, while she tried to copy Revna's grace and controlled the speed at which she consumed the delicious food. The Second Kingdom's food was incomparable to anything she had ever eaten.

So many different spices and flavors danced on her tongue, she could not help indulging in a taste of everything the Kingdom had to offer.

Once the plates were cleaned, Hagan spoke to his mother. "So, what's father got going on that's more important than seeing his son after five years?"

Maeve's eyes widened, and she flitted her gaze to Elias, who shook his head. Revna frowned, but Hagan did not falter his commanding gaze.

She answered. "You know your father. War, strategy, and the kingdom. He never stops working." A bored expression covered her true expression, disappointment.

Quickly changing the subject, she glanced at Maeve. "What are your thoughts on the kingdom, my dear?"

Maeve smiled softly, happily averting the conversation. "I think it's the most incredible place I have ever been, I'd love to see more."

Revna smiled at that. "I'm sure my son would be happy to escort you for a tour. I hope your accommodations are suitable, it is the best we could do on short notice. I assure you your estate will be returned to its former glory as soon as possible." Hagan nodded but gave his mother a wary look. He looked at Maeve, his eyes brewing with what appeared to be worry.

Maeve did not know what to say, she did not quite understand Court hierarchy, but she never thought Sergeant would grant her all of the riches that it had. She simply nodded, managing a few words of gratitude. "Thank you, everything is perfect."

The Queen's eyes flitted to Mikael, and she smiled coyly. "I see you're still trying to hide that crooked nose, Mikael darling."

Maeve almost spit out her water, and chuckled. "I noticed it the first time I met him." Giggles still rumbling in her chest.

Revna turned to her, her brows furrowing for the slightest minute before giving her a warm smile. "Now that is intriguing." Revna said softly. They returned to chattering for almost an hour when finally, Hagan spoke to her. "I must attend the meeting with Father after this, but I can show you around tomorrow if you'd like. Would that work for you, Maeve?"

She half-smiled, half-grimaced. "I don't have anything else on my social calendar."

She caught him rolling his eyes.

CHAPTER 23
THE KNOWLEDGE

She was in a curious mood. There were so many new things to learn and places to explore, and if she were going to live in the Second Kingdom palace for the foreseeable future whilst her estate was being prepared, she wanted to look around.

After brunch, she decided to walk around the palace. Other than a few servants fluttering about, she had the Great Room to herself. She started there, eyeing the downward spiral of the grand staircase. She descended, stopping at the floor beneath where a long corridor led to a few chambers and doors beyond. Down the corridor, she began hearing muffled voices beyond a broad hardwood door. She slowed her steps, walking in near silence as she came up to the door. Near the crack between the door and the stone wall, she put her ear to listen.

A deep voice spoke, his words sounding like he was grinding rocks together. "The Rebels are not giving up. There have been uprisings growing in some of the faraway towns, even some as far as the Port of Smiths. The Divide was not enough for them, now they must disrupt our way of life." He sounded annoyed, but not concerned.

Hagan spoke. "We sent a single survivor from our time in the foothills to send a message to their Leader. My *cleasiera* Sergeant was extremely convincing." A single survivor? Lie. They allowed many to live, even if the number they killed was still too many to her. The Forge still burned too bright. But why would he lie?

A thunderous voice spoke next, and an odd familiar shiver fell over her as she listened to his voice. "Generous. My son is so generous, so kind. But this was the last time. We have given warnings, we have punished the many that defy us. It is clear to me that is not enough. They are mostly *ganera* anyways, the Smiths did not take their time and care to create them. Not like us." She heard a faint sipping sound, and a long pause as the meeting remained silenced. "The Dorcha Mountains were a Gift to them, something even the Forge would not grant them. And they disrespect that Gift by rebelling against the written words that drew the Divide. That divided us from the lesser." He spoke with such confidence, with a knowledge that no matter his plan it would work in his favor. His Forged Fate was set. "War. We must go to war." He said with finality, an emotionless echo in his voice.

She inhaled sharply.

Silence made the room feel empty. Until the gravelly voice spoke in a low tone. "Lucius, check the hall. My ears are old, but I believe I heard something. This is not the conversation for ears outside of this room." She did not know of any Lucius, but she did not plan on meeting him then.

She panicked, and tiptoe ran to the end of the corridor. All she could think in her head was *Fuck. Fuck. Fuck.* in rhythm with her toes hitting the stone ground. There was another large hardwood door at the end of the hall that was ajar, and she slipped through it noiselessly. Her curious mind almost cost her dearly.

She turned, hoping not to see someone's chambers. But she did not. In fact, she saw something far more exciting. A library. If she could even call it something as simple as that. The room was six-sided with multi-story ceilings that shot into the rafters of what she assumed was the top of the palace. It was more of a tower, with wraparound black frame windows on three of the six sides. They looked out into the courtyard and mountains beyond.

The other side housed shelves and shelves of books that ran nearly to the ceiling.

The libraries of Geneza were nothing like this. One wall of books in a small shop along the main square. Many of the editions were torn, had missing pages, or smelled of mold. Nothing like this grand library, that had to have thousands of books that looked as if no one touched them. Preserved and beautiful and full of knowledge.

A staircase went around the perimeter of the room, leading to spaces with desks, couches, and more books. She decided to go up to the second floor, sitting on a couch as casually as possible. As if she had been there for hours.

She had not noticed before, but it turned out she was not as alone as she thought.

"Beautiful, powerful, and intelligent? You must be joking." Mikael whispered from behind her. He lounged in a deep cushioned leather chair, his legs laying carelessly over the side. A book sat in his lap, his usually perfect coiffe of blonde hair turned messy. A smirk sat on his full, rosy lips.

"What is that supposed to mean?" She asked, making sure to equal his volume.

He looked away, an amused eyebrow shooting up. "Well, why else would you be here other than to gain more knowledge? The Second Kingdom's library pales in comparison to the Fifth Kingdom's, but I suppose you could learn some things from these shelves." His hand gestured about the room.

"How about let's not concern yourself over why I'm here. There is something I was curious about though since we're here. About you." She attempted to subtly avert the subject that she was just minutes ago listening to a secret war meeting. What better way to distract Mikael than with his favorite topic, himself?

He sat up, swinging his legs effortlessly to sit upright. "My interest is mildly piqued. What is it you desire to know, Maeve darling?"

"Why did you leave the Fifth Kingdom?" She asked.

He tilted his head, something like pain flashing across his face. His gaze burned into hers, and a soft buzzing radiated up the back of her neck into her skull. He squinted his eyes, features softening. "Alright." He stood, striding over to the couch that she sat on. She scooted over to one side so he could take up the other. "I trust you'll keep this to yourself, love. But I did not leave the Fifth Kingdom. I was exiled."

She turned toward him fully, mouth slightly agape. "How?" He smiled mischievously. "Well, you know how I grew up. What you don't know is what I did after I left the childhood home. Many knew of my Gift, of how it had only grown stronger as I grew bigger. There are certain opportunities for such Gifts in the Fifth Kingdom." He leaned in, adding dramatic effect. "I was recruited by the King consort. Though Sebastián was King at the time. Before Flora fucked everything up."

She listened, while attempting to make her wild curiosity seem subdued. As much as she regretted thinking about it, Mikael was damn interesting.

"Ah, now I've got your attention. Yes. I worked directly with the King and Queen of the Fifth Kingdom. Sebastián had a certain skillset, and I was one of his tools. He's a *spaidera*, you know. So, his hunger for knowledge never ceased." He looked around quickly, making sure no one was within earshot. "My hunger for him never ceased, either. I worked as his spy, one of which he has scattered throughout the Five Kingdoms and beyond."

There was no hiding her interest then.

"Yes, you heard that correctly. Bash and I were lovers, and for the longest time Flora did not know. We were to run away together; he did not care to be King if he could not be with me. Which, he couldn't. His power was vast, so his obligation to Flora to create an even more powerful Born to rule in her stead was the only thing that held us back. For obvious reasons, our affair had to end. Flora found out; she nearly made the entire palace overgrown with weeds from her anger." He rolled his eyes, annoyed. "Bash convinced her to spare me, to allow me to still dwell in this world. Alone, but alive." His eyes reflected a deep sadness. She understood Mikael a bit better now. He was broken, and the shards of him left were sharp.

"You loved him, didn't you?" She asked, a strange companionship forming between them.

"More than there are drops in the Aeriös Ocean." He said truthfully. She sensed his overwhelming sincerity.

"Then you will be reunited once more." She said simply, leaning in to give Mikael some level of comfort. "I believe that the Forge creates someone for everyone, and that in our Forged lifetimes we are to come across that one. I don't think the Smiths would be so cruel as to create us to be alone."

"When you have caused the Forge to burn as I have, perhaps the Smiths take away such luxuries. I can control many things, but in this I am powerless." He stated, and she felt something other than confidence in his demeanor for the first time. Something completely uncharacteristic. Guilt.

He raked his hand through his hair, taking a deep breath. And like that, his shield was up once more. "His cock was perfect too. It's such a terrible shame."

She rolled her eyes but laughed softly. "Remember what I said. I still believe."

He gave her a breathtaking smile, then spoke softly. "Beautiful, powerful, and intelligent." He stood, heading toward the downward spiral of the staircase. He turned to speak once more. "Go pick up a Smith's damn book so you can be all three." A wicked laugh followed.

"Dick." She said under her breath, then went to explore the library more. On the third floor, she discovered a section fully dedicated to history. History fascinated her. To know what has happened as far back as words could be written. They were like stories to her, something she wished to have. A story written about her, but only if the details of her life were interesting enough to be told.

A dark blue book stood out to her, the golden writing read, 'A History of the Five'. She sat at a near desk, which was mahogany with a leather chair assigned to it. On the front of the book, the shape of Ignisiem was outlined in white, the title once more in gilded letters. She laid the book down, opening to the Table of Contents at the front of the book.

Scanning down the lines of the page she saw sections dedicated to 'Before the Five', 'Dorcha', 'The First Kingdom'. She stopped there. The First Kingdom was no doubt the most interesting of them all. This Kingdom sat at the top of Ignisiem, signifying the status of living there. The grandest, most fruitful Kingdom. They had the most land, the most Gifted citizens, and the most powerful King. The Mind King. He was a *cleasiera*, the most Gifted one on record.

The Kingdoms are known as such so the citizens always know where they belong. Naming them based on rank, even if some would argue the rankings weren't true. From what Mikael had said about the Fifth Kingdom, it seemed far more exciting than the Second. Then again, she had always preferred warmer weather, and the Fifth Kingdom was a perpetual beach.

She turned to the section of the First Kingdom, noting the grand scribing of the first letter T. This book was like a work of art, each letter carefully printed to be read. Though the dust would indicate that it had not been touched in ages.

Quick footsteps patted down the stairs, and her attention was brought to them immediately. Although she thought the danger had passed, the freshness of it kept her wary. A female was walking down, she was holding three large books which appeared overly heavy in her small hands. She was shorter than Maeve, with a curvy frame. Her skin was dark, the color of rust. The reddish-brown color meshed beautifully with her dark eyes, black brows and lashes surrounding her expressive eyes. She had a long plait of shiny black hair, braided back into an intricate formation. Her outfit stuck out most, she wore the uniforms of the Kingdom servants.

The female looked up, startled. "Oh, hello! I'm sorry, I am not used to having too many visitors." The female smiled, her youthfulness evident in her glow.

"It's no bother. I have just been reading about the First Kingdom." Maeve gave her a soft smile. "I'm Maeve, by the way. And you are?" She asked, which seemed to visibly surprise the servant.

"My name is Jolee, I spend most of my free time here in the

library. Many of the servants don't go to places in the palace like this, except the Queen gave me an exception. So long as I kept the place organized. But usually, I work in the Queen's Garden. I'm a *nadura*." Jolee said, her stiff back easing as Maeve smiled.

Jolee radiated kindness, and she felt the need to try and be her friend. "Sit with me, Jolee. If you can spare a few minutes from your organizing."

Jolee smiled softly, then obliged. "You are *helbredera*."

Her brows scrunched. "How did you know that?"

"All of you always have such a glow about you. It feels healing to be in your presence, even. This is true for all of the *helbrederas* I have met, excluding one or two." Jolee explained. "What are you reading?"

Maeve nodded. "It's a History of the Five Kingdoms. I am currently on the first but have not made it very far. There is much to remember." She patted the book, which sat three inches high from the table. "What do you usually read?"

"Indeed. The history of the Five is long, and usually terribly one-sided as well." Jolee rolled her eyes, as if she felt comfortable enough to speak candidly. Maeve was happy to meet someone who was completely themself in the palace. "But I usually read romance. Love stories." She blushed slightly, and averted her eyes from Maeve.

Maeve grinned, realizing that she was in need of talking with someone other than the three males she had been sharing most of her time with. "And do you have someone in particular you think of when reading about the males in your romance novels?"

Jolee laughed, a charming cackle that brought her comfort that she wasn't being too intrusive. "Oh, I don't know, Maeve." Jolee's eyes flashed, and Maeve felt the lie did not come naturally to her. "Well maybe someone." Jolee admitted with a sigh.

"Who is this lucky male?" Maeve asked, her excitement growing for her new friend.

Jolee blushed even brighter. "He is very handsome. Tall, dark, and his eyes are the dreamiest part about him." She looked off, fantasizing. "They are a beautiful golden color. He's *bhiastera*, so they are not your normal brown gold of the common male.

They are like hot, liquid gold." Jolee groaned, throwing her head back in faux despair.

Elias. She was clearly infatuated with Elias. "What's stopping you from pursuing Elias? He is unattached, as far as I know."

Jolee startled. "Do you know of him? I didn't mean to fantasize so much about his King's Sergeant. Just my thoughts running away from me."

"What are you talking about? We just work together. We're both in the 22nd Brigade. Honestly I'd call him one of my closest friends." Maeve said.

"I see. Well, you know it would be improper for me to pursue him. He is far more Gifted than I am." Jolee said, a shade of sadness darkening her features.

"That's fucking mad. What does it matter? You're clearly in love with him, you need to do something about it. You are so beautiful, and so kind. I think you should do it. Why not?" Maeve asked. She could not believe those in the Second Kingdom truly believed that they could not mate 'above their station', as if they were racing horses trying to birth the next champion. "Love is a Smith-given Gift. I would argue it's far more powerful than the abilities we are granted. Love is eternally powerful, while our powers will one day be turned to ashes of the Forge."

Jolee smiled ear to ear, her eyes wide and hopeful. "Well put. Maybe I will."

She smiled back, her words echoing inside of her own head. Love is a Smith-given Gift. A Gift she wanted so desperately to feel for herself.

Jolee stood, taking Maeve's hand. "It was wonderful to meet you, Maeve. I do hope our paths cross in the near future."

"Me too, Jo." Maeve said, causing a confused look to cross Jolee's face. She thought it was a good nickname for her new friend. With a nod, Jolee walked gracefully down the stairs and out of the library.

She listened for others roaming the library, but sensed no one.

Privacy. She carefully put away the history book, then turned to ascend the stairs to the third floor. A private library and a section full of romance novels, she could think of no other place she would rather spend the rest of the day.

CHAPTER 24
THE COFFEE

"This must be a lot to take in." Hagan observed.

They started in the Great Room, at the largest hearth she had ever seen. The fire was roaring inside of the midnight black, marble fireplace, warming the entire space. Brown leather couches sat in conservational patterns around the room, many blankets and pillows strewn throughout. This space was built for comfort and sitting around a fire together for hours. A family, that is.

"Indeed it is." She sighed, gazing around the room. It felt odd to do something as normal as a tour of the palace after their journey so far. She went from being covered in blood, the spoils of battle haunting her memory to living in a palace with a male she had an ever-growing fondness for. She was still brewing over the way he left things the other night, but she did desperately want to see the rest of his home.

"Me and my friends growing up created many memories here. When I was a youngling, this was my favorite place." Hagan said, his large hands sliding across the smooth leather of one of the couches. His eyes seemed far away in thought.

"It's beautiful, everything looks so comfortable," Maeve said, then threw herself upon the nearest leather couch. She groaned.

"Okay, tours over. I'll stay here for the remainder of the day."

Hagan chuckled. "Your propensity for comfort is rather strange for someone of your upbringing."

Maeve feigned shock. "You mean for a peasant. Yeah, well I've got to say, I would have preferred to grow up in a place like this. But then maybe if I did grow up with luxury and status, I wouldn't be who I am today. And I like her."

Hagan shook his head. His face turned more serious, and he said, "Beauty is not real. Perception is. Things are not usually what you believe them to be." He paused. "I like her too."

She scrunched her nose inquisitively. "Like who?"

"Who you are." He replied, referencing her previous statement, pure honesty in his clear gaze.

She smiled softly, looking down at her hands as she turned to sit up on the couch. Before she could reply, he began. "In any case, I have learned to make my own family. Sometimes even the Born do not have what they want in a 'family'."

"I am starting to see that for myself. You and your father, there's a rift between you?" She asked, in as nonchalant a tone as possible.

He sat down beside her, leaning against the other edge of the sofa. "He is a complicated male. I may not always agree with things he does, but everything he does is for the Kingdom." She sat up, facing him, and listening.

"When I was young, he was stern. I am his heir, and I am that before anything else. Even his son."

She sighed. "Do you think he always has the Second Kingdom's best interests in mind?"

He glanced at her, green eyes narrowing in question. "Of course, I do. He isn't a nice male, but he has brought this Kingdom to new heights. We are stronger than ever."

She didn't know if she agreed, but she also did not want to push him further on the issue of The King. Even though she did want better for the Second Kingdom, especially when it came to the treatment of non-Gifted Fae.

Brushing a hand through his dark locks, he stood. "There is still much to see."

Maeve snorted, rising from the couch. "What's next, Prince of Infinite Wisdom?" She raised a playful eyebrow.

Hagan rolled his eyes and led her to the front of the palace, where the throne room was in it's own wing off of the front door. Pushing open the large dark hardwood doors, they strode into a round room with three story ceilings. The ceiling was composed of transparent glass, exhibiting the sky and clouds overhead.

Hagan saw her gawking at the glass sky. "My father likes to flaunt his Gift, so if he's angry or disappointed with someone in this room, the sky will let everyone present know of his feelings."

He rubbed the back of his neck, as if brushing off a memory. She nodded. She wandered to the two thrones that sat at the back of the room. The wall was glass and looked out at snowcapped mountains that jutted into the sky near the thin clouds. The King's throne was evident, as it was the color of a terrible storm looming overhead. The dark grey was accented with gold edges, an elegant balance of thunder and lightning. Seated on the King's right was a deep, black-purple throne that was plain in comparison to the King of Thunder's place. The place of Queen Revna.

She touched the smooth marble of the King's throne and felt her spine go stiff, closing her eyes to steady herself as her body swayed.

Opening her eyes, she observed a male sitting on the King's throne. He appeared middle-aged, his Gifted lifespan making his face appear to be entering mid-life. He could have easily existed for four hundred years. His cloudy grey eyes darkened when he saw her, he sat back and scanned her up and down for a few seconds longer than she would have preferred. Just his stare gave her deep, rattling chills.

His crown shone in the light of the throne room, the platinum stark against his shoulder-length dark brown hair. His features were sharp, similar to Hagan's but also completely different in the way he carried himself. He was in a state of constant dominance, his mouth never turning into a smile and his eyes never flickering with amusement. Power surged throughout the room, it felt ancient and dark to her, as if it had existed and thrived in this world for longer than she could fathom.

The King of Thunder rose from his throne and stepped toward her.

"You are quite the prize." His voice was as deep as the rumble of an earthquake.

She was vibrating with fear, but gave him a soft toothless smile and lowered her eyes as she swallowed down her shivering breath. The King approached her. His eyes were glued to her, searching her for imperfections. His mouth changed into a terrifyingly handsome smile that she did not think was possible on his serious face.

The King reached out, his ice-cold hand brushed her cheek right beneath her green eye. He grabbed her chin with two fingers, tilting her head up slightly to look deeply into her eyes. Thunder clouds loomed curiously overhead, and she had to force herself to not cringe under his glacial stare.

The King breathed. "And the eyes…."

The air warmed around her, and she opened her eyes to see Hagan's emerald stare replace the King's deep, dark grey. The ground was cold, and her back ached with the impact of her fall.

"Are you okay?" His brows were knitted together, creating small lines in his forehead.

"I-I don't know…" She said, shivering. Hagan warmed the air around her more, and his scent wrapped around her like a warm blanket. She returned to breathing normally, and after a minute of sitting there staring at the King's throne, she finally got to her feet. Hagan gave his hand to help her, but she rose on her own.

On shaky legs, she turned to Hagan. "Your father… are his eyes grey… like—" Hagan immediately inched toward her, and her body warmed to a comfortable temperature.

"Like storm clouds?" He asked knowingly.

"Yeah, that's exactly what I was going to say," her voice faltered, his presence electrifying just inches in front of her. "How did you…"

These visions were getting strange, each one she felt more than the last. She had never dreamed in such a way that she felt things. Her mind manifested these feelings, but they could not be real. She had to wonder if there was something off here, because something has been different within her since she met Hagan.

Her body and mind are there in the moment in these dreams, as if put there without her knowing. Like it was a trick. As if they were not her own.

She pushed back from him, hands smacking against his broad chest. "Get away from me." Her voice was dangerously low.

"Wh-" He stammered.

"It's been you this whole time."

"Maeve, what are you talking about?" His mouth was agape, his faux surprise making her fire rage even hotter.

"The things that I'm seeing. You're the cause! I thought I was just getting creative, or maybe a little mad, but you're the main thing that has changed. If you could convince that *bhiastera* to do what you said..." Her voice had cracked, to match the small but growing fracture on her heart. "You could have easily put these fucking visions in my head."

"Maeve, please. I did no such—"

"Don't lie." She hissed, her eyes beginning to glow.

"Maeve, I have no fucking idea what you're talking about. What have you seen other than my father?" His voice was desperate, eyes wide.

"You should know, you've been putting this shit in my head. All of this didn't start until I met you." Maeve hissed the last word as her fists clenched.

Hagan looked down at her hands, then back at her bright glowing irises. "Careful, Maeve. There is a lot you do not understand. I did not put those memories into your head."

"Liar." She said, venom on her lips.

Hagan shook his head, and attempted to close the distance between them. "Maeve, please." His hand reached for her face.

A buzzing began at the back of her skull, like a beehive that had fallen out of a tree. "Don't fucking touch me," She said, a command.

And he didn't. His hand reached out but did not touch her. His eyes glowed back neon green, but he did nothing.

Without another word, she stormed out of the throne room.

→→ →→ ←← ←←

After changing out of the form-fitting dress and into something more casual, she decided that she needed to find Petra. These visions or daydreams or implanted memories... whatever they were. If she didn't confide in someone about them, she may go insane.

As she threw on a sweater and leggings, a small laugh escaped her lips. Hagan acted scared of her. Him, scared of her. She could have easily broken his arm when he tried to touch her, but she did not. Part of her didn't want to hurt him. Even if the majority of her did.

Maeve had sent a *ganera* to tell Petra to meet her at the town square. The lift brought her down, the guards and workers greeting her as she left.

In front of the waterfall that secluded the lift, the townsfolk were out and about going to shops and restaurants in the late afternoon sun. She spotted Petra sitting at a quaint table with Lyra, and they sipped coffee as they chatted. Petra's eyes were entranced in Lyra's. She had never seen her look at someone like that.

Maeve walked up to the table, pulling up a third chair.

She released her eyes from Lyra, smiling. "How's the palace Princess Maeve?"

Maeve rolled her eyes at her. "It is... decadent. To say the least."

The third coffee that sat on the table was light brown with swirled, frothy milk. It smelled incredible. "What do they do with the coffee here?" Maeve asked, wary of heavier topics.

Lyra tossed her long hair over her shoulders and replied. "There's an *aimsura* coffee maker, and she heats the milk enough to mix with coffee so it's all fluffy. It's delicious, we ordered you one." Lyra gave a big, expectant smile.

She grabbed the cup and took a sip, her mouth filling with the delightfully warm milk and coffee mixture. It tasted of sweet comfort, contrasted by the bitterness and richness of the coffee. This was her new favorite thing. "Wow."

Upon request, she delighted the females with details of the elegant palace, the Queen with her warm welcome, and every detail she could think of other than Hagan. A swift silence fell over them as she ran out of new things to tell them.

Petra cocked her head. "And your General?"

Maeve looked down at her coffee. She paused for a bit, taking in a large breath. "Not mine, first of all. I thought for a second, maybe he wanted me. I think I was very, very wrong. I have no idea where we stand or what I'm doing."

Petra spoke under her breath. "You can tell us, Maeve. There's clearly something more." Maeve didn't know if she was allowed to say anything, but felt the need to express herself anyways.

Her voice was low, as she leaned in to speak to the females. "Okay. This stays between us." The two nodded, and were focused on her words with dedicated gazes.

"Hagan is not just our General. He is our Prince, like the actual King of Thunder's son. So, yeah it turns out he was actually Born and has two different Gifts. You guys have seen the *aimsura* powers, but I have seen the *cleasiera* side. He can convince someone to do things with almost no effort."

She took a long breath— remembering the night he cursed her attacker in the alleyway in Blarra— and continued. "I've been having… dreams of this guy. Daydreams, night dreams, visions, I have no fucking clue. What I do think is that he's somehow putting that shit in my head, and some of it was pretty dirty."

Petra's ears perked up at that and she teased. "So you're complaining that he's teasing you with sexy little dreams?"

Lyra hauled off and punched Petra in the arm. "He is completely invading her boundaries by doing that, Petra. It's not right." Lyra said, and smirked. "Do you know for sure it was him? It takes a highly Gifted *cleasiera* to change your dreams and thoughts like that."

She shook her head and shrugged. "I mean, yeah, I can't be sure. I kind of… lost my cool before he would confess."

Petra's icy gaze glittered with excitement. "What did you do to the prince, Maeve?"

Maeve looked between the two females, smirking. "I wanted to hurt him, I'll be honest with you. But I didn't. I just called him a liar and ran away to see you guys." A sigh parted her lips, and she indulged in a long sip from her coffee.

Lyra nodded thoughtfully. "Well, you showed great restraint. I have been tricked by a *cleasiera* before, and it feels like an intrusion. He is our Prince, and I respect him, but if he did those things to your mind he was in the wrong. He will apologize, I am sure of it."

Petra scoffed. "So loyal. While I love that about you, Ly, I'm going to have to disagree. Even if the Forge itself willed it, an apology wouldn't cut it for me."

Lyra rolled her eyes playfully, then wrapped an arm around Petra. "Maeve will make her own choices. When he apologizes, and he will, because he is good, she will decide to forgive him or she will not. Its her choice."

Petra laughed. "If he doesn't find his way into her bed first."

"Petra." Lyra warned.

"What? I'd bet that'd be a great fucking apology."

Maeve shook her head, amazed at Petra once again even though her best friend had been saying shocking things since the day she met her.

Lyra quickly changed the subject, clearly wanting to avoid talk of bedding the Prince and her General. "So, Maeve. Have you been acquainted with your estate yet? I hear the Sergeants get a rather lavish piece of land and a large home as well."

After how much she adored her guest chambers, she had almost forgotten. "I have not, actually. I will have to ask... someone about that."

Petra gave her a sly look.

Maeve smiled, and the females sat there and chatted until dusk began to settle on the picturesque village. "I should be getting back. Thank you two for this." She hugged them each, Petra holding on to her for an extra few seconds. Petra whispered, "You're going to figure this out."

Maeve left them feeling renewed.

Night had fully fallen now, and the multicolored stars shined bright against the midnight blue sky. The lift ride was smooth, but the icy breeze as she reached the top chilled her to the bone. The Second Kingdom palace shone a bright white against the darkness.

As she was walking toward the palace entrance, there was an eerie feeling creeping down her back, a tickle, as if someone were watching her. She peeked around, attempting to not be obvious. No one was there besides a few *treaniera* guards and her. Shrugging, Maeve went up to her room, took a quick bath, and went straight to sleep. She laid under the thick blankets, inhaling the scent of the fresh sheets that pulled her into a deep slumber.

CHAPTER 25
THE FOX

Ganera servants milled around the palace preparing for the Blood Moon Celebration that would begin that night. The palace was awash with excitement as the *ganeras* put up decorations that brightened up the palace in rich oranges and reds. Lanterns were being put at the top of the high ceilings, soaking the palace in warm light.

A small breakfast was served in the dining room, where she found Elias casually eating a chocolate pastry. "Good morning, Maeve. Are you excited for the Blood Moon?"

Sitting beside him, she took a bite of one of the strawberry pastries. "I am! However, all of this does seem a bit much. The celebrations back at home weren't so outrageous."

She laughed a bit, and Elias met her eyes. "I do believe you will have a good time. Queen Revna is quite the party planner." His golden eyes looked at her inquisitively "Would you like to take a walk with me?"

Maeve smiled; this was a bit unexpected. "Sure, let's do it."

They left out of the back of the palace, to the courtyard. A sprawling green field met them, overlooking the mountains beyond. Various species of flowers and bushes were planted there; she wasn't sure how they kept it so lush as the weather had cooled to an icy chill.

Naduras.

The Second Kingdom must employ a large number of them to maintain the space. Ezra would have loved this. Her mind drifted there, but she pulled herself back to the present. She would not feel guilt over him and his actions.

They walked through the courtyard, and there were groups of white cottages set at the back of the space. "Those are for the servants, they live on the grounds." Elias said, answering the question she was about to ask. Their lives were truly ingrained in the Kingdom.

Trails and winding paths exited from the main courtyard. Elias led them on one that was shrouded in tall trees with orange and gold leaves. The path curved, and they walked for a few minutes beneath the shroud of color before opening into a small space where the flowers bloomed so beautifully, she couldn't stop looking at all of the different colors. Deep purple, light blues, a hundred different greens, blood reds, more colors than she had ever seen in one place.

Elias grinned, noting her amazement. "This is one of my favorite places on the grounds. The Queen's Garden. *Naduras* work on it every day to keep the blooms as beautiful as they can possibly be."

Maeve smiled at him. "All of this color in a palace that is so monochrome. It's an escape."

She wondered what inspired Queen Revna to have this space created, and then remembered the cold, harsh expression on the King's face. An escape, indeed.

She and Elias sat in the grass at the edge of the garden, where a small outcropping of trees gave them a breathtaking view of the mountains beyond. Elias had brought a bottle of wine and two glasses, and they sipped as they reclined onto the grass.

"How are you fairing here, Maeve? I know court life can be a bit demanding." Elias asked as she laid on the grass beside him.

"It is an adjustment, definitely. I didn't expect it to be easy, but the folk here are just so different. Taking on this persona isn't really my thing, you know? Back in Blarra, I could just be myself. Maeve, the healer. Not Sergeant of the 22nd Brigade."

Elias nodded slowly, his eyes scanning the mountains beyond. "I do understand. An outsider looking in. I haven't told you about how I came to be in the Second Kingdom, have I?" He turned to her.

Maeve shook her head. "Not exactly, I just know you and Hagan have a pretty lengthy history."

Elias smiled, and his golden eyes glittered in the morning light. "In the Fourth Kingdom, Hagan and I got into a bar fight. For lesser Gifted Fae, this wouldn't have been a big deal. A few broken chairs, a couple of bruises maybe. Well…" he chuckled. "For two Born Fae, it was destruction. We ripped apart the entire bar and proceeded to bloody each other up and down the town's street until we were both completely worn out."

A breath escaped her lips, this was not the story she expected.

Elias continued. "We had both had a fair amount to drink, and I had approached the female he was with. Flirtatiously." A smile played on his lips, and he gave her a quick wink. "After all of the carnage was finished, she was the one who approached me. She actually wanted me to join them, because it turns out he was the Prince of the Second Kingdom, and she was his betrothed. Really, we should have been put on trial for our actions. She was the only one of us who had any sense at the time."

He leaned on one elbow; his side stretched out. His tunic came up just enough to see his hip bone and toned abdominals. "Now Hagan and I have saved each other's skins on the battlefield too many times to count. We're family."

Maeve shook her head, her mind buzzing with questions. Who is the female? Is Hagan still with her? This was just getting weirder. Despite her initial thoughts she decided to ask. "You said for two Born Fae. So, you were Born?"

Elias' expression darkened, something like pain flickering in his eyes. "Yes. It's true. Both of my parents bore the Gift I was given. I grew up in the Fourth Kingdom. At court, no less."

Elias waved his hands, like growing up in court was no big

deal. She could tell this subject was sensitive for him. Why did he live at court? Were both of his parents bearish *bhiasteras*? So many questions.

He smiled admiringly. "I know it may come as a shock, especially when you saw me in my other form. I am a rather large beast, after all. My mother was bearish, my father something else. I take after my mother, obviously."

She laughed, imagining a small bearish *bhiastera* cub with his mother. "What happened to them?" She asked hesitantly, aware of the shift in his demeanor.

"They are alive, if that is what you wonder. I have not been to see them in many years. They are still in the Fourth Kingdom, living their lives, as I live mine."

She turned to face the mountains, her brows scrunching in thought.

"What is it that troubles you?"
She smiled softly, turning back to meet his speculative gaze.
"It's a long story."

"It appears we both have the time." He popped open the cork of the second bottle of wine with a loud pop as the cool wind rustled through her loose auburn locks.

"He is your best friend. I would not want to speak badly of him to you. It seems unfair to unload it on you."

Elias faced the breathtaking views and said. "Hagan is honorable. He is good, for a Prince at least." Elias smirked sardonically, and refilled their glasses with a bubbly white wine. "However, I am one to see the good and the evil in all of us. I believe that the Forge creates us with both, even the Born."

She nodded and lowered her head, watching the bubbles fizz in her sparkling wine. Elias eyed her expression, and spoke in a whisper.

"It is Hagan that has your thoughts, you can tell me if you wish. I can see the weight it bears on you."

Maeve looked up at him through her lashes. Though she had really just begun to get to know him, his friendship had caused her to trust him almost as much as Petra. "I'm confused, Elias. Hagan does not appear to be who I thought he was."

She shrugged, and Elias patted her shoulder. "What did he do to cause you such confusion? I thought you two were getting along fine, like something was blooming between you, even."

His dark brows were furrowed, and she layed on her back on the grass to look at the bright blue sky.

"So, being that you know he is Born, you must also know that he has the *cleasiera* Gift."

He nodded, acknowledging his knowledge of Hagan's lineage.

"I have been seeing things... in my dreams. Sometimes I just lose myself and see others and have interactions, but then I wake up or open my eyes and I'm here again. It may happen in my dreams; I may imagine something while standing on my feet. Either way, I am seeing things that were not there before. Things that I do not know of."

Elias stilled, his eyes zeroed in on her. "L-Like what?" His voice was low, and his tone turned serious.

She felt heat on her cheeks. "A lot of Hagan... which made me think it was him."

Elias' eyes squinted, confusion evident on his face. "So, you did not confirm that it was him?"

She shook her head. "I suppose I did not, but who else would be capable of that? It's been happening since I met him in Blarra."

Elias nodded, taking a deep breath. His face returned to its normal, kind expression. "Hagan would not do something like that, I assure you. He prefers to not use those Gifts if he can help it." Maeve nodded, and then remembered the *bhiastera* that attacked her. He may not use it often, but he sure had the taste for manipulation.

"You're sure of this?" She asked.

"I am. I say it with the utmost confidence because I have known him for many years. He has been brutally manipulated in the past, and I assure you he could not do the same to you."

Before she could speak, a pair of *naduras* stepped into the clearing, presumably to work on the garden. One of them was a male with ebony skin, but his eyes were a leafy shade of green. She was delighted to see who the other was, Jolee. Her new friend. Her dark hair shone in the overhead sun, her servant's clothes unnatural looking on such a beautiful female. Jo's dark eyes darted between her and Elias, lingering on Elias' stretched out physique.

Jo walked over with a few flower cuttings, and they were the most vibrant lavender tied together with a silver ribbon.

She smiled at Jo. "Good morning, Jo, I see our paths did in fact pass again. Thank you." Jo handed her the small bouquet, and smiled from ear to ear.

Elias looked between them. "I did not know you two had been acquainted. Jo is a wonderful *nadura*. She is incredibly talented, as you can see." Maeve nodded and looked up at Jolee's warm smile.

"These are truly incredible. Lavender is my favorite scent, you know." Maeve said, then inhaled the relaxing scent of the bouquet. Jo smiled and returned to her duties. She stole one glance back, but Elias averted his gaze to avoid it. When she turned to go to work, Elias watched after her. She sensed his admiration when watching Jo. If only he knew she wanted him just as badly. They would make quite the handsome couple.

She gave him a wry look, and he rolled his eyes. "Not a word."

Curious, she kept her voice low. "And why not?"

"Because it is none of your business, that's why."

With a nod, she assumed it best to change the topic. But she had to make one last comment, as a dedicated matchmaker. "If you were to be interested in Jo, I do think she would be interested."

He sighed, abandoning the subject.

Elias and Maeve sat in the garden, chatting about anything and everything before they headed back up to the palace. Elias went off to the kitchen, but she stopped when she saw The Great Room was now covered in fall leaves. Real trees shot into the tall ceilings, creating an enchanting forest inside of the palace. Lights and candles were strewn all about, creating a romantic aura that drew her in. Tables were organized around the room under the full trees that appeared to grow right out of the white marble floors.

Two thrones had been set at the front of the room, for the

King and Queen to watch over the festivities. *Ganeras* and *naduras* scurried about, putting final touches on the Blood Moon preparations.

She was so taken aback by the room that she didn't notice when Queen Revna walked up behind her. "Do you like it, dear?" Revna asked, and Maeve whirled around to meet Revna's gaze.

"Honestly... It's way more than I could have imagined. Back in Blarra we celebrated the Blood Moon with a few drinks and a bonfire. Nothing like this."

Her eyes met Revna's, and Revna smiled as small crinkles at the end of her eyes formed. "I am glad. What do you plan on dressing up as?"

Maeve stilled, and embarrassment flooded her cheeks. "We're supposed to dress up?"

Revna chuckled, and brushed Maeve's arm with her petite fingers. "Come with me, dear. We will find you something of mine. I have worn a different costume every year for centuries." Revna took her hand and led her up the stairs to her bed chambers.

The Queen's chambers had a large hardwood door that was guarded by a bored looking *treaniera*. She straightened, eyes alert. "My Queen," she said curtly with a small bow. Revna nodded to the guard and led Maeve into her bed chambers. A large hearth made of dark purple stone took up the corner, with an oversized plush couch in front of it. Books lined the back wall, an entire library for the Queen. Her canopy bed sat in the corner, and an archway opened to a massive closet.

The closet was the size of Maeve's room, walls were lined with dresses, shoes, elegant fabrics, jewels, and more. In the center, a glass chandelier glittered as it refracted small rainbows all over the walls. A white haired *ganera* scurried into the room, bowing to them both. Her name was Yuna.

Revna explained. "Yuna knows where my things are better than I do. She will assist you, please do feel free to borrow anything you like. I must attend to the preparations, but I am excited to see what you choose. I'm sure it will be stunning!"

She smiled warmly at Maeve, and strode out. She wasn't sure

what she did to get such approval from the Queen, but she was glad for it. Her kindness and generosity reminded her of Lady El, but much wealthier.

"You are looking for a costume for the Blood Moon, Sergeant?" Yuna asked.

Maeve cringed. "You can just call me Maeve, and yes. What do we usually dress as at these parties?" She walked down the rows of clothing. "Back in Blarra, no one felt the need or had exuberant funds for costumes." They just got drunk.

Yuna answered. "Um, all sorts of things really. Beasts, flowers, warriors, princesses, anything you want to be for the night."

Maeve nodded, furrowing her eyebrows as she took a moment to think. "Okay, well what options does the Queen have?"

Yuna smiled, then brought down three garment bags from the wall. "I have been in the Queen's employ for two centuries, and these are my favorite looks so far. She always dazzles, you see. She commissions a different costume every single year." Yuna's pale blue eyes glittered with pride in her Queen.

She smiled, then opened the three garment bags.

Yuna spoke softly, pointing to the different bags. "The Sunflower look was incredible, the most skilled *naduras* grew a crown of oversized yellow petals for the headpiece. There is the warrior, the best metal workers from the First Kingdom created custom armor for her highness. This last one here is the Fox. This one may be my absolute favorite, because of the furry ears and mask. I think it would look lovely with your hair color."

Yuna pulled out an intricate headpiece that looped through the hair to give the wearer furry orange ears sprouting from the skull. The front was covered in white fur, and shaped right around the eyes and cheekbones of the face.

"Well, I am not much of a warrior. And I couldn't trouble the *naduras* to grow me a new headpiece. I will try on the Fox mask then."

She tried on the mask, looking into the large round standing mirror. The mask fit her perfectly, and Yuna helped her tighten it around her head, concealing the ribbons. Maeve smiled from ear to ear, looking at herself in the mask. Foxes were her favorite animal; she had always loved how curious and mischievous they could be. "This will be perfect." Maeve said, her voice giddy.

Yuna nodded, smiling up at her. "Wait until you see the dress…"

→» →» «← «←

She took a long bath, with all of the fancy soaps and smells she could find. An *aimsura* was assigned to help her get ready, the stunning brunette was named Sky. Her eyes were the actual color of the sky, so she thought it fitting. Stepping out of the tub, she quickly covered herself with a towel and sat on the stool at her vanity.

"Allow me to do your hair, I have a couple of tricks up my sleeve." Sky smiled. Maeve took in the details of the *aimsura*'s face, she had freckles across the bridge of her nose that scrunched when she smiled. Her dark hair was in a short bob and straightened to perfection.

She felt the air heat around her head, and she flinched. "No worries, milady. I am simply heating the air around strands of your hair to form it. Trust me." Sky said, and she relaxed as the *aimsura* finished her work.

"Stunning." she finally said, stepping back to admire her work. Sky had set pieces of her hair into big, beautiful curls. Maeve's hair was voluminous and fell down and around her face in a way that brought out her sharp chin and cheekbones.

Maeve smiled, amazed at the skill. "Thank you so much, Sky. It's incredible." She couldn't stop touching the curls, bouncing them around with a swish of the head. "Do you know how to do makeup as well?" Maeve asked, and Sky grinned with a nod, going to work on her face.

"If it's not too much trouble of course, I know you must have other things to attend to," She said tentatively.

Sky scoffed. "Oh, please Miss Maeve. I am assigned to you, and this beats heating bath water for Mikael any day. He likes it strangely hot, near boiling." Her lips quivered with a laugh, but

Maeve's chuckle escaped first.

They laughed together, and Maeve could not help but think that she and Skye would become fast friends at the expense of Mikael.

Sky worked quickly, pulling all sorts of colors and brushes out. Maeve sat there with her eyes closed while Sky worked her magic.

"What do you think?" Sky asked, as she looked at herself in the mirror, lamp light flickering against her amber eye.

Now she looked and felt like a fox.

Sky had taken dark brown and black shadows and brushed them on and up her eyelids, creating a sharp effect on her eyes. The contrast caused her eyes to be extremely vivid, glowing back at her in her reflection. More shadow was drawn on the angled lines of her face, causing everything to look sharp and perfect.

She was amazed, and she turned to Sky, meeting her gaze. "Thank you, it's seriously beautiful."

Sky leaned down, to her ear and whispered, "Just wait until he sees you. He will bow before your beauty." and with a bow, she left the room.

Did everyone know about her and Hagan? Really, they were nothing at this point. She was still much too unsure about his intentions, but deep down she couldn't deny that she liked the idea of Hagan bowing down to her.

She shook the thoughts from her head and slid into the dress that was laid out on her bed. The dress had thin straps that loosely tucked on her prominent shoulders, and the neckline plunged below her sternum, revealing the small crease between her breasts. The back of it plunged just as low, exposing most of her back. Her skirts started at her navel, where the dress cinched in and puffed out multicolor silks that fell to the floor. The colors were like a fox— golds, browns, creams. A fox-fur shawl was left in the bag, and she draped it around her arms after donning her mask.

She closed her eyes and took a deep breath to compose herself before looking into the mirror.

The night was extremely cold, and she wrapped her fur shawl further around herself in an attempt to warm herself. She was standing on a balcony that overlooked the heavily snow-covered mountains beyond. She shivered, but felt the air warm around her as a male presence wrapped her in heat. The scent of him filled her, and he was behind her, arm wrapping around her waist. She tilted her head back, feeling his strong chest and shoulders press into her back.

"A fox. I could not have chosen a better costume for the Princess of Mischief." Hagan whispered in her ear. "But did you have to make it so revealing, it's driving me fucking crazy." He growled the last word, and she shivered from something other than the chilled air.

He squeezed her tighter, and she sighed. "One day the Queen of Mischief." She turned to face him.

His arms remained around her, and he smiled upon her with a glow in his emerald eyes. "Patience, my love. Our time will come." he said softly, and planted a swift kiss to the tip of her nose. She felt his warmth, his strength, it was as if they were molded together. Welded together by the Smiths.

When she opened her eyes and saw herself, her breathing was labored. Frantically, she searched around the room, out onto her balcony, and in her bathroom. It was just her. She shook off the daydream, her head in a hot daze. It can't be Hagan putting these images in her mind because they are perfectly crafted for her. Every time she sees him like that, she just wants him more and more. The distinct details of these visions were exactly how she would have wanted them. Maybe it was just her own thoughts, like Elias had told her. She would have to find out when she confronts Hagan tonight.

Finally, she put the finishing touches on her outfit and donned some strappy black heels Revna left for her.

In the mirror, she did not see herself. She cast her eyes upon mischief and beauty. Burnt orange, sienna, cream, and various browns cascaded down to create her bountiful skirt. The low-cut dress showed off some of her more desirable features. Her petite shoulders and chest were on full display, as well as the defined lines of her back. The skirts bundled at the hip, giving her an even more dramatic curve of the bottom. Her mask finished the ensemble, the sharp fox features gave her an air of mystery. She felt a different part of herself rise to the surface, a confident part that wanted to embody the spirit of the fox for the night.

The Queen of Mischief.

CHAPTER 26
THE BLOOD MOON

The Great Room looked even more magnificent when the sun began to make its descent behind the mountaintops. Warm candlelight filled the room, and autumn leaves gently fell from the towering trees overhead. Many Fae milled about, talking at tables, eating, and admiring each other's costumes. Elegant, sensual music was drifting through the hall, and many of the crowd swayed to the lovely sound.

Maeve walked down the stairs slowly, looking around to see all the costumes. Her face warmed and noticed almost neon green eyes pierced hers as she strode down the stairs as graceful as a fox. She kept his gaze as she descended the steps. Despite the many whimsical costumes around her, the only one she could notice was his.

He had fur wrapped around his neck and shoulders, exposing most of his chest and powerful abdomen. Leather pants covered his bottom half, and he had a large broadsword strapped against his back in dark leather.

A Warrior Prince. He could not have chosen a more attractive costume.

Her blush deepened as she realized her eyes were trailing along his body a little too long. She pulled them up to his face, where she found him smirking. His eyes burned bright.

She walked deeper into the crowd, the nobles from the town had been invited, as well as some wealthier families in the surrounding lands. Many dressed as animals, she spotted a few owls, many wolves, as well as too many felines to count. A well-dressed *ganera* offered her a glass of amber liquid, that looked similar to the whiskey she drank with Hagan the night in the fancy Inn. She took a sip. It had the same honey vanilla flavor that she adored.

Maeve inhaled the scent, causing her mind to wander to the thought of how it tasted on his lips and tongue when it came from Hagan. She downed it, and felt the soft burn start to dissipate the thoughts of her insane daydream.

"Enchanting."

She felt Mikael's velvet voice run down her spine. She turned to find him dressed in all black, including a velvet mask that accentuated his delicately carved facial features. His lips were lined with blood red lipstick, while black liner turned his eyes bright blue. He was simply wearing black cat ears and an expensive looking fitted black suit.

"Great costume." She said dryly.

Mikael smiled, and stroked the furry feline ears that sat lazily upon his coiffed, blonde hair. "Everybody loves a pretty pussy."

That caused her to choke down a laugh.

"A drink?" Mikael offered, and he summoned a *ganera*. She and Mikael took two glasses filled with a clear liquid. They clinked glasses and shot it down. Despite the sharp smell, to her amazement, it tasted like strawberries. She met Mikael's bright blue eyes. A strange sensation tickled at the back of her skull.

He chuckled. "Delicious, wasn't it? Well, at least I made you think it was delicious."

She gaped. "Quite the parlor trick. While I am impressed, do not fuck with my mind."

Her eyes flashed in warning, and she pushed her Gift outward for him to feel.

"My apologies, darling. This spirit is just awful." He frowned.

She gave him a soft smile. "Just a warning."

Mikael walked off to grab two more shots and returned with a smile on his lips. "Another drink, love? I promise I won't interfere. Red is a delightful color on those lips, by the way. If you need to freshen the color up, I have plenty on my lips to share." He lowered his gaze to her lips.

She rolled her eyes and sighed. "I'll pass on the generous offer. As for the drink, I am now in desperate need of that."

They laughed, and she glanced over at where she spotted Hagan. She shot the drink back, and it tasted like poison. Her face pinched in disgust.

Mikael whispered. "Regretting your decision?" He strode off toward a voluptuous brunette female dressed as a promiscuous wolf. Maeve chuckled to herself, feeling the bubbles start to take over.

She found herself strolling down a barren hall, her mind awash with names of Fae she would likely not remember. The marble against her exposed back felt cool as she leaned against a wall of the unoccupied hallway. The hairs on her arm rose, a scent of smoke filled her lungs, and the air became alive with static.

A deep, familiar voice echoed in the hall. "I do not believe I have met you. I do think I would have remembered."

The King stepped into the dim light of the hallway.

"I do not believe we have met." His thunderous voice echoed in the empty hall. He looked exactly as she saw him in the throne room. Except now, he looked older. His dark brown hair was greying, slivers of silver obscuring the sheet of dark. That silver matched his grey eyes, a color she would never forget. Lines creased his handsome face, the face that looked so similar to Hagan.

She stiffened but gave him a soft bow. "Good evening. My name is Maeve, I am the new *helbredera* for the 22nd Brigade."

The King examined her closely, his stormy eyes flitting back and forth between her bi-colored irises.

"Hmmm. You may just be much more than that, sweetheart. I must say, if I am not being too bold. Your eyes please me." Maeve managed a half-smile, but her fists were still clenched behind her back.

"Thank you, your highness."

He nodded, reaching out to touch a lock of her curled auburn hair. "A lovely shade."

Her breath caught in her throat, and she felt bile rising from her stomach. Before he could grab the lock of hair, she heard a demanding male voice.

"Father," Hagan said, almost a command to the King.

The King of Thunder pulled his hand back, and turned to Hagan. "My son. It is so good to see you." A sneer spread across The King's face. "Your Sergeant is lovely."

Hagan glared, and his eyes glowed a deep green.

Maeve shivered.

"It's been five years, Father." Hagan said through his teeth.

The King laughed, it's rumble echoing through the hallway. "What is five years in three centuries? Do not be so sentimental, son." He examined her like his next fine art purchase. "Maeve, darling. I do hope you enjoy your time here. I have no doubt our paths will cross again." The King strode off, patting his son on the shoulder as he went.

Hagan's presence at the other side of the hall was deafening. If his glowing irises weren't enough, she felt his power rumbling deep in her bones.

Her head was spinning, she needed fresh air. She strode, heels clicking, past Hagan and through the crowd to the large terrace beyond.

Cool night air chilled her exposed skin, but she welcomed the focus it gave her. The King had properly rattled her, she felt far too exposed under his dark grey stare. Finding a glass of white wine, she downed it in a few gulps.

The night was dark, and the moon shone so brightly she had to squint her eyes. At this point, it had turned a soft pink. The Blood Moon's vibrancy had not yet made its peak. Once it did, and the moon's color mirrored fresh blood, the real party would begin.

More drinking, dancing, and sex would fill the night until the Moon passed. Almost as if the Moon awakens the souls of the dead, allowing them to partake in the living's mischief. With how pent up she had felt lately, letting loose with someone might just cheer her up.

Warm air surrounded her, and she saw a large male presence in her peripherals.

Turning her head toward him, she snapped. "Don't. I like the cold."

Her eyes glowed, anger fueling her power. He was the one she wanted to let loose with, to explore the transgressions of Blood Moon with. Despite those desires, she still needed answers from him.

Hagan frowned, and the air cooled back to its original temperature. "You're angry with me."

Maeve's eyes flashed.

"No shit, Hagan. I'm angry, confused, overwhelmed, and on top of it all I have fucking visions in my head that were not there before." She felt frustrating tears pool in her eyes but bit them back.

Hagan's eyes softened as he sighed. "I have missed your filthy mouth, but it still comes as a surprise to me when you speak in such foul terms. But I understand your frustration."

Her face scrunched in confusion. He missed her after two days?

"Do you really think I am capable of putting those... so-called visions in your head?" His face turned serious, almost hurt.

She looked down into the lush courtyard below. "You're a *cleasiera*, and not to mention they started when I met you.... And they're usually about you." Her face heated, and she bent over the railing.

Hagan leaned out beside her and whispered. "Allow me to set your mind at ease, Maeve. I am not responsible for those images. Although, part of me wishes that I was responsible for the one's about me. Assuming you enjoyed them, of course." His voice caressed her soul, and she somehow believed him.

She turned to see his face, all seriousness except for a flicker of heat in his emerald irises. He was absolutely breathtaking in the moon's soft pink light. Her eyes darted to every corner and angle of his perfect face.

Hagan's eyes followed suit, examining every aspect of her face.

"Do you swear?" She asked in a whisper.

He returned his gaze to her eyes, nothing but sincerity on his face. He took his thumb and forefinger to her chin to gently lift her head to deepen their gaze. He was a mystery to her, but she did not doubt his honesty.

Her heartbeat quickened, despite the cold air, her body vibrated with heat. She did not know if it came from Hagan's Gift or herself.

He took his thumb and brushed it down her lower lip. "I swear." He whispered.

She breathed in the cool air, closing her eyes to take in his scent and allow the freshness to fill her lungs. It made her drunk. He took a half-step forward, closing the already tight distance between them on the balcony.

"I need you to know that I would never take advantage of you." A smirk surfaced on his full lips; his eyes locked onto hers. "In almost every way."

She laughed, and her eyes twinkled in the moonlight. In that short time, the Moon had darkened significantly and set a sensual reddish glow over them both.

She asked, her voice shaking. "It's funny you think there's any way that you can take advantage of me."

He lowered his eyes to her lips as she brushed her lower lip with her teeth. "We shall see, Queen of Mischief."

Her eyes widened, but before she could ask how he knew of that nickname, loud noises came from the Great Room.

The music and voices poured out of the open doors to the terrace, and in a few seconds the space was crowded with costumed Fae. Maeve retreated slightly, and Hagan's dark gaze said everything. *We will continue this chat another time.*

Almost everyone at the party was on the large wrap-around balcony as the Moon's color deepened to it's most vibrant shade of blood red. Cheers, dancing, and music filled the air. *Ganera* flitted about with shots of every variety, and she grabbed two shots of amber liquid.

She set the two shots on the balcony, Hagan watching her carefully. "I know I may be a hypocrite for asking this." She grinned up at Hagan, and amusement flickered across his face.

"I'm intrigued." He smiled from ear to ear.

"Mikael did this thing where he made this taste sweet, like strawberries." She offered Hagan one of the shots, and his glowing green eyes contrasted the red glow that was settled upon them both.

"I think I know what you mean. Cheers." His lips formed a sly smile, and they downed the liquid.

She tasted something so decadent she let out a soft groan. Chocolate, with a hint of something else... mint. It may have been the most delicious thing she had ever consumed. She looked up to him, and the satisfaction on his face was evident.

"So?"

Maeve laughed, bubbles multiplying in her mind. "That may have been the best fucking thing I've ever tasted."

Hagan stepped forward. "No taste compares to yours, darling."

Her body was immediately burning in the cold night air. Many Fae were dancing and chatting around them. A few stole glances toward them, noting and giving casual bows to the Prince.

Her chest ached. "And how would you know that?" She whispered against his neck.

His breath tickled her ear. "I just do."

Her blood felt as if it were boiling. A delicious heat pooled at her center, and she could not stop her hands moving to his arms. His skin was both soft and rough, and his muscles rippled underneath her cool touch.

She felt so twisted up, too warm around all of the other partygoers. Her mind was at a crossroads. While she was extremely attracted to him, she always got the feeling that he was hiding something. He speaks in riddles, but she wants nothing more than to solve them. The pull between them was something not of this world, something so electric it would be silly for her to fight it.

Her gaze met his, and he understood. They needed privacy.

Hagan nodded curtly, and grasped her arm to nestle it in the crook of his own. He led her through the crowd, and Maeve could not help but notice the many eyes watching her. She pushed her embarrassment down, replacing it with a tilt of the head and a sway of the hips as she walked with The Prince.

Inside, many of the partygoers had started retreating to dark corners or guest rooms with various lovers. Hagan surprisingly took them to the back exit, and into the courtyard beyond. The same familiar, twisted path came into view and they walked through it toward the garden.

Tension that could only be cut with the sharpest of knives filled the air that they breathed as they arrived at the Queen's Garden. The reddish hue that shadowed the already dark garden made the space look like it was bathed in blood.

She heard rustling throughout the space, whispers were so quiet she could barely discern them. They were not alone, but it was still quite private. Finally, he led them through a few hedges to a hidden clearing.

She squinted through the dark red dim light.

The clearing was lush with much vegetation, but a large tree sat at the center. Moss and flowers hung from it, some parts almost touching the ground below.

"This is one of my favorite spots in the kingdom." Hagan said. He led her underneath the tree, where she stumbled along the moss and flower covered ground. Too much mint chocolate alcohol, apparently. She followed him, the heat from his arm keeping her fire from the balcony blazing.

She still felt so unsure of him, of the entire place. There was one thing she knew for certain. She wanted to be alone with Hagan. She needed it.

CHAPTER 27
THE GARDEN

Beneath the Blood Moon, the only color was red. Under the mossy tree, it looked as if blood flowers rained upon them where they stood.

"I used to come here often, to sneak away. On this bed of moss, looking up at the stars. Believe it or not, one-hundred years ago this was but a fresh-planted sapling."

Maeve could only make out the basic lines of his face, but she could see him looking miles away. She looked up at the many stars overhead, and kept her neck achingly bent as she took it all in. The sky was a strange shade of red-black that made the stars look subdued. However, with no clouds in the sky, the monochromatic atmosphere was breathtaking.

"It's beautiful." Tilting her head back down, she stilled at Hagan's intense gaze.

"Yes, it is." His hands reached out, and he removed the fox mask from her face. "Even better." Hagan smiled.

Her entire body ached. Awash with emotion, she felt the slightest pang of unease. She could not understand how he looked at her. His eyes spoke a million words and yet she could not speak the language.

Her body felt betrayed, but her words needed to be spoken.

"What is this?"

She backed away slightly, as she furrowed her eyebrows. Since they met, he conquered her mind and her thoughts. He could frustrate her to the wildest of ends, and then melt her frustrations away with a few words. She needed to know for sure what was happening between them.

Hagan's mouth was half-gaping, his eyes searching hers. "I-I wish I knew." He broke her gaze and strode toward the base of the tree. He sat down, and pushed his hand through his dark brown hair. "I cannot seem to control myself when I'm with you. As much as I try, just being around you pulls me in."

Maeve's already pink cheeks were enhanced by the Blood Moon's glow.

"So, what's the problem? Why are you resisting this?" She motioned between them and sat down beside him. The ground was surprisingly soft from the moss and flowers.

Hagan only looked down at the ground. "It's inappropriate." He looked up, and she saw the uncertainty cloud his gaze.

"What? Because I'm your Sergeant? After the moment we shared in that Inn, I know you don't care about that. I may as well have thrown myself at you, and you left me." Desperation leaked into her tone. She thought of how hesitant Jo was to pursue Elias, simply because she felt like she was not enough. "Is it my... status? No title, only twenty-five years Forged, from Blarra, not nearly as powerful as you. Average." Maeve almost spit that last word.

Her fists were clenched at her sides, but she breathed through the urge to break his nose. On that last word, Hagan's head shot up.

His eyes glowed as bright as they did the night he compelled the *bhiastera* in the alley way of Blarra. He lunged, and before she knew it, she was being crushed by his large torso, his arms caged her to the ground. Hagan was on top of her, his scent wrapped around her. His breathing was rapid, each breath sent shivers reverberating down her body to her core. Powerful legs trapped hers, forcing her open.

Sweet heat was gathering between her legs.

He breathed, "Don't." His eyes were glowing neon, he stared into her very soul. "You are exceptional. I don't want to hear you speaking of yourself in that manner ever again."

It was almost too much to handle. She fluttered her lashes and glanced at his parted lips.

"Those fucking eyes." A low growl came from deep within Hagan's chest.

He hardened against her stomach. Her eyes flitted to his, and a gasp left her lips. Hagan crashed his mouth against hers. His lips were soft, yet firm.

Urgency bloomed between them.

Hagan's strong hands held her head in place, his forearms on the ground as his hands kept hold of her face, his thumbs latching to her jawbone. She opened for him and found his delicious tongue. Their tongues danced and writhed against each other. Her body was on fire. She explored his muscled back, her hands making their way to the back of his head where his soft locks tangled between her fingers. She pulled lightly, causing him to groan against her mouth.

He stood them up in a sweep of strength which set her head spinning. She was suddenly pushed against the large tree, and their mouths found each other once more. The bark scratched her exposed back, but the ache was nothing compared to the pure need that dripped from her core. His hands explored to her waist, then her round bottom. He squeezed, pushing her up against him.

He released their kiss to whisper, "You dare to call that average?"

Maeve let out a soft moan as he trailed kisses and licks down her neck to her collarbones. She tipped her head back, letting him explore as far down as he wanted. The fabric around her breasts felt tight as they swelled, and her nipples peaked through the silk.

Hagan skillfully slipped his hands underneath the dress to shift and expose her petite breasts. Maeve managed to look down, and saw dark green eyes staring hungrily back at her. She squeezed her legs together, the anticipation was too much.

His mouth closed around her nipple, she whimpered. Her legs

felt weak, and she could feel the twisting pleasure low in her stomach already gathering. He exposed both breasts and massaged them, plucking over her nipples as he went.

"Perfect," He whispered against her sternum.

He continued down, and kneeled before her. "The only person I kneel for is you. I do not kneel for '*average*'." Maeve looked down at him, the tip of his mouth was turned upward, his raw gaze peeking beneath his thick lashes.

His hands were exploring her thighs beneath the silky dress that now felt almost itchy against her skin. His hands glided up to her bare ass, and he squeezed. Continuing their journey, his hands found her hips, and electricity sprung from every place where he touched her.

Maeve gasped. Without warning, Hagan snuck under the fabric of her dress, still kneeling before her. She was backed against the tree, and she welcomed the support as her legs trembled. He peeled down the underwear she was wearing, and each breath against her front made her body ache with desire.

She felt his lips against her stomach, kissing and licking until he was almost at the apex of nerves between her thighs. Grinding her hips up, she hoped to lead him the rest of the way.

A small, breathy laugh escaped Hagan. That laugh vibrated against where his lips almost touched.

He paused.

She could barely take breath, desire blurring her vision as she attempted to look around them under the crimson moonlight.

She saw nothing, no disturbance.

Hagan struck.

He lapped at her, his tongue exploring her flesh. She cried out, and pushed herself further against the tree to support herself. Hagan's hands found the back of her thighs and he lifted her effortlessly, letting her legs fall on top of his broad shoulders and down his back.

She felt like she was floating.

He drank from her, and she groaned as he thrust his tongue inside of her. The pressure inside her was building, and his grip tightened around her as he focused on her bundle of nerves. He swirled and swirled, a torturous dance as she twisted so tight she thought she may snap. Her head fell back, mouth open as her breathing labored. He tortured her for what felt like hours, giving and taking away pleasure until she couldn't take it anymore.

He sucked on her, and she whimpered, pleading with him.

Hagan's tongue swirled with purpose against her, and he pushed her harder against the tree as he swirled faster.

Maeve's breath hitched, and her core twisted until release found her.

The pleasure that exploded through her felt like an explosion of feelings and emotions, vibrating and warming her entire body. Her back arched, and her head was thrown back to face the stars overhead.

Hagan dug his fingers harder into her thighs, and held her in place as he drank from her endlessly. He gave a final lap up and down her sensitive skin, and sucked on her clit in a way that made her body lurch.

He set her down gently as he found his way out of the silk of her dress. He rose to meet her gaze, her body feeling limp against the hard bark of the tree.

His voice was labored. "No taste compares."

He kissed her, and she tasted herself on his lips. She was oddly sweet. Her eyes felt heavy, and her head light as he kissed her, passion rippling through the air. Her legs were still shaking, and she released the kiss as she tried to catch her breath.

Maeve lost her footing, and the already dark night went black.

Cold.

The icy wind that cut into her skin shivered her to the bone. She was riding through the night, with nothing but a thin cloak to shield her from the freezing temperature. She heard hooves beside her, galloping at a rapid pace that she was struggling to keep up with. Her body ached, the forest sliding past her in a blur of dark blues and greens.

She managed a glance to her right, and saw a female riding beside her. The darkness shielded her face, but she caught a glimpse of porcelain skin against dark hair. She rode so elegantly, atop a midnight-colored horse who reminded her of Callistus with its shiny silver mane that whipped in the wind.

A warm female voice sprang into her thoughts.
"Keep going and do not look back. Be well, my dear."
The female's voice was like music, and the melody was impossible to ignore. She felt her body respond, and she pushed the horse harder into the night as the presence of the female felt farther and farther away.

Heat surrounded her, and strong hands held her head away from the mossy ground. She opened her eyes to see his inquisitive eyes staring back, a hint of concern furrowing his brows, creasing over his straight nose.

"I have to say, that's never happened when making a female cum." His voice had the faintest hint of amusement.

A flush spread across her face. She stood up, Hagan steadying her.

"The fainting is new for me too, must be because I haven't eaten anything." Hagan smirked, and helped her brush off her dress and adjust the exposed parts of skin. "We should get going, we may be missed at the party."

She furrowed her brows but agreed. She wasn't used to being seen as any type of important, but she supposed he was. Despite the bliss she had just experienced with Hagan, she could not keep her mind off the female in her dreams. Something about her felt so powerful, her words causing Maeve to act without hesitation.

Hagan and Maeve walked through the dark garden, and she heard noises that echoed into the night. Hagan took her hand, guiding her with his firm grip. They turned a corner toward a small clearing of rose bushes and she felt the breath leave her lungs.

The scene in front of her was something out of an exotic brothel. Blarra did not have one, but she had heard rumors of Fae of all sexes and walks of life that would gather to give and take pleasure. She and Petra had joked about going to try it out, but never actually did it.

She was comfortable with one partner, but she had never thought to include another. While she usually preferred males, the idea of a female in her bedroom always intrigued her.

She could never tell Petra that.

Her shocked eyes were set on three Fae laid out on a blanket, all engaged with each other. Their bodies were so passionately entwined, they barely noticed her and Hagan.

Glowing, wide blue eyes met hers, and the sharply defined features of Mikael came into focus.

Maeve breathed; her body felt frozen.

She could not take her eyes away. He was laying against the back of the female of the group, thrusting into her from behind as they both lay on their sides. Smells of mint and musk filled Maeve's nose, the passion leaving a sweet taste in her mouth.

The female's eyes were closed, her head lolling back against him as he went slow and sensual. The male that joined their entanglement pleasured the female, lapping at her and worshipping her body from the front.

She moaned and sighed; her body writhed in what Maeve could only imagine as ecstasy. Mikael's eyes didn't leave Maeve's as he went, and an arrogant smirk on his lips entranced her for the shortest of seconds before Hagan pulled at her hand.

She shook her head, following him into the courtyard and party beyond. "That was something." She muttered as they walked through the courtyard.

Hagan cleared his throat. "Mikael takes many lovers. I could have gone without him looking at you though, the bastard could never keep his hands to himself."

Maeve giggled. They clearly had a history.

She and Hagan strode together into the back entrance of the palace, and much of the party had returned to the Great Room, where the King and Queen now sat upon their thrones.

They merged into the crowd, where the King was speaking.

"What a joyous Blood Moon it has been, but we must remember the true purpose of this night. The drinks, the laughter, the dancing, and the after-hour festivities..." The King raised a sharp brow, an expression of charm that did not suit him. "Those things mean nothing if we do not have the dead on our minds. We honor them on this night, we celebrate them. We honor our citizens, so threatened by the radicalistic Freed Fae storming our lands, taking our livestock, and killing the ones we remember on this day. As we enjoy the luxuries of our bountiful Kingdom, we must not forget that the war is real. The Savage who calls himself their Leader dares to pillage and take from our land, and he must be stopped. Our Kingdom does not honor the dead of the Savages who call themselves a Republic. We celebrate those lives that were given for the Kingdom of Thunder. Happy Blood Moon to you all."

The crowd cheered, but Maeve kept quiet as she stared at the thrones. A throne built upon half-truths and cruel intentions.

With a wave of the hand, the music began to play anew, and dancing commenced. She watched the King's speech but felt nothing from his words. Has he not seen the Freed Fae face to face? Does he not know that they are weakened and are no match for any Gifted Fae in a fight? What they used as a dwelling was already dilapidated, even before the Brigade had destroyed it. Nomads of the Freed Fae were simply using the Second Kingdom's land to survive.

The King was merciless. She had to remember that, as Hagan had warned her that her kindness could be severely punished when it comes to the King's enemies. He was spinning a web of lies, and everyone there was caught in it. She had witnessed what the Freed Fae were, and she could not possibly call them 'savages'.

Grey eyes met her, the dark diminutive eyes scanning every particle of her being. His endless stare seemed to strip her bare, violating her. Managing to rip her gaze from his, she set her eyes on the Queen, who briefly met her gaze.

Shadows of concern clouded Revna's expression for a moment, before returning to watching the members of her court dancing.

Hagan looked down at her, eyes glittering. "You want a drink? I can guarantee the party will be going on for another few hours."

She sighed. "What would you normally do at a soirée such as this, your highness?"

His mouth turned up. "Get otherworldly drunk." His grin widened, revealing a boyish smile that made her heart drum.

A laugh bubbled from her. "Drunk it is."

She grabbed two bottles of champagne from a table nearby. Golden eyes captured hers, and Elias smiled and waved at her from across the dance floor. He strode forward to greet them. "Looking to get into a little trouble?"

She smiled, welcoming the distraction. Weird visions, confusing males, frightening Kings, and being a Sergeant of the 22nd Brigade? It was past time to let loose.

Hagan frowned when he saw Elias, who was swigging from a menacing bottle of dark brown liquid and smiling drunkenly. Maeve spotted Lyra, then Petra beside her. They seemed to be together all the time now. Petra had never settled down with someone before, she usually didn't even sleep with the same female more than once.

Smiling to herself, she waved her hand up to get Petra's attention. Her icy blue eyes met Maeve's, and she immediately dragged Lyra with her to meet them.

Maeve hugged her friend, and pulled back to see her outfit. She chose a wolfish costume, the fur bodice and ears were a light blonde color, accenting her rich skin color, and her breasts were pushed up almost to her collarbones.

Glancing at Lyra, she could not help but smile. She wore a black furry mask. She was a saber-tooth, and her mask had long fangs coming out from each side.

Now she understood, they were dressing up as each other. "You guys want to get drunk?"

Petra giggled, holding onto Lyra for support. "I think we want to get drunk-er. The drinks here are no joke…"

Hagan spoke to the group, surrendering to having company with them. "I think I know the place."

CHAPTER 28
THE WATERFALL

Elias, Maeve, Lyra, and Petra sneakily followed Hagan through the crowd to the back side of the grand staircase. They went downstairs, three flights of stairs passed before they reached the bottom floor.

Petra and Maeve pulled back from the group, slowing their steps.

Petra asked. "You and Hagan did something. Didn't you?"

Her eyes widened, Petra's audacity never seeming to amaze her. "How do you know?"

Petra smiled, leaning in. "I can smell it on both of you. His breath, to be specific." The two laughed, and Lyra shot her a look of disapproval as they reached the bottom of the last flight of steps.

Cool grey stone covered the floors and walls, and the air was chilled, as if a light breeze came from beyond the hall.

Elias laughed. "Wow, it's been years since I've been down here. So many memories." He took a swig of that amber liquid, then passed it to Maeve. She took a large drink, waiting for the burn that did not come. The liquid tasted of something sweet, yet sour. Blueberries.

Hagan glanced at her sideways, eyes just a bit brighter than normal. He shrugged. They walked through the cavern tunnel, which echoed with their whispers and laughter. A cool breeze found them as they walked out to a large patio that overlooked the mountains.

Maeve froze.

This was the exact place that she dreamed of, when she imagined Hagan completely naked. He was dripping wet from the large infinity pool that now spanned the length of the cave opening the group stood on.

Faint roaring of the waterfall below filled her ears.

Petra ripped off her clothes and mask, and Lyra followed suit. Lyra was toned, years of hunting and fighting defining the lines in her stomach and arms. Black ink patterned her upper arm, bands and symbols wrapping around her toned bicep. Her blonde hair cascaded down her front, halfway shielding her perky bosom.

Lyra screeched, her giggle echoing against the stone as Petra slapped her ass and pulled her into the water. The two females groaned as they stepped in.

"How is this mountain water warm?"

Petra's icy blue eyes were wide with surprise and wonder. She glanced at Hagan, whose eyes were glowing in the barely lit room. Lyra tipped her head back and sighed, the water teasing her collarbones.

Elias laughed. "It's quite the party trick of Hagan's. Welcome to the world-renowned *aimsura* hot springs."

Elias joined the two females, stripping his clothes as well.

She was still standing there, mind running in a million directions. She had never been here, never seen this place yet she somehow imagined every detail just days ago. The mountains, the blue tone of the water, the sound of rushing water.

Everything was the same.

Hagan approached her, extending his arm to hers. "Is something wrong?"

Maeve huffed a laugh at that. No, nothing was wrong. She could only see the future now. At least, a lot of what she has seen was a future she would not mind having. Either that, or she was mentally ill. More reasons to get drunk.

"This is breathtaking." She attempted to recover from her strange behavior.

She shook her head, but Hagan looked as if he did not fully believe her. He seemed to push that thought aside, and brushed her cheek with his hand.

"You want to get in?" The glow of his green irises beckoned her to forget about all of her worries.

Sighing, she gave in. "I do."

Hagan stripped off his shirt, revealing a rippling stomach and defined lines. She tried to not watch him, but could not resist as she shimmied out of her dress. The air was chilled, but she felt incredibly warm as Hagan pulled off the leather warrior pants he had been wearing, revealing the shadows of his manhood in the dim light.

Maeve caught a gasp before it escaped from her lips. She pulled her eyes back up to his, warmth pooling low in her core. He looked at her bare body as if he was starving and she was the last morsel to be served.

She smiled, a shy blush creeping over her freckled face.

Elias hollered, words slurring. "Do you two need a moment?"

The other two females in the water laughed as they floated around together in the now steaming water. She could only guess what was happening under the line of the water as they creeped farther into the darker corner of the endless infinity pool.

Maeve stepped into the warm water; Hagan close behind. The warmth set her mind at ease, and she sunk down to cover her exposed breasts. She swam over to where Elias was leaning against the edge, bottle in hand, gazing out at the mountains.

He swigged from the bottle. "What d'ya think?" His glazed-over golden eyes glanced at her as she swam to the edge.

The end of the pool was soft stone, raised up about ten feet from where the waterfall descended down to the grand city below. The view was truly breathtaking. Looking around, she took in the sizes of the mountains, some big and small, and some capped with snow. Sounds of the waterfall rushed through her mind, setting her at ease. The stars overhead were bright, the sky a canvas of swirling purples and blues with speckles of bright white stars and a soft pink moon. Just like her dream, excluding the Blood Moon's pinkish hue.

She sighed. "It is tranquil, beautiful. I could swim in this pool for hours."

Hagan swam up beside her, wrapping his strong arm around her back. Static buzzed where he touched her, but she welcomed the delicious heat that it brought. Hagan took the bottle from Elias and drank deeply. He offered it to Maeve, and she obliged. Taking a quick swig that now tasted like chocolate cake.

Hagan smirked down at her. "This place is something special. It has existed as long as my line has existed in this palace. Nearly a millennium."

Maeve had a lot of questions, she had limited knowledge of Kingdom history.

She began. "Who ruled before your mother and father?"

She was not familiar with the histories past the current rulers of the Five Kingdoms.

His lashes lowered, eyes set on her. "Before the King of Thunder was the King of Fire, Asos. It was unheard of to have such a power, but around nine-hundred years ago, a male was Forged by the Smiths, an *aimsura*, who could harness living volcanoes. If he wanted, he could've burned every Kingdom to the ground. Most *aimsuras* can control simple things like rain, lightning, cold or warm, and sometimes earthquakes. History states that he did almost burn all Five Kingdoms, in the hope of ruling them all. That all changed when Asos met the Lady of the Frost, Eira. She is painted with hair as white as snow, and she was Forged with the power over the cold. She was said to be kind and merciful, but she refused to marry him knowing that he wanted to destroy so many innocent lives. She was dedicated to serving the Smiths and the Forge, and such death would surely upset the balance created by them."

Her eyes never left his, this story entranced her like a youngling reading a mythical tale. "In the end, he loved her enough to sacrifice his pride and ambition. They married, and after one hundred years of trying they managed to have a child.

A male, Frey. Who would one day become the King of Thunder." Hagan's eyes hardened.

Her brows furrowed, and she looked out toward the mountains. Her voice was low. "How did Frey seize the throne?" She was afraid of the answer that she was almost certain of.

Hagan's gaze went distant, and Elias whispered. "Once our King truly harnessed his power, he... took the throne by force. He struck them both down with lightning."

Her eyes widened, and she could not help her mouth falling open.

Hagan sighed, despair creeping across his handsome features. "I was not yet born, but there are servants who have worked for this Kingdom for hundreds of years. Growing up here, you learn things."

Elias continued. "Many believe that our King found his father Asos' actions weak, that love was not a fair enough motivator to give up power."

Maeve nodded. She could not imagine what weight this knowledge must carry on Queen Revna, Hagan, and the higher-ranking Fae like Elias who must know of the twisted past. King Frey already made her uneasy, but now she had a much more distinct flavor of hatred for him. He was power hungry and evil. She had only known Hagan for a short time, but she wanted to believe that he was not capable of such malice as his Father had committed in the past.

Elias, Maeve, and Hagan sipped from the bottle, the conversation lightening up after each sip. Petra and Lyra joined them after a while, and the group laughed and drank until the sun began to peek out from the mountains beyond, turning the sky the faintest orange. The bottle was empty, and the group felt the dizzying exhaustion settle over them all.

Petra kissed Maeve on the cheek, saying goodnight. Or, Good morning. She and Lyra said their goodbyes and stalked out of the water— shifting into their *bhiastera* forms, their clothes in their jowls, to dry off and make the trek to the town below.

Elias strode out of the water, his muscled ass on full display for all to see. He stretched, his large muscles flexing with the effort. He glanced back, golden eyes flashing at her, who was accidentally staring.

"Enjoying the view?"

She scoffed, rolling her eyes. Hagan glared at Elias. "Go to bed, El."

Elias glanced between her and Hagan. "Be careful, Prince."

A wary expression crossed his face. He slipped on his pants, and padded his way up to his room. Maeve immediately felt how alone they were. She turned to him, and he was gazing at her in a way she couldn't quite place. His eyes glittered, and a soft smile made him look much younger.

A smile crept upon her lips. "This was quite the night, definitely the best Blood Moon celebration I've ever been to."

Hagan swam closer, and Maeve backed to the edge of the infinity pool, hoisting herself up by her elbows. He smiled, which caused her blood to heat a few degrees hotter. He had faint lines there that stretched up to create the most stunning smile, his full lips framing his straight teeth.

"It has been too long since I have been able to enjoy myself. Your presence just…" He looked down, his lashes brushing his cheek. "I'm just so glad that you are here."

Maeve lowered her eyes, she felt so many hidden words underneath what he chose to say. She wanted to ask what else he wanted to say but was refraining from doing so. He had feasted upon her in the garden just hours ago, causing her pleasure she could have never imagined, and yet he seemed to hold so much back. Looking down at the water, she suddenly felt his presence just inches from her, his body almost pressing against hers at the edge of the infinity pool.

They were both bare, the small hairs on her neck and arms standing up in anticipation. His eyes were lowered, looking at her lips. His finger tilted her chin up, and her eyes were forced to his as he whispered against her lips.

"Do not hide your eyes from me. They are the most stunning thing I have ever seen. Every time you honor me with your gaze, I feel that my lungs are full, and my mind is clear. It pains me that I have gone so long without seeing them."

Maeve could barely breathe. Not just from his strong body against hers, but from the words. Has he really waited his entire lifetime to see eyes like hers? Was this real? She never imagined a male like Hagan would want her.

She didn't care.

Her body. Her mind. Everything responded to him. In this moment she did not care that her mind was fooling her with visions of imaginary things, or that she still could not decipher what was real or who was good in this foreign kingdom. With his whiskey-coated breath inches from her lips, she did not worry about his true intentions. While she did not yet fully trust him, she wanted him.

She just wanted to make some of it real. With him.

He brushed his lips to hers, and she tipped the extra inch up to connect them. The whiskey they were drinking coated her lips, and the taste drove her mad. He pressed into her, now holding her at the edge of the pool, head falling back into the open air. His lips felt warm as they glided over hers, his tongue tracing them before opening her wider. He claimed her, and she returned every ounce of passion that he gave her.

His hands stayed in her hair, keeping her in position to explore her mouth as he pleased. She groaned, the slight pinch of her hair being pulled awakening her. She grazed her teeth against his lip, and he kissed her deeper. She felt his hardness against her, so close to her core she could nearly feel it inside her.

A deep, throaty sound came from him before pulling away. They were both gasping for air, a hot flush spread across her face, chest, and arms.

Her green and amber eyes were wild.

Hagan cleared his throat, eyes not leaving hers. "We should get going, we both need rest. The Brigade will be leaving in three days' time."

He turned, and she followed him out of the water. "Uh, what the fuck was that?" Her voice was low, but vicious. She thought the games were over after what happened in the garden and the words he said to her just moments before.

Hagan averted his eyes and slipped on the leather pants he

was wearing the night before. Maeve did the same, careful to allow herself to dry a bit before donning the Queen's borrowed dress.

Fury flowed through her. "Why do you continue to fight this? The ups and downs, the hot and the cold— this game you are playing with me is sickening." Her eyes burned, she hated how much his rejection ripped her apart inside.

Hagan brushed a hand through his thick brown locks, then focused on her. Anger began to flood his eyes, turning them a dark green. He closed the distance between them.

"You have no idea how much I have to fight. How much I have to fight my urges. After all this time, it is killing me. I let things go too far, and I am sorry. There are… things that need to happen. As it stands I cannot take you in that way. As much as I want to." Hagan's eyes were wide, pleading with her to understand.

She scoffed. "Then what was last night? Is it because of where I come from? I'm not well-bred like you. I did not grow up in a fucking castle. I am no Princess. I'm from Blarra, and I'm just a healer. I'm not Born, I'm not worthy."

His eyes flashed neon green, a muscle ticked in his sharp jaw. "I fucked up, Maeve. When you walked down those steps in that dress, in your fox mask," He shook his head. "it felt as if my entire body would burst into flames. I needed to pleasure you, to worship you in some way. I meant what I said last night. You are a Queen, and I am not even close to worthy. It just— it can't happen like this." His eyes pleaded with her to understand.

She was shaking, the tears burning against her eyes. She bit her lip to distract her from the pain in her chest. In this short time, he had managed to twist and pull at her heartstrings and she was tired. His mystifying words just simply didn't make any sense to her, and she did not believe that the connection they shared was so complicated.

"Do you want me?"

He exhaled, the feeling of defeat sagging his shoulders. "Yes. But it's just not that simple."

"I don't want to hear 'but'. Find me when you know without

a doubt what you want, Hagan. Good night." Her words and body were stiff as she turned from him and marched up the stairs to her bedroom.

A loud crackle of thunder erupted above the palace.

A KINGDOM OF MISCHIEF & MEMORIES

CHAPTER 29
THE INVITATION

Dawn's pale light cast itself upon the mountains that morning, making the snowy tops reflect silvery white. Her room did not seem to welcome her in the same way as it had on her first day in the Second Kingdom, and she knew she needed to find something of her own. No more borrowed things, she needed to go to her home. Whatever that would be.

When she rose from the bed, she noted a slight ache in her temples. Everyone had overindulged on Blood Moon, and not just in spirits. Recounting the previous night, she knew there was still so much that was uncertain between her and Hagan. She gave him an ultimatum, but also made the mistake of forming her words to say that she would wait for him to make up his mind. Her heart spoke before her head.

Laying at the base of the door was a small letter, a rosy-hued envelope no larger than the palm of her hand. Picking it up, she peeled open the small seal and unfolded the fragrant piece of stationary.

Miss Maeve,

*I would be delighted if you joined me for morning tea at my
cottage tomorrow. If you travel out of the capitol and into the first town to
the West, my home is at the edge of the wood at the farthest corner. It is
the smallest home in the town, you won't be able to miss it.*
It will be my pleasure to see you when dawn breaks.

With gratitude,

Clover

She smiled at the formal invitation and felt excitement at the
prospect of seeing her kind little friend. If she was being honest
with herself, she could use some of the sunny attitude that the
nymph seemed to always have.

⇥ ⇥ ⇤ ⇤

Packing her small bag of belongings, she took another look at
the grand guest chambers and sighed. She would miss the tub the
most. Finding the nearest *ganera*, she began asking around about
the existence of her promised estate. Finally, after milling
through five other servants, she got an answer. Her home was
just outside the capitol.

Quickly going into the dining room, where a light brunch was
served, she grabbed a muffin and left without greeting the guests
who were casually eating.

Heading out to the courtyard, she murmured the directions
that she had been given by the servant who hesitantly gave her
the key to her estate. A large bronze key sat heavy in her hand,
the nervousness beginning to be eclipsed by her excitement at
having her own home and privacy when she took leave from the
Brigade.

Down the lift, leave the capitol from whence you arrived.
Then, travel past the field of wheat to—

She had forgotten the rest.

"Where are you off to, Maeve?" The kind voice of Revna was at her back as she neared the entry hall. Hagan's mother was truly Gifted with the art of surprise.

Turning, she smiled softly. "Good morning, my Queen. I am actually going to see my estate. I have not yet gotten to visit it."

Revna nodded, a hint of uncertainty flickering in her bottle green eyes. "I see, well allow me to at least send you with an escort. It will not do well for you to venture from the capitol alone."

Spotting Elias leaving the dining hall, she called out. "Elias!" Causing him to look around quickly before spotting her with the Queen. Sauntering over, he looked mildly annoyed.

"Fine morning to you, my Queen." He said with a short bow. "What is it you need from me, Maeve?"

"A favor." Revna cut in. "Would you be a gentleman and escort Maeve to her estate? I would ask my son, but I have not laid eyes on him since early in the evening last night."

Maeve smiled awkwardly; an escort seemed like far too much effort. But she would not refuse the offer of a Queen.

Elias smiled in a faux gentlemanly manner. "Of course."

"I do hope the estate is to your liking, it has not been touched in years but it is a lovely little home nonetheless." Revna said, her gaze warm when she looked at Maeve.

"Thank you, I am sure it will be wonderful." She replied, eyeing Elias and the exit of the palace.

With a soft bow, she and Elias walked out of the palace.

"You do know I'm not in need of an escort." Maeve said, brushing her hair aside.

Elias smirked. "So, you know exactly where to go?"

She rolled her eyes. "I had an idea."

He laughed warmly.

Together, they boarded the lift and descended to the capitol square. Past the waterfall, the town was alive with many Fae going about their daily errands. She noted a vast number of younglings, surprised at the number of them. Elias glanced at her, seeing her gears turning.

"You are not accustomed to seeing this many younglings with parents, I take it."

She smiled, meeting his gaze. "I have seen many children come and go. In Geneza, if they were Gifted they would easily be adopted or sent to different courts to live out the rest of their lives. I have just never thought about where they go."

Walking in silence, she thought of the younglings whom she lived with. The looks on the *ganera* children's faces when they were not chosen to be adopted, which happened more often than it ever should have, tore her up more than anything. She felt that struggle, too, but found solace in comforting and taking care of the ones who were hurt. Whether that was her personality or her Gift, she could not tell the difference.

They walked down the smooth flagstone path toward the town center. Overhead, the sun was obscured by fluffy white clouds, promising rain in the near future. A damp chill filled the air, and she pulled her thick travelling cloak further over her for warmth.

Elias turned to her as they neared the entrance of the capitol. "I will get the horses. Be back shortly." He jogged toward the stables at the other side of the road, waving toward a female *ganera* servant who immediately sprung to her feet from the large bale of hay she was sitting on. Maeve walked over, greeting the *ganera* kindly.

She extended her hand, but the *ganera* bowed before her.

Shaking her head, she smiled kindly at her. "Please, there is no need. I'm Maeve. And you are?"

The female appeared young, just out of childhood. "Georgia, ma'am. It is wonderful to meet you. I'll fetch your horses."

Elias inclined his head in thanks. "Georgia is the lead horse handler, she has worked here far longer than I have been alive."

Maeve scrunched her eyebrows. "But she looks very young, how old can she possibly be?"

He shrugged. "The Forge must have Gifted her with a lengthy lifespan. Some would consider that something far greater than true Gifts like ours. Others may consider it a curse. I suppose Georgia used her time to master horses."

She nodded, her lips turning into a thin line. "Gifts don't have to mean power, Elias. She is truly Gifted as well."

His gaze shifted a bit, turning contemplative. Finally, his lips curved in a smirk as he looked down on her with his golden gaze. "I have never thought of it that way."

Georgia returned, the tethers of Callistus and a huge golden horse around each arm. They followed her with full obedience, and she could have sworn she caught a glimmer in her horse's dark eyes.

Thanking Georgia, they mounted their horses and set off.

Callistus neighed, which was followed by a sudden scoff from Elias. "That is quite rude of you to say, horse."

Maeve whipped her head in his direction. "What?"

Callistus huffed. Elias turned to her, a grimace on his face. "It appears your steed has quite the foul mouth. She's up to the same antics as before. Do you want me to tell her what you said, horse?"

The midnight horse set off in a trot, and Elias willed the golden horse to catch up.

Maeve laughed aloud, still amazed that Elias could converse with animals. She stroked Callistus' mane. "What did you say to him, girl?"

"She wondered, rather loudly, how Ray here could possibly hold a big, fat bearish ass like mine." His expression turned pouty, and she could not control her roaring laughter as they trotted toward the southeast, along a well-worn path toward a field of wheat.

"How far out is it?" She asked, eyes peering around the expanse of hills and valleys. Much of the green had begun turning, leaving many shades of tan and brown.

He replied. "Just over the hill, here." As if on cue, Callistus galloped faster along the path, up the hill. When they reached the top of the hill, she pulled hard at the reins, sucking in a sharp breath.

What Queen Revna had called a 'lovely little home' was nothing short of a mansion. Brick was painted bright white, going up two stories to a dark sloping roof. Wide, black-framed windows contrasted the stark, white brick. Connected to the home was a large wraparound porch, with double doors leading to a balcony coming from the top floor. Behind the home, a small field of bright purple sprigs of lavender shot up from the ground in wild disarray. If she could have imagined her dream home, which she had never really taken the time to do, this would have been it.

"What do you think?" Elias asked, shocking her out of her amazement.

"I-I am overwhelmed." She could have easily been having another vision, but as the icy wind whipped her hair across her face, she knew this was real. All of this was hers.

CHAPTER 30
THE HOME

"Did you want to stand here in the cold, or do you need a few more moments of staring aimlessly at your estate?" Elias asked, humor dancing across his face.

The mist clearing from her thoughts, she glanced at him and dismounted from Callistus. "Let's go then." Reins in hand, she began walking with Callistus to her new home.

"You go ahead, Maeve. I'll be heading back to the palace. The door is unlocked."

She turned, facing him. "What? You don't want to see my new house?"

He laughed and began turning to leave. "I have seen it plenty. Go on now and enjoy. You deserve it."

Waving him goodbye, she turned back to Callistus. "I guess it's just you and me." Together, she and Callistus walked toward the door, on the rough path that soon turned to cobblestone. Besides the clattering of hooves, she heard nothing. It was peaceful there.

Surrounding her was a field of green and brown grass, left to be wild and beautiful leading up to the steps of the porch. Within her sight, she could not see another home. All that filled her vision was pure serenity. Cerulean skies, wispy grass, and bright sprigs of lavender leading to a home of her dreams.

Her thoughts were calm, with no worries of her next expedition with the Brigade, her duties as *helbredera* Sergeant, or what was between her and Hagan.

When they reached the wooden steps, she let Callistus into the field to graze, giving her a soft caress through her mane and across her snout. Hesitantly, she climbed the steps and reached for the knob on the dark hardwood door. Taking a deep breath, she opened the door and stepped inside to explore.

Stepping in, she noted dark hardwood floors contrasted by shiplap walls painted a calming white-grey. Beneath her feet, the floors creaked quietly, whispering a *Welcome Home, Maeve*. To her left, a curved archway led into what she assumed was the kitchen.

To her right, a small entryway lined with built-in bookshelves led to the living room. Caressing the spines of the endless book collection with care, she stepped through the hall and into the large living space. Smells of fresh bread and fruits met her first, intoxicating her. She had not yet realized she was hungry. A floral fragrance met her next, like the luxurious lavender soaps she had always indulged in. The scent of fresh rain met her last, and she knew who awaited her through the hallway.

Laid out on the hardwood was a greyish-white thick, fur blanket. Atop it lay a silver tray with baked bread, fruits, cheeses, and a bottle of bubbly white wine paired with two drinking glasses. Surrounding the feast were candles of every height, all lit and flickering in the subtle breeze of the open windows. The black framed windows that filled the back wall engulfed the room in the day's dim light, the clouds keeping the bright rays at bay. Each window was opened ever so slightly, to let the perfect amount of cool into the room.

Laying on the fur blanket, his sleeves pulled up to reveal strong, tanned forearms, was Hagan. He looked at her with a strange mix of admiration and fear, a hesitant Prince who had laid out a picnic in her home for her. The sunlight gleamed off of his emerald eyes, his tanned skin close to glowing. His pile of dark brown locks was ruffled in the light breeze, and he looked much more casual than she had ever seen him. As if they were just two Fae having a romantic picnic in her living room.

She stood there, and he watched her, waiting for her to say something as she took in the surprise of his presence in her home. After the events of the previous night, she was not sure how she felt. She knew she wanted him, she knew that there was an undeniable connection between them that could not be explained, but was that enough?

"Hi," she said, the only word she could manage as her thoughts ran in two different directions.

"Hello," he said, glancing down at the tray of food awkwardly. "Would you like to join me? I want to talk." She brushed her hair over to one side, eyeing him contemplatively.

She sighed. "Alright, fine. But only because I'm starving." She sat down on the far side of the fur blanket, facing him. "This is quite the spread you've brought all the way here."

His eyes glimmered, and a smirk spread across his lips. "I may have had some help." He smiled shyly. "I am hopeless at apologies, but I know you deserve one."

"Oh yeah? And what is it you'd like to apologize to me for?" Laying on her side, she scanned the choices of morsels and decided upon a thick slice of cheese. The sharp, tangy flavor filled her mouth as she took a bite of sweet, sliced apple. The pairing was delightful.

He laughed softly. "Where do I start? My actions have been unfair to you. I see that I have played with your emotions, hidden secrets, and not been my full self around you. I am truly sorry, Maeve. You deserve better."

"This is all true. You've been a complete asshole to me." She said, sitting up and crossing her legs out in front of her. Taking a sip from the bright, bubbly wine, she took a minute to think. "However, you quickly found the way to my heart. I love cheese."

"I know." He said, smiling. "The combination of sweet and savory is a true Gift from the Forge."

She laughed, a joyous laugh that released her mind of the previous tension. "Indeed."

He took his glass, drinking deeply from it. "So, what do you think of your home?"

She paused, taking a long moment to slowly examine every inch of the room ostentatiously. Raising an eyebrow, she returned her gaze to his. "It will do."

He nodded but furrowed his eyebrows. "We can have something different set up for you, if you would like something grander…"

"Hagan." She said, which caused him to focus directly on her. "I am only kidding. This—" she said as she gestured around the room, "—is the most beautiful home I have ever seen. I can't imagine something more perfect for me. Thank you for setting this all up."

His cheeks went a soft reddish tone, and the boyish smile that crossed his lips made her heart nearly stop beating.

"Oh, I see. Sometimes I forget about your charming sense of humor." He smiled, licking his tongue across his teeth in that excruciatingly sensual way. She assumed it was just a habit, but if he knew what it did to her, he would certainly be sure to do it more often.

Her smile nearly reached her ears as she grabbed for another morsel to nibble on. Deciding on a slice of bread with jam, she took a bite. When she looked back at Hagan, he was watching her with a thoughtful gaze. The green of his eyes was bright, but not the neon stare of power or intensity, they were a Spring green that calmed her as much as the scent of lavender and a hot bath had done before.

"How long have you been working on all of this? I cannot imagine you could have had this home built and furnished in the time since we met," She asked, as she took in the dark brown wooden stairs that led to the yet unexplored upstairs.

He sat up, brushing his hair back as he chewed the food he was eating. "This house was previously owned, we simply did some refurbishing and cleaning to make it yours. All of the land, until about a ten-minute horse ride each way, is yours. The land isn't much, simply wheat and grasses, but it is private. I know you must miss privacy living in the palace. So, I got a horde of servants to come and help me breathe some new life into this place. When word got around that you were trying to come here, I raced here as soon as I could with the help of Yuna and a few others to finish things up before you arrived. All the servants adore you, for obvious reasons. They wanted to make this place special for you."

Listening to him, she realized her heart felt like it was going to burst. Lowering her gaze, she felt a single tear fall down her cheek.

"Are you okay? Why are you sad?" Hagan asked, rising to sit beside her on her side of the blanket.

She did not know exactly why she cried. What she did know was how much love she felt in that moment. The *ganeras* had adored her so much for simply treating them as equals, which was how they should have been treated by everyone. Then there was this male, this male who had in a matter of a few weeks completely changed her life. The love she felt from him was real, palpable.

She and Hagan had shared so much in such a small amount of time, and she could not ignore her feelings bubbling to the surface. He pulls her in, pushes her away. He gives her so much unbelievable pleasure, but won't let them share a bed. Despite her heartstrings being pulled in every direction, she knew deep down that she would keep waiting for him for forever if it meant that she could have him.

Disdain and desire, a dangerous balance of the heart.

She did not want to be complacent; she did not want to wait. Every gleam in his eye, every touch that passed between them, every time his anger flared up when she was threatened by another, and every kiss they shared told her what she needed to know. Just like the place they were sitting together. Another sentiment of how he felt.

Tilting her head up to meet him, her eyes watery, she knew what she saw in those same eyes that intoxicated her from the moment she first saw them in the tavern of Blarra.

Love. She loved him.

Their faces had gotten so close, if she just leaned in, she could kiss him. His scent enveloped her with the sweet embrace of a dewy morning. She loved the Prince of the Second Kingdom, even though she was a simple healer from the outskirts of the Five Fae Kingdoms. She was no one, but nonetheless she felt the love that he had for her. Even if he would not say it.

He smiled, the crinkle of his eyes warming her cheeks. "I would give away all of my riches and all of my power just to know what you are thinking right now."

"If only you could read my mind." She said playfully, winking at him with her amber eye. Her brows furrowed. "Wait, you can't read my mind, can you?" She asked, now concerned about all of the mischievous things she had thought of him.

He leaned in, a sensual smile on his face, eyes flashing bright for the slightest moment. "You flatter me, Princess. However, that Gift is given to only a few *cleasieras*. I have tried, believe me. But I cannot read yours, or anyone's, mind."

Curiosity taking over, she rested back on her hands and asked. "What is the difference between taking over someone's mind, and reading it? I would think the control would be more complex than simply knowing their thoughts."

He nodded, thoughtful. "It is hard to explain, but I will try. Willing someone to do something is like playing with puppet strings. You grab onto the strings, then bounce them up and down until they have done what you commanded. It is a clumsy skill. Taking that a step further, with even more power you can make those strings dance for eternity. This is more tactful. That is what I did back in Blarra, the strings repeated their dance on and on until his mind no longer had a body connected to it and the strings would collapse anyways." He paused, taking a sip of his wine as he gazed out of the tall windows. "Thoughts are different. A thought is like a singular miniscule fiber from the millions wrapped into one string. To be able to grab at something so small, so difficult to see, is a separate Gift entirely. Sifting through the snow to find one single flake. Few *cleasieras* are so blessed by the Forge, and my mother whom I get my Gift from was not Gifted with such a skill."

She nodded, processing the unfathomable act of controlling someone else.

He added, smiling. "Of course, there are ways around this. I have found success in ensnaring the mind to tell me what they are thinking. With varied success. I don't think the Forge appreciates cheating fate. And I am not fated to know the thoughts of others."

"Have you ever met anyone who could?" She asked, not thinking about the possible ramifications of her question in her own heart.

He looked into her eyes, focusing between the two colors. Left. Right. Green. Amber.

"Once." He said, glancing down at the small crumb of bread twiddling between his fingers. "She was equal in power and grace. She was both darkness and light when one needed the other. Not to mention, she was beautiful."

The female that Elias mentioned in the Garden, the one that had recruited him. "What happened to her, Hagan?" She asked, pushing down the ache that she felt just by talking about her. Knowing that she probably pales in comparison to this lost female.

"She was taken from me, from the Kingdom, the night before our wedding day."

A gulp stuck in her throat; shock evident in her wide eyes. "I am so sorry."

His lips turned up on one side, and nodded. "All is well now."

Shifting herself to face him, she grasped his wide back and pulled him forward, in a soft but firm embrace. She squeezed, letting her Gift wrap around him in a light echo of a glow. A comforting, healing cloud around them.

He sighed, feeling any sore muscles loosen up or overused joints momentarily healed of their pain to feel nothing but the good. He groaned, the soft healing touch interrupted by Hagan pulling them both to their feet.

"Are you ready for a tour, then? There's a few things I want to show you."

"I am."

CHAPTER 31
THE TRUTH

They started behind the staircase, where he took her hand and led her to a pair of black-framed doors leading to the back porch. "This is one of my favorite parts of the house. I feel like we could feel truly alone here, with no distractions. Just beauty."

We, her mind echoed. He said *we*.

From the back of the house, there was nothing in sight besides wheat, grass, and lavender plants sporadically planted near the home. The landscape was pure splendor. Her whimsical side wanted to roll around in the soft grass down the hill and explore the vast countryside.

The porch had a metal table and chairs, where she could imagine enjoying morning coffee when she was on leave. Pulling her back in the house, they made their way through the living room area, down the entry hall, and through the archway into the kitchen. Hardwood floors greeted her throughout, leading to numerous shelves lined with bright silver pots, pans, and kitchenware that she had no idea how to use. Cabinets lined the bottom half of the wall, painted a deep navy-blue color with bright silver knobs. Above the sink, a black-framed oriel window opened to the front side of the house. The mountains of the Second Kingdom dominated the scenic views, storm clouds creating a shadow upon the peaks that darkened the outline of the landscape.

"What do you think?" He asked, leaning against the white marble countertop beside the sink where she stood.

"Hm. I think it is a spectacular view. But knowing that the Second Kingdom always lingers above our heads," she let out a long sigh, "it troubles me."

"I see." He said, inclining his head toward her. "I want to show you something."

She squinted her eyes at him, clueless at how he could possibly have more surprises on top of what he had already shown her. He took her hand, his long fingers entangled with hers, and led her through the kitchen and small dining room to a quaint sunroom at the back of the home.

The room was made of the black framed windows, giving a complete surrounding view of the fields and valleys beyond. A long workstation bench was set against one wall, stocked with herbs, decanters, and all of the supplies to create natural remedies. The other side was furnished with a cushioned table for healing those in need. She let out a small gasp, amazed at the detail that had been put into this place. "I figured you may miss healing townsfolk, so I thought you could have a smaller version of your Apothecary in your new home. To help with homesickness. Do you like it?"

She laughed, a joyous sound that filled her body with a delicate flutter. "Hagan. This is everything I could have asked for that I didn't even know I wanted. Did you think of this?"

He smiled, his grin reaching his ears, his eyes creasing with both happiness and a sense of pride in his surprise. "Yes."

"Thank you." She pulled him into a tight embrace, her head nestling between his chest muscles. "You are forgiven," She whispered against his torso, and she felt his head lean down to nestle against the top of hers.

They pulled back, hands still wrapped around the others, and locked eyes for what felt like hours. Finally needing to blink, she pulled him in for one more embrace and closed her eyes.

His strength enveloped her, his tunic soaked underneath the river of tears coming from her. He squeezed her so tightly that she could barely breathe, but she welcomed the cocoon of comfort he was for her.

"It is not your fault." He said against her hair, his deep whisper vibrating against her skull.

She pulled back, looking at the line of concern his brows drew above his nose. "I did those things. I did terrible things to living, breathing beings. I cannot reverse it. I cannot take it back. I am dark, I am broken." Her voice broke on the last word, a sob beginning to build in her throat.

He picked her up gently, cradling her in his strong arms as they walked up the dark hardwood steps of her home.

Opening her eyes she felt him, his presence in the now. There was no sense behind what she had seen, but if it truly had been the future, and she had been manifesting what she wanted in her mind for weeks. She needed to act upon it. She needed his comfort. She needed everything that he could offer her. Not as a Prince, but as Hagan.

Her friend, lover, and protector.

Looking into his eyes, she watched them begin to glow, their powers surging between them. Tilting her head up, she met his gaze and looked into the depth of his endless green eyes.

"I want you," She said, a near silent whisper that stilled the air between them.

Hagan stilled, but kept his eyes glued to hers. "You want me?" He asked, desperation evident in his stare.

She did not want him to feel so desperate, she did not want him to be alone. She knew without a doubt that they wanted each other equally and she was not going to settle for disappointment again. "I'm not going to say it again, your highness."

His eyes lit up like molten spring.

Their mouths collided, an explosion of passion that caused her legs to dissolve. He beckoned her mouth to open for him, tongues swirling and thrashing against each other. She reached for him, his cock firmly in her grasp. He was already hard in her hand, as she had suspected he would be. He groaned, and she rubbed him with her hand, feeling his hardness straining against his pants.

He brushed her off her feet, keeping their lips connected as he walked out of the Apothecary and up the stairs to the top floor. When they reached the top, he momentarily broke their connection to set her down gently on her feet. "There's one more thing I need to show you." He said, a sensual spark in his stare.

"I'm hoping there's a few things," she said, a smile forming on her lips.

With a growl, he took her face in his strong hands and kissed her, his passion obvious as he pushed her back through an open door. Turning her around, he held her in front of him, pressed against his hard body and warmth.

Her eyes took in the room, a bedroom, her bedroom.

A small stone fireplace sat at the back wall, the fire lightly crackling to warm the space. Black trimmed doors opened out to the balcony facing the mountains, the light dimming as the darkest clouds veiled the sky in grey. In front of the fireplace, sat her bed. Silken duvets covered the wide feather mattress, dyed the color of lavender, which was becoming her favorite hue. Fluffy pillows lined the back of the bed, the white canopy swaying in the light breeze coming from the cracked window.

Turning back to him, she tilted her head up to speak to him, clutching the sides of his tunic with her fingers. "It's perfect."

"I'm glad you like it all."

He really had chosen furnishings and design choices exactly as she would have wanted them. He knew her favorite color, which he may have guessed from her favorite scent, and he chose things that were cozy. She preferred comfort over fashion any day. It was truly a home that was made for her, the only thing that would make it better was...

"Is there a tub?" She asked, biting her lip with excitement.

"Go look for yourself." He said, his hands grasping her around the hips, turning her toward the archway of her connected bathroom. He walked behind her, hands on the bones of her hips and front against her back as they made the few steps toward the bathroom. She felt him against her, his arousal impossible to hide against her back.

Through the archway, a shiny black metal tub sat in front of the tall window looking out to the lavender fields below. Bright white stone floors made the glorious bathtub stand out even more, and she wanted nothing more than to climb into it. There was something else she needed to do first.

Removing his hands from her hips, she turned around to meet his gaze. His eyes were aglow, neon pools of desire basking her face in their light. She stepped up on her toes to brush her lips against his, then fumbled backward and stood in front of him. She ripped off her thick tunic, exposing her bare breasts to him.

He stood there, gazing down at her, looking in awe of the lines and curves of her body. She watched his manhood press against his pants, leaving stark lines against the fabric. The open window brought in a brisk chill, peaking her nipples to their breaking point. He lunged, giving in to the temptation of her.

His mouth explored her body as he pushed her onto the bed. The silky purple sheets wrapped her in a subtle embrace as his contrasting hardness pressed her body into the feather mattress. Trailing kisses down her neck and chest, her body lurched when he closed his lips around her nipple and pulled. Heat pooled at her center, and he grinned against her breast. Massaging her breasts, he took turns licking and sucking her nipples until they felt raw in the cool air.

She whimpered, a soft plea.

"Always so impatient." He muttered against her bare skin.

He continued his exploration until he reached her navel, and his hands found her wide hips, pulling them toward him. Pulling at her leggings, they glided from her with a strong grace. She sat up, tilting her head to meet his neon stare.

"We seem to be unfairly matched." She said, glancing down at his tunic as her fingers found the edge of it, brushing the skin of his abdomen. He shivered but allowed her to undress him. Beneath was his tanned torso, the strain of his muscles evident in the strong lines of his chest.

She bit her lip, returning her gaze to his. She reached for the waistband of his pants, pulling gently. He gave her a tempestuous smile, his eyes crinkling at the edges.

"I prefer having the upper hand in battle." With a light squeal, he pushed her back down on the bed. He made his descent further down toward her navel.

Brushing his nose through her reddish-brown fuzz, he kissed the bundle of nerves between her legs. She cried out, the sensation beginning to build deep in her stomach.

He sucked on her, taking the sensitive skin between his lips. Her back arched, begging him to taste. Grasping her hips, he drove his tongue in her.

A gasp left her, and she arched her back further as her toes curled in anticipation. He began drinking from her, his groans vibrating against her hot flesh.

His tongue lapped at her center, each stroke like a wave of sweet heat building in her core. The coils in her stomach tightened, and her release built as he drank endlessly from her. His emerald gaze met hers as she looked down at him laying his head against her bare thigh, and he struck once more. The sight of him was too much.

She came around his mouth, pools of heat ebbing from her as she moaned, the sound echoing through the rooms of her home. Her legs squeezed, the sensation making the muscles in her body stiffen so tightly that she thought she may break.

She collapsed further into the bed; her body languid from the intensity of her climax. He crawled up to meet her, his lips were glistening, wet from her.

He had never looked so stunning. His eyes were neon pools of wonder, taking in every inch of her face. The soft light from the window accented the intricate lines of his face, the wind rustling in to cool them both down. She smiled softly, but her eyes looked at him hungrily. She felt their combined power filling her bedroom with urgency, a mix of dark storm clouds and the yellow-white light of healing swirling together into one.

She tilted her head up, wrapping her arms around his shoulders, and kissed him. This kiss wasn't the rough, intense clumsiness that took them before, but a passionate exclamation of how she felt for him. She forced his mouth open, dancing her tongue against his as she reached down and felt his hard length against his pants. It pressed against her stomach, teasing her as she rubbed against it. She pulled again at the hem of his pants, and he surrendered to her. He stood quickly, stepping out of his pants.

He was a masterpiece, every inch of him a copy of what her fantasies had drawn. The Smiths perfected their art, giving her everything that is masculine in him.

He crawled over her once more, caging her in his strong arms as he enveloped her world. She tilted her head to him, lips brushing his earlobe. "Do I have to ask you to fuck me, Hagan?"

His breath hitched against her mouth, and he pulled her even closer, his body hard against hers.

"I will no longer refuse what you want, Princess." His voice was rough, his glistening tip poised at her entrance.

He struck, filling her with one graceful stroke.

He filled every inch of her, his delicious fullness pressing her open. She squeezed against him, and they moaned, their mouths colliding once more as he grabbed her hips, sitting back on his heels and pulling her against him. Over and over. His sweet rhythm was addicting, the rushes of pleasure pumping through her with each stroke.

His hands were on her ass, squeezing her hard as he thrust into her again and again. Her head lolled back, sweet release building deep within her once more.

Leaning down, his lips brushed her nipples and then up her neck. "You are perfect." He whispered against her neck, then filled her to the deepest parts of her core. She kissed him, her arms pulling him in as he paused inside her.

Groaning, she grazed her teeth down his lip.

A guttural sound left his lips, and he thrust deep inside her.

Thunder then struck overhead, and the house shook with the force. A storm had been rising, the patter of rain loud against the roof. Bright light flashed from afar, the storm growing, especially above her home.

His breath labored, he pushed inside her, his pace quickening with every breath. She moaned, on the edge of another climax.

Digging his fingers into her hips he thrust faster, slamming into her until they both found release.

A loud crack resonated from the sky.

They came together, moans escaping her lips until the ebbs of pleasure died down and she was left dripping from him. He groaned with a final thrust, releasing every drop of him into her. Her body was floating in a sea of emotion and pleasure. Weightless, frozen in the moment of ecstasy.

Their eyes connected, and she felt a different type of release as she gazed up into his neon stare.

She remembered.

CHAPTER 32
THE MEMORIES

Flood. That is the only word I can describe for what I was experiencing inside my head. My mind is awash with so many feelings and memories that my senses are overwhelmed. I have lived two lives.

I am not me.

I am much, much more. I am nearly two hundred years old. I am a Princess, heir to the Third Kingdom throne. My mother is a powerful cleasiera, *one of the most Gifted in the realm. My Father is a* helbredera, *but only uses his healing powers to hurt. I was engaged to Hagan, Prince of the Second Kingdom.*

Hagan.

I was brought to his kingdom to be with him, to one day marry him and hope the Smiths would bless us with long lives that we would spend together, ruling his Kingdom and siring an heir that would be able to harness the mind, body, and weather. A power move.

At first, I was unsure. I did not like not having a choice in the matter, and he seemed to share the same sentiment. It was not love at first sight.

We fell in love slowly, but then all at once. It began with subtle compliments and gazes that lasted just slightly too long. Brushes of the hand, a shared laugh. Before I knew it, we were training our Gifts together, learning how the other worked and how to defeat them.

Our minds began tangling, and our joys were found together.

Together we would spend days exploring the woods, entangled under the stars. Living in the Second Kingdom, I felt at peace. I was surrounded by those who loved me. My best friend Jo, who was so desperately infatuated with my other best friend, Elias. They played a perpetual game of cat and mouse. I got to share my life with Hagan, who I knew deep down would one day be my husband. His scent brought tingles down my spine. Fresh rainwater became the smell that would fill my senses every night as we lay together in his bed, passion driving our skin to touch.

He taught me passion, he taught me confidence. I gave myself to him, in every way.

His voice was my favorite song. His laugh an encore. His face was a masterpiece that no artist could replicate. His body was my sanctuary, always there to take me when I craved release. He was everything in my small, fragile world. We were going to make our world tremendous when we became King and Queen.

Finally after a few decades, when the rivers of our love had begun to overflow, we sat together for a picnic under the tree with flowers and moss that cascaded around us. Servants brought us the best wine, cheeses, and desserts in the most luxurious spread I had ever seen. We sat together under the warmth of the Spring sun, every flower in his Mother's garden at the peak of their brightest bloom. The scents of the garden were nearly overwhelming, and surrounded me with a blanket of sweet perfume.

I closed my eyes, lying on the picnic blanket with the love of my life beside me, soaking in the sensations of a perfect day. When I opened my eyes to the bright sun and allowed them to adjust, the glitters of a bright ring met my gaze.

The ring was nothing short of brilliant. It was a thing of pure beauty. A large pastel purple rock sat in the center, the millions of sparkles nearly blinding her in the bright light. Surrounding the gem were smaller gems of white opal that all sat on a silver ring.

"Marry me," Hagan said, giving me the widest, silliest smile, I could possibly imagine on his perfect face. I faltered, as I always liked to tease him. Our eyes were locked in that long moment, and concern began to darken his emerald gaze when I finally gave him my answer.

"Yes," I whispered, and he kissed me with so much heat I may have melted beneath him. We made love in the open air of the garden that day, no

concern of who would find us in our post-engagement bliss.

Safety. That is what I felt when I was with him. If we were together, no one could stop us. We would play games, drink wine, and explore each other's bodies under the watchful eyes of the stars in the night sky. The Smiths had blessed us with happiness, and that happiness came to a halt when my Mother arrived for her yearly visit on the day before our wedding.

"You must not marry him." My mother declared, as we sat together at my favorite coffee shop owned by the talented aimsura *baker. Sipping my frothed coffee, I nearly choked on the semi-sweet liquid. I stared at her, in complete disbelief as she was the one who brought me to be with him in the first place.*

"Mother, I love him. We have been courting for decades and now you decide that you do not approve?" My voice was shaky, she would not take this joy away from me.

Her warm voice turned cool and dangerous as she kept her words at a near whisper. "There are things about this Kingdom that you do not know. There was once a time when you were safe here. Now, I do not believe you are. Not truly."

I was utterly shocked. Her supple lips were pressed in a firm line, and her green eyes were as hard as stone. "I refuse. I am marrying Hagan tomorrow and there is nothing to be done about it. I'm happy, Mother. When I am with him things are easy. Why would I want to give that up for reasons you won't even tell me?"

"You must believe me, my darling." The Cleasiera Queen's eyes were pleading with me to obey. "It is not safe for you here, or at home."

I flinched, swiftly getting up from the table to leave. "This is my home. Hagan, Elias, Jolee, the Queen, they are my home now. I have lived here for almost fifty years, Mother. I will not be forced to leave my family."

But I would be forced to leave. Everything.

That was just over twenty-five years ago, when I thought I had been Forged. The memories from that time no longer felt real.

Like a hurricane of color manifesting in my mind, my memories were returning to me in waves, but Mother's final words to me as I walked away from her were clear.

"I did what I had to do to save you once, and I will not hesitate to do so again."

CHAPTER 33
THE PRINCESS

Rushing water filled her ears, as if she were drowning. Hagan pulled from her, lying beside her as she cradled into a ball, her thoughts beginning to slow their rush into her mind. She covered her ears, breathing heavily as her memories stopped coming back so quickly, relief blossoming against her temples. He may have been speaking to her, but she couldn't hear. Memories still worked their way back, but they slowed as she tried to think back on all two-hundred years. Tears fell from her eyes, the green eye glowing so bright that she could see it's shine over the bridge of her nose.

Hagan pulled her in, his arms wrapped so tightly around her to comfort her. Her mouth wanted to scream, but nothing escaped her lips. He flipped her around to face him, their naked bodies side by side as the tears blurred her vision even more.

"Maeve?! Maeve, what's happening?" His arms were still around her, stroking her back and hair to calm her.

Her breathing was labored, her glowing eyes distant as everything came back. Tastes, smells, experiences, knowledge. Things that she could have never imagined were true but were without a doubt what she knew.

She knew who she was.

Her eyes slowly drifted to his, and for the first time since the night in the tavern she really saw him.

Hagan.

His eyes searched hers, and finally, she spoke.

"Hagan," A smile grew on her lips, and her eyes burned with the forgotten tears.

"What is it? Are you okay?" Concern scrunched the lines in his face as he spoke in a soothing voice.

"Better now."

His eyes widened, and he pulled his hands to either side of her face.

"M-Maeve… do you remember me?"

She gave him a breathtaking smile and felt her love for him fluttering in her chest as her heart beat a slow rhythm against her rib cage.

He kissed her, and everything she now knew made sense.

Her name was Maeve, Born of the Third Kingdom. Daughter of the Bone King and *Cleasiera* Queen. Brought to the Second Kingdom, where she fell in love with Hagan, heir to the Second Kingdom. Not Forged by the Smiths, but brought into this world by their grace two centuries ago. Gifted with the powers to ensnare the mind and to heal the body. Born with two colored eyes, one from her Father and one from her Mother.

Her Mother.

Tears crept into her eyes, and she gasped for breath beneath his passionate kiss. He pulled back, looking into her reddened eyes.

"Hagan, is she really gone?"

Realization cooled the fire from his gaze. She knew the answer but needed to hear it from his mouth.

"My love, I am so sorry." His eyes burned with newfound tears, and his brows furrowed. He watched her, waiting for her to respond. When she did not, he continued.

"Maeve, your father… he found out. He found out about all of it. When you were brought to my Kingdom, it was to protect you from him. Your Father. She made him forget you Maeve, and later on when she came to visit for that last time, he figured it out. I don't know how because she made me forget you too. Maeve, I would have searched for you for the rest of my life if I knew you existed. For twenty-five years, I was oblivious. But your Father, finding out, drove him over the edge. In his anger, he broke her. And he went completely mad after that. Smiths, I am so sorry. Please, Maeve." His voice broke slightly, his emotions taking control of his usual stoic demeanor.

Her father, the merciless Bone King. The male who had killed her mother.

Unable to speak, she recollected her Mother. Dyvina, Queen of the Third Kingdom. Her smile could melt the frost, and her wit could charm the most stubborn male. A true Queen, she was the opposite of her Father. She loved her subjects, and she loved her daughter. So much so, that she made her forget. Her mother made her forget everything about her past life to start anew. She made her forget Hagan.

Finally, she found her words. "Why did she do this, Hagan?" He sighed, rising, and pulling her to him. "Oh, my love. We have so much to talk about."

She pulled one of the blankets around her, sitting up and against the pillows.

"Why didn't you tell me who I was?" He had mentioned not knowing before, but all this time he must have known. Amongst all her emotions, anger bubbled to the surface.

Hagan let out a deep breath. "Maeve, there is so much I wish to tell you. I thank the Smiths that you have returned to me." He raked his fingers through his rustled hair. "I wanted you to discover on your own. There were times where I wanted to tell you so badly, my heart ached every day since I saw you the first time in Blarra. But then I realized that you did not know me, and my heart broke all over again. The night at the Lake, I knew that you remembered something about me. I saw it in your face, but you just did not know what it was you were remembering. I refused to force you into something you did not truly know was real. It felt wrong for only one of us to know."

His eyes gleamed in the low light, and she recognized honesty in his words with the odd sense of humor she had loved.

The subtle humor that cracked a smile on his usually serious tanned face contradicted the downtrodden expression. His dark brown curls sat heavily upon his forehead as he lowered his chin. A single tear fell from his eye and drifted down his cheek.

His voice broke, and she reached to wipe the single tear from his cheek.

She nodded, a sense of understanding and forgiveness washing over her like warm water. "All that matters is that you did find me. You found me Hagan, and now that I remember we can pick up where we left off. The love we shared was beautiful and glorious. Let us find that again, let us forget about what my mother did." Her voice was soft, but he hung on every word, his lips parted. "Well, maybe we don't forget, but we forgive. I would like to think my mother did so for a good reason, but I just cannot begin to understand what it was." She took in a deep breath, sitting with her legs crossed.

"I knew there was something so special about you, it just took me some time to figure it out. You have no idea the frustration I caused myself, wondering how the fuck I could fall for someone so quickly. Now it makes sense." She laughed sardonically, and a small smile played upon his lips.

"Fuck, if I would have realized bringing you to bed would have made you remember..." He realized, his eyes widening in astonishment.

"I tried, Hagan. You're the one who was fighting it."

"Smiths, I have missed you, Maeve." Hagan said, his eyes glittering with admiration. "You knew all along, a part of you knew and wanted to show me."

Beneath the newfound happiness she had found with Hagan, there were still many questions in her mind that needed answers.

Her face turned serious. "Why did my mother do this? Was the Second Kingdom not safe in her eyes? Why?"

His face turned to stone, creasing the lines in his forehead. "I do not know. You were promised to me, if I kept you safe. We spent years together, and your mother would visit you every few years, to check in. One day, during one of her visits, she was different. She spoke of treason against her husband. Devious things about my Father. Then, that night, she took you. She controlled your mind, and made you forget, I'm guessing. It was by far the worst day of my life."

Maeve's head was aching, all this information too much for a single night. According to Hagan, her mother had betrayed her Father and Hagan. She remembered how deeply her mother loved her, something had to have changed for her Mother to make such a rash decision. Her Mother stole the memories of her life away, but for what?

"What did she say about your Father?" She asked, knowing that the King of Thunder was very capable of nefarious acts.

He shook his head. "No, what she said was insanity. My Father can be cruel, but what she suggested was absolutely ludicrous."

"Hagan." She warned, needing him to communicate honestly with her. Now that things were beginning to be real, she wanted it to stay that way.

He groaned in irritation but relented. "You already know what atrocities everyone knows about your Father, the Bone King. Well, she suggested that my Father was even worse. That he was kidnapping females Forged with great power to mate. To create a more powerful generation of Born Fae. Forced mating. As if he could do anything like that without others noticing. Someone's daughter or wife would be missed. Especially ones so Blessed by the Smiths." He shook his head, as if the idea was completely preposterous.

What if it wasn't, though? The King looked at her like a piece of meat, at best a bartering chip, how would he look at non-Royals? She knew how. But she would not spend more time dwelling on that topic while so many questions still floated about her mind.

Her mind. Her mind had the powers only given to her, the Gift her mother gave.

She was Born, she was a *cleasiera*.

The familiar tingling in her healing fingertips was contradicted by the humming presence of her mind. That humming radiated from the base of her neck to her temples, begging to be used. She had felt it before, and now she knew why.

Any time Mikael or Revna tried to touch the tethers of her mind, they warned them to stay away. She could see the memory differently now; she saw them poking and prodding around her head when she conversed with them. But her tethers were sharp and whipped at any possible intruder. Her guards were up for twenty-five years.

She cracked her neck, and the humming strained against her skull. Pushing it out toward him, she felt the Gift as if it were an old muscle that had not been exercised in a long time. While nothing was visible to the eye, she could still sense the tethers of his mind. Or according to Hagan's analogy, puppet strings.

Hagan's tethers were like smoke, but dark red in color. They swirled around his head, challenging her to reach out.

"Maeve, go slow." He warned.

Her eyes shot open, and the green of her left eye cast his face in a subtle glow that was noticeable in the dim night. He looked back at her, his emerald stare glowing in defense. He must have been trying to hold her mind back from his.

"Do you remember the Battle of Wits?" She asked, attempting to change the subject and forget her existing anger. For the moment.

In the time before, they participated in what they called 'Battles of Wit', which consisted of each of them trying to push into the other's mind and make them do something silly.

He smirked. "I particularly remember you often winning."

She laughed, pushing down the tethers of her own mind. "My favorite was when I forced you to wrestle Elias, in bearish form."

Her instant connection with Elias was not without reason. He had tried to remind her, in the garden. He spoke of the female that he flirted with in the bar, how he met Hagan. She now knew that was her. He was one of her dearest friends, and she had hitched a ride on his bearish form many times in the past. They rode together to battle, their bond something Gifted to them by the Forge. A true allyship. They were both outcasts from their respective courts. He was the heir to the Fourth Kingdom, where his Father, the Hybrid King, rejected him for not being hybrid

270

too. He only took after his mother but gained the rare Gift of talking to animals as well.

He did not bother to fight the Hybrid King, as a beast of both wolfish and saber-toothed would be impossible to encounter on the battlefield, and win.

Those dark days brought Elias to the Second Kingdom Court, where he became the most trusted advisor and friend of the future King and Queen of the Second Kingdom. One of which he tried to wrestle, often.

A smile broke across his mouth. "I do. I also remember you patching me up after, and how many times you apologized. Twenty-two, if I'm not mistaken."

Elias had not tried to hurt him when they wrestled, but he had ridiculously large claws that had been particularly sharp that day.

Their conversation turned to chaos, trying to reminisce on old times while also clearing up details of the others' life, all while avoiding the time in which they were apart. Time that was important, time that changed them both in real ways. She did not want to breach that subject when she was still trying to figure out who she was. How could she be both old Maeve and new Maeve, a result of two completely different lives?

They talked for hours, until sleep snuck up on them both and the darkness turned to day.

CHAPTER 34
THE TEA

"Good morning, you stunning, mischievous thing."
Hagan stood near the fire, only wearing his pants loosely
around his hips. In the morning's soft light, he looked like
a sculpture adorning the hearth.

"How am I mischievous? You're the one who woke me
two times last night, with your mouth in unspeakable places."
She teased and pouted her lips as she looked up at him.

"Ah, well if you remember When I get to wake up to your
beautiful face again after twenty-five years, I simply cannot be
expected to refrain. You, my love, are irresistable."

She blushed bright red.

More memories had flooded into her mind today,
seemingly awakened by the small bit of rest she got while
sleeping in her bed with Hagan. She could pinpoint certain
parts about her time in the Third Kingdom. She remembered
the way it looked, and the way it made her feel to live there.
The Third Kingdom sat on the cliff of the vast Aeriös Ocean
that went on for eternity into a foggy abyss of nothing. Into
what felt like hopelessness. There was darkness there. The
more she thought back to her time growing up in the Third
Kingdom, the darker things were.

Some memories were completely invisible in the darkness, much like the Fifth Kingdom across the Ocean.

Really, the Fifth Kingdom lay beyond the channel, but the eerie fog around that land never allowed her to see it. As if it was out of reach. She had never ventured on a boat to visit, even though her curiosity did make her want to.

The Fifth Kingdom was the only Kingdom ruled solely by a Queen. Queen Flora, who had a husband King Sebastián, the sole ruler of the land with her husband as her consort. The *Nadura* Queen inherited the land from her Father, who had only sired her with a random *ganera* female, leaving Flora to be Born with only one power and a bastard of the previous King. Rumors say that this *nadura* power was strong, which was reflected in the brush and vines that surrounded the land. Her floral fortress was a sound reason to leave her Kingdom alone.

The spies of the Fifth Kingdom were vast, they had been controlled by the *spaidera* King Sebastián, who gathered the intelligence for the Fifth Kingdom. Mikael had been one of them in the past. The most brilliant minds in the realm of Ignisiem reside there, where the Temple to the Smiths lies on the island far out in the Aeriös Ocean.

Hagan came to sit on the bed beside her, pushing her hair behind her sharp ear.

"I wish I could spend the day with you," He said softly, planting a light kiss upon her lips. "I know we still have so much time to get back."

"Well, why can't you?" She asked, leaning in to touch her nose to his.

"Preparations." He said grimly, a dull look in his eyes. "Though my father will be making all of the decisions anyways, he wishes me to be there to plan the ins and outs of our next trip. More Rebels rousing in the Second Kingdom who need to be dealt with." His wording made her flinch, hating what it meant to deal with the Freed Fae.

The things that they did to commoners and servants were routine in the time before her memory was taken. She would take minds left and right, they would do it together. On the battlefield, at court, and in training they would combine their minds to do great things. Her training was varied since she was able to control the mind and the body. This power had endless opportunities, and at the time she loved wielding her Gifts.

Like mind training.

Her promised mother-in-law was a kind soul, but a strict teacher. While Queen Revna was not Gifted with tremendous power, she did know how to utilize what she was given. They would sit at the coffee shop in the town below the Second Kingdom and sip frothed coffee, surrounded by hundreds of Fae and the tethers of their minds.

The game was simple.

Revna would choose someone within the crowd, and Maeve would have to make them do something. While it was not ethical to her now, Maeve enjoyed the training then. Her mind had to be clear, and she had to remain completely inconspicuous. On a specific occasion, Revna happened to choose a burly red-haired male with muscles on top of muscles that sat on top of his muscles.

When the male began to do a funny little jig in the middle of the crowded town square, Revna nearly spit out her coffee from laughing so hard.

The Queen she had always had a love for. The opposite could be said for the King.

She thought back to the conversation she had overheard in the halls outside of the room where his meeting took place. Before she even remembered who the King really is, before she knew the extent of his evil.

"Do you believe there will be war?" She asked.

He looked mildly shocked, but answered her. "I do not know."

Lie. She knew based on the meeting and her knowledge of the true wickedness of the King of Thunder that he had every intention to hurt others. To start a war.

She acted as if the response sustained her, even though it did not. Too much on her mind to muster a real response, she decided on something simple. "I hope that we do not, the Forge need not burn so bright over simple land discrepancies. Don't you think so?"

"I do." He said, and leaned in to press his lips against her neck. She was glad their beliefs aligned in that respect, but was not sure he could be completely truthful when his allegiances still lie with his Father.

She sighed, smiling up at him. "You're going to be late. As am I." She noticed the dawn had broken over the mountaintops over an hour ago, which meant she was late for tea with Clover.

They each grabbed their horses from the stalls in the back of the house, which she now remembered were always there. Callistus must have figured it out on her own after the thunderstorm Hagan had caused in the night.

In front of the steps of her home, she and Hagan stood in each other's arms. "When I get back, I promise we will keep talking. You are different now, not quite the Maeve of before. But I do not care. We will begin again, keep going from where we left off. I love you, my Queen." He said, as if picking up from the day before their wedding twenty-five years prior. As if nothing had changed. As if they hadn't changed. He pulled her into a soft kiss, then released her and promised, "I'll be back as soon as I possibly can."

With a nod, she mounted Callistus and trotted off to the West.

→» →» «← «←

The ride was not long, the well-worn path easy to navigate. It was still early, and many of the usual travelers were not on the roads yet. When the village came into view, the path turned from dirt to well-lain stones. Hooves clacked against the hard stone, the sounds and smells of the village reaching her soon after.

When she reached the first couple of buildings of the village, she dismounted and walked with Callistus through the main road to the far side of town. A thick wood began there, the once orange hues turned to brown with the cold.

What Clover had written in her letter was correct, she

immediately saw the house that could not belong to anyone but her. Surrounded by three- and four-story estates of the town was a one-story, light green dome-shaped dwelling with a light wood door. The color reminded her of leaves, which was fitting for the daughter of a powerful garden nymph.

Clover's past was tragic, and she felt an obligation as both her Sergeant and her friend to be there for her. She found Clover's life so interesting and regretted the way others thought of half-Fae Nymphs or Nymphs in general. Like *ganeras*, they were lower. Even someone like Clover, who had much power in her blood, was seen as less.

She remembered how her views used to be, growing up as a Born. But she refused to retain that part of her old self, to allow her past to dictate how she acts in her future.

Tying Callistus to the short fence that surrounded Clover's home, she patted her snout and walked up the stone path to the quaint home. The height of the place was odd, the ceilings could only be as tall as Hagan. It must feel relatively normal to Clover, maybe even a luxurious height to her.

She knocked at the wooden door, expecting Clover to take longer to answer it. However, she opened it one second after knocking. She was certainly excited to see her. Clover's bright lavender eyes looked up at her, their whimsical nature making Maeve smile.

"Hello, Clover. May I come in?" She said, tucking her traveling cloak further around herself in the chilly air.

"Yes, of course milady." Her voice squeaked.

She stepped inside, the immediate warmth making her take her thick cloak off and hang it on the spindly coat hanger at the entrance.

The space was definitely small but was decorated with every color of the rainbow. Every piece of furniture was a different color, and the brightness of the space was contrasted by the clutter of many things collected over Clover's long life. Trinkets filled every shelf, which lined all of the walls of the small space. In any space that knick-knacks did not reside, a plant did. Leaves, flowers, vines, and other exotic plants filled the space as well. A bright blue door interrupted the many shelves on the far wall, to what she assumed was the bedroom.

The kitchen had light pink cabinets, and a wood-burning stove held a brass kettle that was screeching. Steam burst from it, making Clover scurry over to attend to it.

"Please, feel free to sit." Clover said, preparing the tea into two small yellow teacups. She seemed anxious, like she was nervous to serve her tea in her tiny home.

Maeve chose a fluffy purple chair that she pulled from the white table, which was decorated at the edges with small painted flowers of pink and purple.

Clover sat down across from her, the small metal tray of teacups shaking in her frail hands. She managed to set it down without spilling and spoke. "It is so good to see you, Miss Maeve." She said, taking a sip of her tea. "Please, enjoy. I added a touch of lavender, for the aromatics." She smiled, the smile not quite reaching her semi-pointed ears.

"It is lovely to see you too, Clover. Thank you for the invitation," she lifted the yellow cup from the tray, pinching the small handle in between her thumb and forefinger. The serving was much smaller than she would have usually drunken.

She wafted the fumes to herself, smelling the slightest hint of lavender.

She blew on the cup, watching the cloud of steam billow off the surface of the leafy tea. Bringing the rim to her lips, she took a deep sip from the teacup. It tasted almost sweet, not quite like tea at all.

Clover's eyes remained staring at Maeve, a glimmer of an emotion that she could not place passing in her soft purple gaze.

"What is in this tea? It's sweet, so sweet..." Her mind drifted off, unable to form the words she wanted to say. Her lips numbed, then her hands. She felt the teacup slip from her fingers first, then the slight burning sensation of the hot tea spilling on her legs. Her body began numbing all over, but the last to follow was her mind. She tried desperately to reach for her Gift, to somehow grab at the strings of her own mind, but something else made the strings dance as she fell into darkness.

CHAPTER 35
THE DAGGER

The bright flashes of light and carriage noise came through the darkness, but she couldn't quite wake up. Her head was pounding, a sharp ringing beginning to plague her eardrums. Blood and dirt singed her nostrils, accompanied by a sickeningly sweet, floral scent. She had to stop herself from scrunching her nose.

They were in a wagon of some sort, the bumpiness of the ride making her feel a bit nauseous. She noted two others, but did not want to risk opening her eyes.

Her hands and feet were bound by something rough, she imagined it was rope. If she could only touch them, she could easily hurt them and escape. With little noise, she strained her wrists against the bounds. They were not going to budge.

Afraid to open her eyes, she focused and listened. She did not want to reveal that she was awake. The familiar hum of her mind reminded her of her not-so-new *cleasiera* powers, and she took advantage of her captors thinking she was knocked out.

Past the sound of wooden wheels against rocks and dirt, she heard three distinct breathing patterns. A female voice spoke, her tone reminded Maeve of a viper.

Sensual and dangerous.

"The nightshade turned out to be an excellent choice, Lukas. A few drops of my poison in her tea and she went right to sleep." The female's voice rang through the small carriage.

A rich voice that must be Lukas spoke, a rough, guttural accent in his words. "She made herself an easy target. Overconfidence is often the downfall of Royals and Borns, and she is both. Too bad her lover wasn't with her. I would have loved to feel my blade go through his Born skin. I bet it slices the same as mine."

By the Smiths.

She needed to try something. Anything to get out of this mess. With her hands bound, her *helbredera* Gifts were useless. However, the hum of her mind answered her call, which was a struggle against the resounding pain in her head.

With as much restraint as possible, she allowed the threads of her mind to explore, weaving around the heads of the two sitting in front of her. While she could sense the two, she could only see one of them in the confines of her head. The female's threads were dark green, like vines that wrapped safely around her consciousness. The male, she could not sense. His mind was invisible to her, as if the threads of his sanity did not exist. Then, she felt something else. Beside her, the mind of the third captor. Hers were pastel hued tethers, all strewn about in a chaos of color.

Clover.

Clover was one of her captors, and she had likely been the one to use the viper female's poison in her tea. Clover was the reason she was in this situation. She betrayed her. But over what? She thought back to the little conversation they had over the past few weeks, and something that always came to mind when she saw her surfaced. Her Mother's tragic death.

A garden nymph who was nymphean royalty, raped by a *helbredera* to create her. A *helbredera* from the Third Kingdom, someone with the power and influence to get themselves out of the situation. Someone of status. Her Father.

Clover was her half-sister, and she betrayed her. But she had nothing to do with it.

Refocusing, she attempted to snake her way into the mind of the viper, weaving her way through the imaginary vines in an attempt to take control.

That was a mistake.

The venomous voice spoke once more. "It appears the Bone Princess has graced us with her presence."

Maeve flinched, and slowly opened her eyes. She was lying on her side on one side of the carriage, and saw a male and female torso.

"Careful, Princess." The male voice warned.

"It would not end well for you if you tried to take my mind from me, Born one." The female voice slithered down her spine, and the ropes around her hands and feet tightened.

Not ropes, vines. A *nadura*.

She slowly sat up, her vision clearing as her head throbbed.

She looked over, seeing Clover looking at the floor. She did not even have the courage to meet the gaze of the one she betrayed.

He continued, "What a beautiful thing you are. It is a pity that such an alluring female is so rotted inside."

Taken aback by the insult, she scoffed at him. The vines tightened, nearly breaking the skin of her wrists.

Maeve took in the two Fae before her. An ebony skinned female sat to the left, her voluptuous curves accented by the red corset and leather pants that squeezed her in all the right places. Her hair was in long elegant braids, with two silver ones framing her heart-shaped face. Angled brown eyes met hers, and nothing short of hate glittered in them.

Her beauty was strangely alluring, yet every fiber of her being still screamed *Run*.

Beside the female was a rugged-looking male. His hair was almost black, half of it tied in a knot on top of his head. He was a beast of a male, and if they were standing, he would surely tower over her. His shoulder length hair framed a strong, bearded jaw and sharp cheekbones. He'd be considered devastatingly handsome if it weren't for the long scar across his brow, which reached down to his jaw.

Not to mention the menacing look in his grey-blue eyes.

His eyes looked as if they did not belong on his face, a low dark brow making them appear even brighter. The swirls of grey and blue watched her, waiting for her to do or say something. A strange mixture of distaste and curiosity in his stare.

When she sat up, he moved, revealing a long black dagger that was sheathed across his back. His battle-hardened muscles rippled from the movement, but for such a threateningly large male he moved with an unbelievable grace. A warrior.

Black tattoos wrapped around both strong arms, illustrating his skin all the way up to his neck, peeking through his semi-sheer tunic.

Before she knew it, the tip of the dagger was digging into the base of her throat.

She took in a sharp breath and looked him dead in those allusive eyes. She uttered the first words that came to mind. "Untie me and make it a fair fight."

His lips tipped up in a smirk, and his scarred brow raised in an arrogant gesture. He pressed the dagger in further, almost drawing blood.

"Hitting females isn't usually my style, but I've seen what you can do with those hands, Princess. I wasn't going to take any chances." His bronze skin glowed in the low light that showed through the darkened windows of the carriage. He had full lips that pulled to the right when he spoke, revealing a single dimple.

He spoke like she had done something to him, but she had never met this male. While she was still remembering the earlier parts of her life, memories that were coming back to her a few at a time, her mind would have remembered him.

"I have no idea what you're talking about. Who are you and where are you taking me?" She asked, her voice turned hoarse. The tip of his dagger was dangerously sharp, and if he pressed any further, he would penetrate the soft skin of her neck and easily kill her. She pressed herself as far into the seat as possible, away from them. Her body felt completely useless, her strongest weapons bound behind her back and the tethers of her mind unable to reach him.

His lips turned into a surprisingly breathtaking smile, the angle of his eyebrow promising wicked intentions.

"You are on the way to your end, Bone Princess."

Dreams had tricked her before.
Book 2 coming Fall 2022.

GLOSSARY
THE WORLD OF IGNISIEM

Gifts

Cleasiera: (cle-see-air-uh) One who can harness the mind of another. This Gift can be as innocent as changing perspectives or as deadly as sending someone to their death.

Helbredera: (hel-breh-dare-uh) One who can heal others. They can morph and change the body of another to remedy injury or illness.

Aimsura: (ame-su-rah) One who can control the weather and climate. This Gift can be as simple as heating water to as complex as scorching the land with the explosion of a volcano.

Bhiastera: (bee-uh-stair-uh) One who can shift into the body of a predator. Those with this Gift wear two masks, one as a Fae and one as a beast.

Nadura: (nah-due-rah) One who can have power over the earth. This Gift gives power over all plants, a master of nature.

Spaidera: (spy-dare-uh) One who can gain knowledge over all others. This Gift makes all learned things simple, intelligence is the sixth sense.

Treaniera: (tray-nare-uh) One whose strength outweighs all. Those with this Gift could lift something as light as a boulder, or as heavy as a home.

Ganera: (guh-nare-uh) The many. The ones without Gifts.

The Kingdoms

The First Kingdom: The home of the Mind King, the most powerful Fae to ever be Forged in a millennium.

The Second Kingdom: The home of the King of Thunder (*aimsura*), and his Born son, Prince Hagan, mothered by the Queen Revna (*cleasiera*) and Gifted with *cleasiera* and *aimsura* powers.

The Third Kingdom: The home of the Bone King (*helbredera*) and the deceased Queen Dyvina (*cleasiera*).

The Fourth Kingdom: The home of the Hybrid King (*bhiastera*), who takes two forms, a wolfish and saber-toothed, and the Bearish Queen (*bhiastera*).

The Fifth Kingdom: The island kingdom ruled by the Queen of Flora (*nadura*) and the King Consort Sebastián (*spaidera*)

The Villages of the Forged: Equally owned by all Five Kingdoms, these small villages and territories are for the Forged who are brought to this Realm by the Messengers.

The Republic of Freed Fae: The lands beyond the Divide, into the Dorcha Mountains, where those who separated from the society of the Five Fae Kingdoms, led by their Leader, the King with no Title.

ABOUT THE AUTHOR

Shelby Cuaron is an American author who lives in Colorado Springs, Colorado with her husband and two dogs. Her dogs are Mad-Eye Moody and Lily, after her insane love for Harry Potter. She started her writing journey on Instagram, where she found the "Booksta" community. As an adolescent, she had a passion for reading and doing anything in the realm of creativity. As an adult, she uses reading and writing as an escape from reality. With too many ideas in her head, she decided to put her thoughts to paper. Those thoughts turned to stories, and those stories turned to novels. Welcome to her world. There is so much more to see.

Printed in Great Britain
by Amazon

78973693R00167